CLARA

ALSO BY KURT PALKA

Rosegarden

The Chaperon

Equinox

Scorpio Moon

KURT PALKA

CLARA

a Novel

EMBLEM

McClelland & Stewart

LIBRARY AND ARCHIVES CANADA CATALOGUING IN PUBLICATION

Palka, Kurt
Clara / Kurt Palka

Originally published with title: Patient number 7. Toronto :
McClelland & Stewart, 2012.
ISBN 978-0-7710-7132-4

I. Title. II. Palka, Kurt. Patient number 7

PS8581.A49P37 2012   C813'.54   C2012-904050-9

Published simultaneously in the United States of America by
McClelland & Stewart, a division of Random House of Canada Limited
P.O. Box 1030, Plattsburgh, New York 12901

Library of Congress Control Number: 2013938801

Translations from works by Hermann Hesse and
Rainer Maria Rilke are by the author.

Typeset in Van Dijk by M&S, Toronto
Printed and bound in the United States of America

McClelland & Stewart,
a division of Random House of Canada Limited,
a Penguin Random House Company
One Toronto Street
Suite 300
Toronto, Ontario
M5C 2V6
www.randomhouse.ca

1   2   3   4   5   18   17   16   15   14

For Heather

"The important thing, Madame, is not to be cured,
but to live with one's ailments."

— *Abbé Ferdinando Galiani (1728–1787)*
to Mme Louise d'Épinay (1726–1783)

ONE

·❖·

THE DAY SHE BURIED her husband, nearly a hundred
mourners filled the Benedictine chapel. She had wanted
just family and friends but then her daughters had taken
over, and the list had grown. Now it included people from
the museum and from city hall, and the defence minister
and military attachés from a number of embassies were
there as well. Even Guido Malfatti was there, the motorcycle dealer who had been shot in the knee in Russia and
had sawed off his own leg with a shell fragment, and in
1945 her husband had saved his life by taking him to Italy.

There was an intense smell from the lilies in the chapel,
and when the doors swung open and the coffin was carried
out you could smell the horses too. Two black Belgians
they were, beautiful horses in leather and brass tackle,
unshod for the occasion as was traditional. When the coffin
approached, they tossed their heads and their breath

steamed in the cold air, and when the coffin was set down onto the cartbed and pushed forward, wood on wood through the thin layer of snow, the springs gave way with the gritty sound of rust.

She stood at the tailgate dressed in black from hat to button shoes. She wore one of her mother's formal coats of black gabardine from the late 1800s, heavy and long, with wide lapels and black velvet cuffs. It weighed her down and bent her at shoulders and back, and when she reached out and placed a bare hand on the coffin none of the mourners could see her face for the veil. But how they stared at her and ate it up, this timeless scene.

When her husband had been alive, few of these mourners had shown much love for him. After all, he'd been famous, and famous men have few friends. In his later years many had admired him, but certainly there were those who'd whispered about his past, even though they had not the faintest idea of the man he had been and of the time he'd lived through. Only she knew, because she'd lived it with him from the beginning.

That day at the cemetery, when she removed her hand from his coffin and the coachman shook the reins and clucked his tongue and said, "Go, girls! Go!" and those enormous horses leaned into the traces and raised the first polished hoof to take him away, at that moment and from that moment on she stood alone.

She stood like the last person in a house already emptied and dark on moving day, and she looked after coffin and cart and horses leaving, and she stood like this for a long time. Finally she stirred. She took a tissue from her cuff and used it behind the veil, and she turned her narrow back in that black coat on all of them and walked away, down the cemetery lane, past nuns' graves and monks' graves, a sea of black cast-iron crosses each one just like the other.

The previous night it had snowed, and now the air was crisp and clean and it smelled of more snow coming. The high mountains around the valley and the glacier were white, but the pine forests climbing the slopes were still green.

She heard steps on the gravel path behind her and then her two daughters were walking wordlessly by her side; Emma, the gentle and studious one, and Willa, never married and a bit wild like her father had been, with her arm still in a cast from when a birthing camel had kicked her weeks ago on a farm in Queensland.

Eventually they steered her around and walked her to the parking lot. On the way there and without looking up she said, "Please thank the Pachmayrs for me. For the horses." And by her side Emma said, "We will, Mom. Of course we will."

The defence minister and the military attachés and their lieutenants stood by her car, waiting, and they held their hats in bare hands and they inclined their heads and murmured their condolences. They drove off in gleaming black Mercedes limousines with diplomatic licence plates, and the car tires ground on the gravel drive and brown oak leaves swirled and settled, and they were gone.

At the funeral meal she sat next to his empty chair and his placesetting with fork and knife crossed on his plate. Her friend Mitzi Friedmann sat at her other side. There was a picture of him, of her Albert before the illness, looking the way she'd loved him all her life, bold and grinning and that cowlick in his hair, and his chin up high.

She noticed she was beginning to pay attention to detail again. She made mental notes of how much she disliked the commotion in the room; the priest, Father Hofstätter, being benevolent and jolly with everyone, and all these relatives like excited carrion birds who hovered and ate and drank and watched her, and looked away when she caught them watching. Some came up and said a few words in praise of Albert, which was nice. Dr. Kessler, the physician who'd taken over Dr. Mannheim's practice and who'd helped Albert greatly during his final days, came up too and bowed and held her hand. "I've lost a friend," he said. "You lost that and so much more."

After the meal Willa and Emma took her to the stone house near the bridge where the river Inn flowed through this old city of St. Töllden, home to her family for generations.

There was tension again between her daughters. She felt it but did not want to deal with it, and so she sent them away. In her bedroom she moved the small hinged silver frame with her two favourite photographs closer to the edge of the night table so she could see it from the pillow. One of the photos was of Albert and the girls, perhaps nine and twelve years old, walking side by side on a sunny fall day with leaves on the ground. The girls were skipping alongside their father on the path by the river, Emma in pigtails and Willa with a single ponytail off-centre high on her head. The picture showed them from behind in skirts bouncing and in sweaters she had knitted and whose patterns she remembered still. Albert's hands were on their shoulders, holding them close to either side of him.

The other picture was of him as a young man before they were married, grinning and confident in full uniform, photographed at the officers' training course in the spring of 1937, before the famous general had called him to his team of field commanders.

She grieved like this for two days, during which she refused to see anyone or speak to anyone other than Mitzi. She spoke not even to Willa, who as usual on these visits from faraway was staying in her childhood room on the lower floor of the house.

When Mitzi arrived she leaned her canes within reach against the dresser and sat a bit crooked in the blue uphol-stered chair by the bedside. They spoke not very much while the sunlight moved from the south window to the west where it flashed on the river and lit up the yellow front of the house opposite and filled the room with warm light before it faded altogether.

Two days later she bathed and dressed carefully in everyday clothes but with a black mourning band on the left upper sleeve of her blouse. The girl from Mitzi's salon came and washed and blow-dried her hair, and left again. She made coffee, and while it dripped she made toast on the old metal toastersheet atop the gas flame.

She ate breakfast in the kitchen and began to think about what she would write, then carried her third cup of coffee into her study. When she was a little girl, it had been Bernhard's room, the younger of her two stepbrothers. There were shelves all along one wall and good light from windows on two sides. She walked around the stack of boxes for the archives, lowered the tablet on the secretary, and sat down on the chair. Writing had always saved her. It would do so again.

A DAY LATER the traditional afternoon visiting began. People sat in the formal living room around the porcelain stove and under the various family portraits and watercolours. The visitors said nothing helpful, but what helpful thing was there to say.

Out the parlour window on these late-fall afternoons you could see the church not far away. You could see the play of sunlight on its stone folds and in its stained pitch chutes and musket slits. At this time of year, every day between four and four-thirty, the sun reflected off the large steeple-cross made of bronze forged from abandoned French cannons and placed there by citizens some time after Napoleon's hordes had come and sacked the city. According to family documents they'd hung the commander of the garrison, Major Ambrosius Herzog, a brother of her great-great-grandfather, by his thumbs from wires above the market square where he died in stoic silence and was left hanging there until his thumbs rotted off and he fell down.

In the living room the visitors sat in their loden mountain clothes and in their city finery. The men turned their hats in their hands and the women turned their rings while she carried the conversation in her strong and formal way. She offered Marsala wine and Cinzano and Earl Grey tea in the good Dresden pot with the butterfly pattern, and she offered biscotti and coconut kisses that tasted of the doillied tins she stored them in.

By the end of that customary week of visiting these same people had stolen all of her husband's war decorations. Gone were his two Iron Crosses, the War Merit Cross, and the various Close Combat and Wound Badges; even his Knight's Cross was gone, the one that the famous general had presented to him in person. They'd also stolen the tank badge from the Afrika Korps, and the silver Edelweiss from the First Alpine Division. They had not seen the Walther pistol because she kept it locked away, but they'd taken his officer's dress sidearm, the foot-long dagger with the ivory handle and silver tassel.

With some of them she'd left the room on a pretence and then watched through the crack between door and frame to see them rise on tiptoes and grin at their wives and put a finger to their lips. They'd opened the glass front of the bookcase and reached in to unpin the piece they coveted, these boy-men from his own family.

She understood that they were after his courage and his eventful life, as if by stealing these bits of tin they could make what they stood for their own, these people who had never done a thing more dangerous than eat with knife and fork. It was interesting to her that those who had snickered at him the most during his life had also stolen the highest decorations.

She thought of it as his final test of them, their chance at redemption, and she kept track of it all not only in her journal, but also in the letters she left for him on his pillow: pages written in blue ink and folded around dried leaves of lavender from the pouches in her linen drawer. On the outside of the sealed envelopes she wrote, *"For you, my Love. Clara."* At first she wrote him a letter nearly every day. As time went by she wrote less often, but never less than twice a week. Her daughters collected the letters like discreet mail carriers and put them away unopened in a shoebox.

Eventually Willa's time was up. The cast on her arm had been removed at the clinic, and she had to fly back to her camels in Australia. On the morning of her departure there was a freezing rain falling, and to see Willa off Clara put on a coat and the black hat with the wide brim. Emma had come, and the three of them walked down the stairs and then slowly on the slippery ground around the house to the front where the taxi stood waiting. The rear door was frozen shut and the driver came around and yanked it open.

"There," he said and stepped back. Willa kissed her mother and Emma, and she wiped her own cheeks with the inside of her wrist, still the same motion she'd made as a little girl.

"Come back soon," said Clara to her. "When do you think we'll see you again?"

"Not sure. I'll do my best. There's often a conference somewhere in Europe or East Africa."

Emma stood stiffly and Willa studied her for a moment, then she reached out and gave her sister another hug.

Finally there was just the harsh sound of the diesel engine under load and Willa's face in the rear window as the car pulled away. The freezing rain had begun to turn to snow.

"Mom," said Emma. "Can I ask? Have you spoken to them, at the museum?"

"About Tom? Not yet. There hasn't been a good moment."

"Just to give him a try, that's all he's asking."

"I know."

Emma stood waiting. "I should go," she said then. "Mark some papers. I'm filling in this week at the college."

"Oh good, Emma. That's good. I know you like that. And thanks for all your help."

They embraced and she stood for a moment and watched Emma walk away, careful on the slippery ground. Emma looked back over her shoulder once and raised a hand in a small motion, then carried on.

TWO

SHE WALKED SLOWLY back around the side of the house, holding on to the rough wall and to spars of the trellis where the last brown leaves of clematis clung to vines.

She stood for a moment and held out her hand to let snowflakes settle on the glove, on the stitched ridges in the black leather and on her fingers as they moved.

Look, she said to him. Snow. The girls were here. But you know that.

She was going to go upstairs but now changed her mind and continued along the garden path, around the house, past the roses with their heads buried in piles of leaves, past the bare apple trees, the bare gooseberry bushes. The wall of the neighbour's house showed yellow through the evergreens. *The garden is mourning,* she quoted Hermann Hesse for him. *And golden drips leaf upon leaf down from the tall Acacia tree.*

The day we met, she said. Was there snow then too? I can't quite remember.

She did not think so, because of the motorcycle and the way they were dressed. She reached and touched a last gooseberry still dangling, and left it there.

I thank you for everything, she said to him. I am so very grateful.

She stood a moment and looked around, then turned back and entered the house and climbed the stone stairs.

On a landing she paused to catch her breath. No, she decided. No snow that night, but quite cold. She remembered that. And Mitzi was along. Evening clothes; she and Mitzi in long gowns, silver opera wraps and peacock feather hats; he in a classic black dinner suit with white tie and stiff stand-up collar. Over it he wore an old leather army coat, a thing cracked with age and split at the seams. Mitzi sat in the motorcycle sidecar that was shaped like a rocket, with her feather hat in her lap, clutching the handrail like a child on a roller coaster. And she herself sat on the pillion seat and held on to him with both hands, her own feather hat wedged against his back. Her teeth were chattering with the noise and the bumpy ride, but she remembered grinning at Mitzi and shouting from sheer wild exuberance.

Late October it was, 1932. In the parks they passed, under monuments to glories and to famous men long gone, the homeless were sleeping in piles of fall leaves, great clusters of leaves, entire families huddled together, lost voices in the dark. A militia truck cruised with dimmed lights; a gang in the pay of some warlord on the prowl for other gangs of other warlords, pale young men huddling on the truck beds with clubs and iron lances pried from picket fences as their weapons. The motorcycle roared past them, with her and Mitzi in their bright outfits like Valkyries flying through the night, and the militia boys' faces turned in unison as if pulled on a string.

The black Norton boomed past all this, past the State Opera House and past the famous hotels lit like spaceships with their doormen in frogged coats, then a right turn off Schubertring and a few more quick turns, rattling on the cobbles, and there was the entrance to the building on Beatrixgasse where she and her other best friend Erika were sharing a flat. Mitzi had a garçonnière of her own on the uppermost floor.

It was three o'clock in the morning. With the Norton shut off, they could hear the hour bell from St. Stephen's.

"And who is he?" her mother said the next day on the telephone at the post office. "Countess Melltrop saw you and she called me. You even left with him, you and the hairdresser. And on a motorcycle!"

"That was Mitzi. You know her. How many best friends do I have? Her and Erika. Mitzi was booked for the evening to look after the singer's hair and makeup, and she brought me along."

"And the boy?"

"*Boy?* He's twenty-six."

"Who is he?"

"He's a captain in the reserve cavalry. Someone we met at our table. He's nice and interesting. His mother was the accompanist for the soprano."

Silence on the telephone. Then, "I thought you didn't like soldiers."

"Not usually. I think he's different. We'll see."

"Different, how?"

"He just is. For one thing he's an officer, from a good family. He listens and thinks before he talks."

"Talks about what?"

"*Mother*," she said.

"All right. Never mind."

"And he's a good dancer. It was fun. You could see how lavishly those monarchs used to live. Gold and velvet everywhere, room after room, and dozens of servants with trays of champagne and canapés. And so many men in fat cummerbunds and ramrods up their asses—"

"Clara," said her mother.

"Well it's true. Even now, in these times. The poverty in Vienna, Mom. Erika is working the parks for the Red Cross, and you should hear her stories."

"You're supposed to be studying. Not spending all night on motorcycles with strange soldiers. Soldiers! And you wore next to nothing, said the countess."

"Don't listen to her. And I *am* studying. I am doing very well. You'll see. If I can, I'll come home on the weekend."

———

SHE DID NOT go home that weekend, nor the next few thereafter. Instead, when her studies and work on the various papers allowed, she went for drives with Albert, for picnics on a blanket on the hard ground under flaming trees, with leaves drifting down. At a store in the first district she spent far too much money on a picnic hamper of wicker with leather corners, like a small suitcase. It was made in England, and it came complete with good porcelain and cutlery and cups and glasses all buckled into compartments.

Sometimes Mitzi came along, or Erika, or his younger brother, Theodor, but more often it was just her and him on the black Norton rattling through the hills around Vienna and through echoing city streets like carefree vagabonds, talking to each other over his shoulder, laughing. It was pure happiness, pure exuberance; pure beingness, she tried to explain to her mother. Wait till you meet him, she said on the telephone.

"What happened to the law student?" said her mother. "The Heller boy. He seemed nice and polite."

"He was. Then I met this one."

"A dragoon on a motorcycle."

"Mother! Just leave it. Wait till you meet him."

The difference with Albert was that with him she felt intensely alive and completely able to be herself. Alive and a touch guilty at times being so happy among the troubles and the poverty and the growing numbers of homeless living under bridges and in the parks. Flying past it all on the black machine piloted by this man in a leather great-coat and aviator goggles, past ancient buildings with green copper roofs and Gothic fronts, and late-blooming roses in the parks still scenting the air.

"MY CAREER AMBITION?" she said to him one day in the palm house at Schönbrunn. It was winter by then, their first. They sat among tropical plants on a white cast-iron bench while small yellow and red birds flitted among palm fronds.

"I am going to be a teacher and a writer," she told him. "That and perhaps a literary translator also."

"A teacher?"

"Yes. A good one." She told him about Mrs. Allmeier, who so long ago had drawn her out of her cave in junior high. Who had given her the courage to stand up and speak, who had been the first to take her ideas seriously and had shown her how to pursue them in linear ways, and when to keep pursuing them and when to drop them.

That kind of teacher, she told him. And a writer, if possible. Her grandfather had been one, she said. And her father had just published a work on the last days of Pompeii. He was an archaeologist and museum director.

In any case, she wanted to be someone following her interests and living by her mind. A portable career that would allow her to have a family also.

She had no doubt whatsoever saying those things. It was what she would do.

They sat with their wool coats open, small puddles forming around their winter boots on the tile floor. Two yellow birds had hopped close to sip from those puddles. It was a Sunday, and they'd walked along Elisabethallee, down Maxingstrasse, and into the park by the west gate. It was snowing. Beyond the glass walls large flakes settled slowly. There was no wind whatsoever.

THE REST OF HER WORLD was ideas then. Ideas of politics hotly debated at the league meetings: Zionism, Communism, Capitalism, National Socialism. And not to forget the importance of other -isms, such as Atheism and Existentialism, that opened one-way doors into the world to come. Fascinating doors that lured you and then snapped shut behind you, and there could be no going back ever.

One of her professors was Dr. Sigmund Freud. He came only when it pleased him, and then he strode the dais in his spats and vested suits, waving a cold cigar and thinking out loud, like a man alone in his study. He followed no lesson plan, no book, no notes; *investigations*, he called his lectures, thoughts on psychology as it related to society and to issues between men and women.

Ludwig Wittgenstein travelled from Cambridge to teach logic and the philosophy of language and the mind. Unforgiving and cynical he was, and he used his intelligence like a sharp knife to slice away unreason and non sequitur and leave nothing other than fact and truth as he saw it. And like a gift for life he gave them his trademark phrase that on things on which there was nothing to be said, one had best say nothing.

"Why?" he asked. "*Why?*" And smiled when the class sat in silence. Wittgenstein moments, they called them. Moments beyond words.

None less than the archbishop's senior adviser gave lectures on the role of Christianity in western art and civilization, and Martin Heidegger came for a period of time, because he liked Vienna, he told the class. He taught Greek philosophy, the philosophy of thought itself and his own concepts of Existentialism.

Once, after a lecture Heidegger had given on *Thrownness*, she saw him sitting on a bench in Resselpark. He looked lost and alone, with not even pigeons at his feet. During the lecture someone had asked him about suicide and he had replied that, while it was a completely acceptable way out and perhaps the only serious question to ponder, it too was completely futile. He stepped to the blackboard and drew a mountain cliff and a stick-figure standing at the edge.

He pointed at the cliff and said, "You leap off whether you want to or not. Thrownness, yes? At the moment of birth, as we've said. Life is an involuntary leap into existence, and by the time you are conscious, you know that all this is rather pointless and will end in oblivion. There is no other possibility. So why then cut your throat halfway down? Why not just wait and enjoy the fall. There must be something interesting along the way. The view, perhaps. The flowers passing, designs in the rockface as you fall. A kiss from some stranger."

He looked away from the class to the drawing and with his thumb wiped away the stick figure and drew a new one in mid-air halfway and head first down the cliff.

"Knowing that may help," he said. "Help with what? Well, with making a game out of it. A game. Something to take your mind off the inherent randomness and pointlessness of the entire thing itself. A project, a coming-to-yourself, being in control of yourself as you plunge, which is the only way to survive. We must live as if life mattered, so to speak."

Heidegger said that it could be seen from this that if Falling Man allowed himself to be distracted by the pointlessness and terminus of his falling, by the anxiety it caused, he would then miss all the fun and all the diversions available along the way.

"Like that kiss from a stranger," he said. "So let's call it As-ifness. To live as if things mattered. Every action, every thought, every word. Without it, we are nothing. *As-ifness.* We'll be talking a lot about that."

But that day in the park he was sitting alone on a bench, looking lost, looking like a fired salesman in an ill-fitting suit, when he could have played his As-if game and made the effort to walk a few steps to the flowerbeds and smell the roses. She stood watching from across the street, stood trying to learn from him while the sun moved an inch in the sky and cars and trucks passed noisily between her and him. Since he was the master, this image she knew must contain something for her to understand and learn from. But she did not understand. Not then.

As it turned out, Martin Heidegger could not complete the lecture series on *Thrownness* and *Beingness* he had planned. The government declared National Socialism illegal, and the university fathers found out about Heidegger's outspoken support of some of the thinking in the party. First he was banned from Vienna University, then he was banned even from crossing the border into Austria.

He was replaced by Dr. Roland Martin Emmerich, a middle-aged professor in workingmen's clothes with bicycle clips on his trouserlegs and shirts without collars. But he had two Ph.Ds and he was brilliant. He taught Søren Kierkegaard in the German translation of his work called *Existenzphilosophie*; he taught Edmund Husserl and Friedrich Nietzsche, and he spun out their ideas until they rang like bells in the auditorium. His lectures turned the crowded hall into something like an isolation chamber within a society still lost in the wreckage of the monarchy and looking to tradition and religion for support.

"It's all so very interesting," she said to Albert. "So . . . *liberating*, that's it! The freedom to think that way. It's fantastic."

It was the first time in her life that she heard a full and tenured university professor speak out loud the notion that God and all scriptures relating to Him might in fact be mere invention in the face of our own irrelevance.

"A mere romantic fiction," Professor Emmerich said to them. "A human wish and yearning in our blundering search for meaning and structure and guidance. Think about it."

She learned that the idea of God, in Nietzsche's terms, had for centuries provided moral structure and rules on how to live responsibly. Now, in the Godless world coming to western society, the meaning in everyone's life was that person's own interpretation. As was the morality of all choices and actions.

It was both liberation and obligation, because Nietzsche had also cautioned, and Heidegger and Husserl said more or less the same thing, that men and women by declaring the idea of God to be a fervent wish at best, a cry for help, had perhaps run themselves off the rails and had doomed themselves spiritually. They had doomed themselves either to hopelessness or to an everlasting effort to rise above their fears and weakness, to become an Übermensch and find other forms of meaning. They had blithely shouldered a responsibility that had theretofore been entrusted to God.

THEN, SOMEWHERE along the course of her philosophy studies, something happened to her. This was not until the Emergency and the night they found the bodies of Mr. and Mrs. Rosenberg on the sidewalk, but as though knowledge had gradually settled into her bones, she came to understand without a doubt that ideas could be firm structures for intellectual and moral support. For survival. From this insight it was not a long step to the thought that moments of inspiration and courage had to be seized and anchored in some form of principle, in a certain inner attitude, if only so that they might be recalled in days of darkness. It was a thought that stayed with her and grew even when unattended, the way certain plants grow best in dim light and without tampering.

"Principles of attitude," Professor Emmerich said when she mentioned it to him. "Not a bad idea, Miss Herzog. Not altogether new, but with lots of work still to be done." This was during one of his open-door sessions, and she and he sat in the unravelling wicker chairs in his office and the note was hung from the door lintel telling other students to wait.

"See where you can take it," he said. "Let it condense, but stay with it. Support it with first-hand insight and with scenes from literature. Look at Yeats, look at Goethe, definitely look at Hesse. Look at Thoreau. Circle it for a while. Talk to me again in six months or so."

The image of Martin Heidegger on his park bench had stayed with her, and eventually she understood it to be telling her that even an existential genius could feel lost at times, could indulge in the sweet sinking feeling, the being-sunk feeling, and that this was all right as long as one had the inner resources to raise oneself up again and climb out of the hole. Like exercising some kind of mental muscle, she wrote in reminders to herself. In any case, once a person had opened the door to the primary existentialist notions of self-determination, accountability, and the life-line of As-ifness, that door could never be closed again.

Fired on by a sense of breakthrough, she enrolled in additional courses in literature. Under Professor Anton Ferdinand she studied the Russian and the American novel for full-blooded characters forced to make difficult choices under pressure. With her friends Mitzi and Erika, and with Albert, she went to readings at the American embassy by authors such as Ernest Hemingway and William Faulkner. And one Sunday in the fall she and Albert took the train all the way to Salzburg to attend a reading by Stefan Zweig. After the reading she stood in line and then asked him to sign a copy of her favourite novel of his, *Twenty-Four Hours in the Life of a Woman*. He reached and took the book from her, and he asked her name.

She told him.

"You like this?"

"Very much. It's so true."

"True?" He looked into the distance for a moment, then he bent over the book. She could see the top of his head, his scalp in the straight part in his hair; his neck in the snow-white shirt collar. He ran the blotter over his writing, closed the book, and handed it to her.

He was smiling. He had kind brown eyes and a moustache, and he looked pale, but there was something else in his smile or perhaps in the way he looked at her and then briefly around at the people in the café; the full tables and the people lining up for his autograph and a word from him; a sadness, she thought, a solitariness even in the midst of so much admiration; a darkness that she could not forget for the next several days.

Eventually she did, and when he and his wife killed themselves years later in Brazil the terror was already everywhere and it was unspeakable but nothing could be taken back.

"For Clara Eugenie," Stefan Zweig had written. *"We have art in order not to die of the truth (Nietzsche)."* And he had signed his name.

THREE

❖

IN HIS WILL Albert had left everything to her, to use as she saw fit. There was a bit of money, and she had the bank transfer twenty-five thousand euros to Willa and she wrote a cheque in the same amount for Emma.

Willa called on Skype from Australia. "You didn't have to do that," she said. "Sending the money. But thank you."

"You're welcome. Spend it. Enjoy it."

"I will. Now, about the Knight's Cross. You mentioned it in your email, so tell me. Who took it?"

"Forget the Knight's Cross. I shouldn't have mentioned it."

"I don't want to forget it. Who took it, Mom? One of Emma's kids?"

"Willa. Let it go."

"I won't. Do you know how few of those they awarded? It's up there with the Victoria Cross and the Congressional

[25]

Medal of Honor. Apart from that it's worth a fortune on eBay."

"I know you are joking. You can't sell those things on eBay because of the swastika on them."

"Well. The *thing*, as you call it, has a history. It was the one medal Dad valued, and you know why. Because of who gave it to him."

"I know that," she said. "But your dad would not want you to cause trouble over it."

"Or maybe he would. One day I'll find out who took it and I'll ask for it back. Was it the snarky one with the tattoo?"

"Willa-dear," she said. "It doesn't matter." There was a silence into which she said, "Willa? I'm fine. There is no need for you to stand up for me. Or for your dad. Really. I miss him of course, and I know you do too." She sat back in the chair and tightened the Sellotape on the microphone, which was a thing of inferior plastic that had broken on the first day.

"Willa," she said. "You have your love of animals from him, you know that. I don't know why I'm saying that." She listened. "Willa . . ." she said gently. "Willa-dear . . ." and she paused and then did not know what more to say.

Next day in the late afternoon, when it was getting dark already and she had turned on the lights in her study, Emma came by to pick up the cheque. Her husband, Tomas, had come along, and Clara made tea for them and she held on to Emma's shoulder as she climbed the chair to bring a fresh tin of Mitzi's raisin cookies down from the kitchen cupboard.

They sat in the living room under the tasselled lampshade and Emma poured tea and talked about school. Tomas sat eyeing the envelope with Emma's name on it, and when tea had been poured and he had munched the first cookie, he reached for the envelope and opened it with the handle of his teaspoon. He took out the cheque and read the amount. He put the cheque back and pushed the envelope with two fingers across the tablecloth toward Emma. Emma blushed. She indicated his mouth and he brushed away a cookie crumb.

"Did Willa get the same?" he said.

"Yes. Why do you ask?"

"Just curious."

"That's all there is, Tom. For now." She did not dislike him, not exactly, but she'd liked Emma's first husband better. As had Emma, she knew. Claude had been a pilot with Air France, and he'd been fun and intelligent, but then something had gone wrong in the marriage. Emma had moved back to St. Töllden and she'd met Tom, a widower with two children. They had three more. He took early retirement when his accounting firm closed over some lawsuit, and he'd been looking for part-time work ever since.

"That's all right," he said. "The amount. We appreciate any help you can give. Thank you. Did you speak to them at the museum?"

"No. Not yet, Tom. I'll wait until they've come to pick up the boxes. There'll be a natural opportunity then."

"There must be something I can do there."

"I don't know. They probably have an accountant already."

"Their archives, maybe. The sooner, the better, Clara. A small favour."

"People study for that line of work, Tom. It is special. They have degrees. Art history, archaeology, library arts. Maybe there are courses you could take to get some kind of qualification. Even just as an archivist."

"Maybe," he said. "Just ask them."

"I said I would."

And Emma, sweet and unlucky Emma trapped here between mother and husband, said, "It's getting dark so early these days. Look at that sky. Tommy, maybe we should go soon."

After they had left, and after she'd cleared away the tea things, the lawyer called.

"Doctor Herzog," he said. "Did your husband leave a firearm of any kind? There's none licensed to him, but you never know. They'll need a declaration from you."

She sat down on the chair by the telephone. "A firearm? Like a rifle?"

"Or a pistol. Any kind of gun. Is there a gun in the house?"

"Not that I know," she said.

"Wouldn't you know if there was one? It would have to

be kept secure, like trigger-locked and in some kind of gun safe. They are strict about that now."

"There isn't one. No gun," she said.

"Good. I'll send a messenger with the form. Please sign it and send it right back."

The form arrived and she stood at the bottom of the stairs in the freezing lobby and read it. The messenger was a young woman in tight clothing and a red bicycle helmet with blue-black bangs sticking out. "I'll shoot it right back," she said and did a clicking little dance step in her cycle shoes.

"It's already dark out there," said Clara. "Be careful. It might be slippery."

"It's nothing," said the girl. "And I've got flashing lights front and back."

Clara signed her name in the box where in bold letters it cautioned her not to make a false statement or risk a penitentiary sentence of seven years. She wondered if that was the biblical seven years, meaning forever.

Because the gun was there of course. The Walther. Upstairs, once she had her breath back, she went to check on it, just to make sure. It was on a shelf at the back in the linen closet, stripped and oiled and the pieces wrapped in cloth and zipped into freezer baggies. Barrel, slide, the cross-hatched walnut grip and magazine, and a box half full of shells.

She would have to find a way to dispose of it. Which was just as well. It was time.

FOUR

✦

IN THE EARLY 1930s they would drink cheap wine and sing student songs like "Gaudeamus Igitur." They'd burn candles and argue sometimes half the night about the best form of government to return dignity and well-being to the nation. Looking back, it made her cringe at how naive and touchingly earnest they'd been, all of them: Monarchists, Jews, Communists, National Socialists.

The Monarchists wanted to roll back history to the way things had been before 1914, as if such a thing were possible. The Communists wanted workers to be in control of all means of production; as the saying went, they wanted not just bread, they wanted the bakery.

The Jews of the Zionist League promised peace and equality, and a society based on reason and spiritual values, like the one they envisioned for Palestine. They did not expect ever to be able to form a government in Vienna, but if they received enough votes they could certainly influence one.

And the National Socialists, whom everyone simply called Nazis because their full name was such a mouthful, promised work and dignity, the two things at the top of everyone's wish list. They had a plan, they said. They pointed north across the border where Hitler's work-creation projects after years of runaway inflation and economic depression were instilling a new pride in people and putting money in their pockets.

So popular did the Nazis and the Communists become with the public that on March 7, 1933, the government in Vienna under Chancellor Engelbert Dollfuss evoked Emergency Rule and threatened to outlaw them. Police raided their meetings and took everyone away in crowded paddy wagons. In the morning police clerks wrote down their particulars, gave them a warning, and let them go.

ALL THE FIRST WEEK of the Emergency it snowed, and it snowed worse in the west of the country. In her hometown of St. Töllden avalanches thundered down the mountain into the valley and one of them blocked the main road from the east. Since the army was busy enforcing the Emergency the road remained blocked for six days and nights, her mother said on the telephone, until locals could make their way through the snow with shovels and horse-drawn carriages.

On the Sunday following she met Peter at Fröhlich's in the first district. Soldiers and police were in the streets, checking cars and pedestrians at random. It was the end of March but still cold and some side streets were impassable with heavy snow.

Peter had arrived before her and when he saw her he stood up and waved. The place was full, and in the salon through connecting doors a violinist and a pianist were playing the inevitable Strauss. She hung up her coat and scarf on a stand and gave him a peck on the cheek.

"Clara," he said. "Have you heard from home?"

She told him what her mother had said on the telephone. They were fine.

"Oh good. I was away in Paris and London."

"For the League?"

"Yes. Everyone's worried about Berlin, and now about the dismissal of parliament here. I'm supposed to be seeing Chancellor Dollfuss tomorrow."

"He shouldn't outlaw those parties. It will only make them stronger."

"Probably."

A waitress came and took their orders. Peter asked for coffee and she ordered hot chocolate.

She grinned at him. "They have the best here. You should try it."

"Maybe next time. What's new? Last time I spoke to our mother she said you're doing well at school. And you have Heidegger and Wittgenstein. That's fantastic!"

"I know. We even have Freud, on a good day."

"And? Come on, let's have it. I hear you're not seeing the Heller boy any more."

"Not really. I'm too busy."

He sat watching her. He smiled. "Too busy. You're blushing. Who is it?"

"Who's who?"

"Come on. What's his name?"

"Stop it, Peter. I'll tell you when I'm ready."

"All right. Did you know any of the students who got arrested? You weren't among them, I hope."

"No. But I do know quite a few of them. If they're outlawed they'll just meet in private homes. It certainly won't stop them."

The coffee came, and the hot chocolate. She made a hole with the spoon in the whipped cream and took a sip of chocolate through the hole.

She held out the cup. "So good. Taste it."

He shook his head. "No thanks. I was thinking, Clara. You should probably keep a journal. In a year or two it'll be all very different. You'll look around and wonder what happened."

"Albert said that too."

"Albert?"

"Oh, all right. You win. His name is Albert. He says this is a groundswell and at university I have a front-row seat and afterwards it's always just a blur."

"He is right. And don't you get caught too. Don't

get a police record. A police record never goes away."

Peter went on to talk about the Reichstag fire in Berlin that Hitler had used to stage his coup. "They all use some sort of excuse. Some sort of phoney emergency and over-night instead of a democracy we have a dictatorship."

She sat holding the warm cup with both hands, listening and thinking and studying him up close. Scrubbed and neat, her big brother in a dark blazer and striped tie. He was fifteen years older than she and his degrees in inter-national law had earned him an enviable job with the League of Nations. He had never steered her wrong.

"I'll think about it," she said. "Keeping notes, I mean. But I'm pretty busy right now."

They sipped from their cups. She caught the violinist winking at her. Out the windows it was snowing. A police car stopped and men in coats and wide-brimmed hats jumped out and arrested a man and a woman on the side-walk. The woman was carrying an umbrella and in the strug-gle it collapsed and broke, and as the policemen were pushing her into the car she beat on them with the wreckage.

"You see?" said Peter. "Even if the Emergency law is contested, they can do whatever they want while it lasts. That's why they evoke it. Your Albert sounds sensible. What's his last name? Maybe I know the family."

"Leonhardt. His father is an estate manager and his mother a pianist. A coach for opera singers."

"I don't think I know them. Bring him around for dinner sometime. What does he do?"

"He is a captain in the cavalry."

"A loyalist. Good. Let's meet him."

In the weeks to follow she called Peter on two occasions. Once, his wife, Daniela, picked up and said he was out of the country, the other time the telephone just rang and rang.

THAT SUMMER Albert competed in a military equestrian event, representing his unit, the 3rd Dragoon Regiment. He won gold in cross-country, ahead of a French major and a German lieutenant. There was a celebration at his parents' apartment in Vienna, and a day later she took him home to St. Töllden, for the first time.

They travelled by train south past fields of wheat and rye, and past ancient farmhouses with thatched roofs and storks' nests on high platforms erected for this purpose. Through the open coach window they could smell the ripening grain and the summer heat on grass and earth. They saw flocks of birds swooping in formations that opened up and regrouped and settled and took flight again. The sun felt warm on her face, and warm on the grainy wood of the folding table by the window; it shone on his bare forearms and on his hands. Through the open window they could smell the hot coal smoke of the train engine.

She was so much in love, all she had to do was look at him and a smile came to her face, and wild hope and gratitude to her heart. His hands, his face, the way he was looking at her. He made her feel loved and cherished, and secure, and of course she took it for granted that her parents would see all that, and accept him and like him too.

But the visit did not go well, and afterwards she would puzzle about it and examine it moment by moment, situation by situation.

"It was so strange," she said to Erika back in Vienna. "Father tried, he really did. He took us to the new Roman dig and we all had dinner and went for a walk, but something felt wrong the whole time. It was mother. I asked her what was wrong and she said only that she had a migraine."

"Isn't that possible?"

"She hasn't had a migraine in years. Well I don't know, but I think it was just an excuse. She was so strange with Albert. Even more reserved than usual. Distant with him, with all of us, and that big straw hat she wore on the walk. You should have seen the way she looked at him from under the brim. Watching him. What was she thinking?"

The answer arrived in Vienna only three days later in a letter written in her mother's hand, the precise and slanted writing the old people called Corinth.

I am sorry if I seemed out of sorts on the weekend, Clara-dear. I'll try to explain, and I'll come straight to the point. I can see how much you love this man and I am happy for you. But I look into his eyes and I am afraid. I will say it just this time and then no more.

Wild men, Clara, bold and dashing men, beware of

them. I know only too well the terrible attraction they can have for a woman. There is something primal about it, something of the cave. A woman sees in his wildness a readiness to defend her and her offspring. She also senses an opportunity through him to go places, and even if they are only places in the heart, they are places she would never tread alone. His wildness makes her feel safe and so very alive; all the more so if the basic man-woman attraction between them is working well, and if his wildness is expressed also in the way in which he desires her. I know you two have this; one can feel it. It is important. It is to a marriage and to a family what a locomotive is to a train, and so I am happy for you.

Your father would faint if he read this, but I know he won't. We are grown women and you know what I mean. You probably also know where my fear comes from. It comes from your brothers' father, of course, my Torben. I know I've avoided talking about him, and perhaps one day I will tell you more. Men like these— Clara, their wildness is so very dangerous because even as their love sweeps us away, these men are also prone to excessive risk-taking and most often the possible gain is not worth the risk. It may be to them, just as Russian roulette seems a worthwhile risk to some in the moment of passion, or a duel for nothing more than a slight. Honour, my God! Clara-dear, men can be such children.

Your Albert; I look at him, I look into his eyes and at his bearing and the tilt of his chin, and I see my

Torben. I recognize what it is that drives these sorts of men. I feel I do, so help me God. But then I can also see and feel your love for each other, and so there is nothing more I'll say on this matter, other than that I wish you both well. But please be careful.

My dear Clara, thank you for your visit. Your father and I are proud that you are doing so well in your studies, and we send our love as always. Mama.

And on a separate page in the same envelope, her father, whose love for her was the purest certainty in her life, wrote:

My dear Clara, I liked your Albert but I hope you will not be neglecting your studies on account of him, and not be rushing into any sort of commitment. Learning sets us free, Clara. It makes us strong and gives us purpose and self-assurance. In any case we must follow both our hearts and our minds. And even if the heart is usually the winner, we must nevertheless weigh them both carefully. You will do the right thing in this situation, of that I have no doubt. I send you my love. Papa.

She showed the letter to Erika, who had known her parents since public school. This was at the apartment on Beatrixgasse, at the end of a weekday with the sky going dark and lights coming on in the city and the windows wide open to let in the cool air.

Erika handed it back with a smile and a shrug, and returned to the kitchen where she soon rattled around in drawers and began scrambling eggs for dinner.

"Is the wild man coming to eat?" she shouted from there.

"No," Clara shouted back. "He's on the horse farm."

She reread the letter, folded it, and slipped it back into the envelope. She took it to her bedroom and put it away in a drawer.

"Are you going to show it to him?" shouted Erika.

She pretended not to hear.

FIVE

❖

THE EMERGENCY CONTINUED but it lost its novelty. In June that year Communists and Nazis had been outlawed, but they thrived underground and the militia was soon back in the streets. Robberies and holdups became common events. In their nighttime shelters in parks and under bridges the homeless had to fear organized gangs swarming them to steal their clothes. Since the bank failures, men in suits and women in good dresses and coats were among the homeless, and always there were those who had even less.

She knew about these developments from Erika. Erika was studying for a degree in Social Sciences, and for an extra credit she worked the streets for the Red Cross by night in a small grey Steyr motorcar that she would borrow from Mitzi and then return in the morning.

Because people's hair keeps growing in times good or

bad, Mitzi's business was doing well; she had given up the shop so as to save the rent money and now she was making house calls. In the evenings the baskets with the collapsible dryer hood and dyes and combs and clippers and towels were replaced with baskets of sandwiches and containers of drinking water, and with first-aid bandages and small brown bottles of iodine all from the Red Cross depot at Hütteldorf.

To help out and to see for herself, Clara on many nights would cruise the streets with Erika. They'd bring cotton blankets and food to families living under bridges; they'd patch wounds and brush iodine on lacerations. One night in early December they came upon two bodies on a sidewalk not far from their own building; a man and a woman, both old and their blood still spreading on the pavement. Moments earlier a delivery van had squealed away into the night.

"Are they dead?" she said.

Erika knelt and put her fingers to the woman's throat. She held her wrist. She let it go. "Try him."

Clara felt for the man's pulse. She put her ear to his chest but all she could hear was her own heart pounding. "I think he's dead. My God, look at the eyes."

The old people lay in the skimming headlights of the car that stood with two wheels on the sidewalk. The doors still hung open. There was hardly any traffic, and no one stopped.

"What do we do?" said Erika.

"We should call the police. You go and I'll stay."

She stood back in the house entrance, hugging herself against the cold. She leaned and peered around the corner. Her first dead. The woman's shop apron and skirt had slid up, and the veined white thighs above the stockings looked vulnerable even in death. The couple lay on the sidewalk in front of the smashed shop window, the tossed brick still in there and plain to see, and the glass raked away probably with iron bars. Empty racks showed. Second-hand clothing had been carried away through the window; a shred of something white still clung to a corner of broken glass.

They were Mr. and Mrs. Rosenberg. She could not think of the woman's first name now, but she had known them, had bought clothes in there, and sold some of her own. Mr. Rosenberg still had a small tack hammer in his hand, had probably come out swinging it, with his wife right behind him ready to poke the thieves with the spike for receipts that lay nearby.

The police car was turning the corner when she took a few steps and reached and pulled down Mrs. Rosenberg's skirt. Marianne, that was her name.

They drove on through the night, the two of them in Mitzi's little Steyr with the broken heater, shocked by what they had seen and now not knowing how to deal with it.

"We knew them," said Erika.

"We did. I bought my black suit there and the yellow summer dress."

"I know."

With strips of bandages she kept wiping the windshield where their breath kept condensing. A spot was hardly wiped when it fogged up again. A line from T. S. Eliot's *Ash-Wednesday* came to her and offered help. *Teach us to care and not to care. Teach us to sit still.* Her hands were shaking and she felt cold. "Where are we going?" she said.

Erika looked in the rear-view mirror and pulled over. "Did you see the side of her face? Mrs. Rosenberg's? The poor woman. And she could hardly walk anyway."

Erika took her hands off the wheel and with her teeth pulled off the knitted gloves, dropped them in her lap, and blew on her fingers. She spat wool fibres and pulled some off her lower lip. "Maybe we can't do this tonight. Can we?"

"We could try at least one bridge. It might help snap us out of this."

They drove on and after they'd done one bridge and handed out food and water, they decided to keep going and do a park.

NOT LONG THEREAFTER, it must have been a Friday because Friday nights were Communist nights, she and Erika and Mitzi met David Koren. Half-way through the meeting at a private home in upper-class Hietzing, a woman student stood up and introduced him as a writer and journalist, and asked him to speak.

"You're just back from a trip to Moscow," the woman said. "Tell us about it."

Koren stood up. He was tall, well dressed in a grey three-piece suit, a solid man with a pale face and dark hair parted on the side.

"It's David *Ira* Koren," he said. "I am Jewish. I was born in Hungary and I grew up here in Vienna. Now I live in Berlin. I know that Communism and National Socialism are the new dreams, but I listen to you speak of Communism, and it's like a fairy tale, this entire roomful of young people in this fine old villa that was probably worked for and paid for by someone's great-grandparents and handed down through generations of privilege. Let me tell you, you have no idea of what you're talking about."

He paused, then went on to tell them about Moscow. What he had seen was most discouraging, he said. The power games and the greed games were in full swing, and in the name of party loyalty the secret police were killing anyone they pleased. The dream of a better and more dignified life for all was just that, a dream. In the meantime, millions were starving to death on account of the famine caused by Stalin's agricultural reforms.

"Millions," said Koren. "Seven, eight, nine million. How Communist is that?"

He said he had not yet made up his mind, but the same dreamy support of an ideal was probably also true for the Zionist Jews and the National Socialists. Certainly the Nazis were doing well economically, but they were also anti-Semitic and anti-Communist. Perhaps it was just human nature, all this fear and greed, and in the end the true divisions were not along the lines of -isms but between people with or without heart and substance.

He sat down.

Erika stood up and told him he was not saying anything helpful. She said they were coming to these meetings even though it was dangerous, but she needed information to help her decide whom to support, the Communists or the Nazis. The Nazis, she said, had interesting ideas on dignity through work and the role of women, and the Communist ideas of equality and human rights were also attractive.

"But you're not addressing that," she told him across the room. "If all you can offer are half-baked generalizations, then come back when you know more. We are still idealists, and there's nothing wrong with that. We believe in some of those ideas and we are searching for solutions. Look around. What else is there?"

There was a stunned silence, which then quickly led to a heated discussion of the core ideas of Communism and how to protect them against corruption and abuse. As tempers cooled, Koren and Erika ended up sitting side by side on a couch, arguing fiercely at first but eventually arriving at some kind of agreement.

"At least, he's interesting," said Erika to her at some point during the evening. "And he has nice eyes, did you notice?"

Koren was staying at a hotel on Thaliastrasse, and the women went out of their way to drive him there. He sat hunched in the back next to Erika, cracking jokes about holding his breath because of the fumes of iodine and hair chemicals in the car.

"Well, would you rather be walking, Mr. Foreign Correspondent?" Erika said to him.

Koren said he would not.

"Just as well," said Mitzi at the wheel. "Might lose your suit and those good shoes and have to walk home in socks. Or are they taking socks too now?"

Koren laughed at that.

They were nearly there when his side of the seat caved in and the steel springs made contact with the battery terminals under the seat. Mitzi pulled over, and they all leapt out, slapping at the harsh smoke in the car. Koren reached in and pried up the seat. There was a smouldering fire among the horsehair stuffing, and they puffed and slapped it out and stood on the sidewalk while the seat cushion lay there smoking. Eventually they wedged it back in and continued with him sitting in front.

After this Koren came to Vienna several times a month. He liked Erika and she liked him. She would pick him up at the railroad station, and within a few more visits Clara made room for them in the flat while she moved up to Mitzi's and slept on the couch there.

Koren saw Clara's desk and the Adler typewriter and all the paper, and one day when she was moving out and he was moving in he said, "I've been meaning to ask you. Are you writing?"

"Well. Just notes, for now." She was pleased to see him

nod as if accepting her into a brotherhood that she very much wanted to belong to.

Koren would arrive from places such as Berlin, Palestine, and Budapest, always with the same brown leather suitcase and a small black Olympia typewriter in a fitted box covered in oilcloth. Like Albert and Peter he liked dressing in suits, sharply ironed shirts, and good English shoes.

She and Erika would go double-dating to nightclubs with Albert and Koren. She'd wear the black suit from Rosenbergs', narrowed at the waist and the skirt down to mid-calf. They'd wear small hats and high heels, and the men wore dark-blue double-breasted suits with wide lapels and striped ties. When Koren got tipsy he'd take off his jacket and roll up his sleeves and slap his big hands together and dance like that, like some bear in vest and shirtsleeves, grinning happily.

In her files there was a picture of them, taken at Mademoiselle in the second district, the four of them sitting close together at a small round table; a champagne bucket on it and the tall flutes, the women's purses and a silver table lamp. Smiles on their faces. Erika with her wavy black hair and those large steady eyes.

Here in each other's company they found a sense of completeness that was similar to the feeling she had riding the Norton with him; riding its rude noise and pounding through dark uncertain strets but together, and with an understood direction of their own.

SIX

❖

THE FIRST TIME she saw Albert's horse farm the day was rich with the colours and aromas of autumn. They'd motored there from Vienna and then stopped and climbed off the motorcycle by the white fence for the military pasture. The estate buildings were just a short distance away; barns and stables with horses poking their heads out over half-doors, all looking their way over the chewed and hard-worn sills, looking and tossing their heads with manes and halters snapping. There was a fenced-off arena at one corner of the pasture, and they walked there in the late sunlight, their shadows long before them on the orange dirt road. In roadside grasses soldierbirds trilled and flew up.

Men in stable jackets and riding boots were exercising horses in that arena, blacks and chestnuts on lunge lines, and the horses stepped precisely and rhythmically. Dust rose in small orange puffs and settled, and horses blew and high-stepped and obeyed minute motions on the line, the turn of a hand, the lowering and raising of the line.

"Would you ride one for me?" she said to him impulsively. "Please, Albert. I have yet to see you on a horse."

"Now?"

"Yes. Why not? It's beautiful out."

Albert surveyed the horses. He waved to one of the handlers, and the man came up to them, leading a black horse.

"Master Albert," he said.

"Mr. Breck, this is Miss Herzog. Mr. Breck is our stableboss."

"Young miss," said Breck and gave hardly a nod. He had short grey hair, a suntanned face with clear blue eyes, and one silver earring.

Albert ducked between the fence rails and reached for the line. "I've got her. Take the Norton, Breck, and bring us a saddle. Bring my own, the English hunter. And reins and my boots."

Albert stood close to the horse and held the line not far from the bit ring. He put his other hand on its neck.

"This is a fine horse," he said. "You won't often see a better one. She'll be shipped off to North Carolina soon. Just look at her!"

"What am I looking for?"

"Ah." He lengthened his hold, stepped back, and considered. He pointed. "Strong quarters, a deep chest and level back. She's fine-boned yet strong, tall with good proportions, a very good neck and legs. See the long face. She has Arab blood." Albert offered her the line. "Want to hold her? She'd love some of that clover by the ditch there."

Clara took a fistful of clover and ducked through the fence. The horse stepped and raised its head.

"Talk to her. Move very slowly and talk to her."

She did, and the horse calmed and soon it stood cropping the clover from her hand. Soft velvet lips brushing her skin, the eyes large and deep brown, nearly black at their depth but filled with sunlight on the surface and with her own reflection and with the vanishing line of the white fence.

The motorcycle came back and they put on saddle and reins, and unclipped the line. She held the horse while Albert pulled on the boots. He was up in the saddle in one fluid motion and moved his hands and heels just a touch and the horse turned and walked off. It quickened its pace.

"Look at him," said Breck. He glanced sideways at her and shook his head and grinned. "He can ride, the young master. See him sit that horse, and she still a bit saddle-shy." He stood holding the coiled lunge line, held it in both hands halfway up as though he'd forgotten it. She saw he had the middle finger missing on his left hand.

She watched Albert and tried to see what Breck was talking about.

"What am I looking for, Mr. Breck?"

"Just watch him sit, that's the first thing you do, young miss. Watch his back. His thighs and knees and elbows. Then watch the horse and see what he's makin' her do and try and figger out how he did that. And you won't see him move hardly at all, like she's readin' his mind. Or he hers. See how high she's holdin' her head? That's a proud horse now."

ON THE WEEKEND before Christmas 1933 she was there again, this time with Erika and Mitzi, and with David Koren. Albert's younger brother, Theodor, was there as well, but their parents were not.

There was snow on the ground and high drifts of snow lay on east-facing roofs. Men were clambering up and down those roofs, roped to chimneys, calling out, "Careful below!" and pushing off snow with long-handled wooden hay rakes.

Breck saw her and nodded. "Cold weather, young miss. Need to wear a hat."

Theodor drove the overland car out of the garage and folded back the top. He waved, and then like some sleigh party of nobility long gone they sat under blankets while he drove them on chained and studded wheels into the hills to the north field, and then down the slope and through windbreaks of trees toward the leeside paddock where the military horses were.

On the way they sipped mulled wine and schnapps from cold stone bottles, and they joked and laughed and ate open-faced sandwiches of smoked boar ham and breast of duck prepared by the kitchen staff.

Theodor looked much like Albert and he carried himself much the same way. He was wrapped in a quilted coat over jacket and leather-seated breeches, and he wore black riding boots. When the coat parted you could see he was carrying a belt knife in a leather sheath.

In the paddocks the snow had been cleared, and the horses were there, chestnuts and blacks working on lunge lines high-stepping and trotting. Theo stopped the car and pointed.

"See those two blacks over there? In the red gaiters. The third Arabian is already gone and these two will be shipped to England in a month or two. Somebody guess what they're worth."

"More than a cow," said Koren. "I have no idea."

"More than a cow is right," said Theodor. "Look at the long bone in the faces. See how they move. This is one of the few places in Europe that breeds them. The count can charge for them whatever he wants." He put the car in gear.

"What count?" said Koren.

"The count who owns it all. Some old monarchist who lives in exile in New York. In a wheelchair."

"It's too good to last," said Koren. "With what's happening in Europe now. You live like Russian nobility here, before the Bolsheviks."

"And we just work here," said Albert from the backseat.

"The Bolsheviks," said Theodor. He turned to glance at his brother.

They drove on. The car raced through snow up to the running boards while at the edge of the wood deer stood like cut-outs and watched them. Later it began to snow again. In sheepskin coats and yardhats they walked out to stock the deer-feeding stations with chestnuts and grain and hay.

Breck saw them and he waved from the barn door. He stomped snow from his boots and called, "More snow comin', Master Albert!" He pointed at the dark skies.

"I see that," said Albert. "So let's cut back on the oat feed and get the shovellers lined up for tomorrow. I want the main paths and all access to buildings kept clear around the clock. And tell the men to use the red lifter and dump the snow behind the north shed where it'll run off downhill."

THAT SUNDAY NIGHT they took the Daimler to a Nazi meeting at a house in the outskirts of Vienna. Theo had guaranteed that there would be no police, and that he could get them in. It was a special meeting. Very interesting, he said. A woman speaker from Germany.

Grim-faced security men stood at both ends of the street, and more patted them down for concealed weapons before they were allowed in.

The meeting took place in the living room and adjoining dining room of a large home. People stood on the stairs and on the landing and craned their necks to see. A slight young woman in a long black skirt and white blouse was in charge. On her blouse, like a brooch, she wore the round party pin with the swastika. She stood against a glass-fronted bookcase, and she gave a report on the economic and social progress across the border in Germany.

While in Austria the government was unable to do anything other than cling to power with force, she told them, the jobs created in Germany were in the millions now; in road construction, in hydro-electric power generation, in home construction, in agriculture, in cars and machinery, and in armaments.

Especially now, with the Communists there defeated, she said, the economy would be improving ever more rapidly. She spoke of a new pride to wipe out the insult of Versailles. And she spoke of a new and important role for women to help form a kinder society. A society where family values came first, where social insurance and health care were available to all. She spoke of hope and dignity; of change, and of a fair distribution of resources and work among men and women; and of financial well-being.

"You are outlawed here in this country because your government is afraid of you. Its politicians and supporters want to cling to power and privilege," she said. "You may have been forced underground for now, but in a way that only makes you stronger. Now you can grow and prepare, away from public scrutiny. We are ready to help you. Have no doubt; you will be forming the next government."

She spoke well, in clear and measured sentences, for half an hour. Then she introduced a man by the name of Seyss-Inquart as the new leader of the Austrian National Socialist Party. It would be his job to prepare the takeover, she said.

Back outside Koren was subdued. He admitted that their platform sounded good. "Too good," he said. "Afterwards, when they're in power they can do whatever they want. I should have stood up and asked her if the Jews are next, now that the Communists are defeated."

"We wouldn't have to adopt all their policies," said Erika. "Just the ones we want."

Koren put his arm around her shoulder. "Really?"

"Well, we wouldn't. In any case I don't think they'll get in. And if they do and then don't deliver, we'll just throw them out at the next election."

At the Daimler Theo wiped snow off the windshield, unlocked the vehicle, and leaned across to open the passenger door.

"But I did like that young woman," Clara said. She moved over in the backseat to make room for Albert. "A woman spokesman. Nobody else has an agenda that includes women."

"She was good," admitted Koren. "I'm glad we came. I can write about that. A moody setting. All those people and that blond little slip of a woman holding their attention."

"And did you hear what she said about Versailles?" said Theo. "Why don't we stand up and do something too?"

"Because we signed an armistice agreement," said Albert. "Breaking it would amount to an act of war."

"Maybe that's what it takes." Theodor started the engine. "The politicians aren't the ones who are hurting. Without an opposition they can just take whatever they want. It's a dictatorship."

"It is," said Albert. "Just about. But you're not hurting too much, Theo. Are you?"

"You know what I mean."

Looking at Theodor from behind and to the side, Clara could see the angry tilt to his head, the jaw muscles working. He raised a gloved hand from the wheel and formed a gun with it. "Start at the top."

"Just drive," said Albert.

Theo felt her gaze and he looked away from the road and quickly at her over his shoulder. "What?" he said.

"Theo," said Albert. "Drive."

THE NEXT TIME they saw David Koren was in January 1934. He had come straight from Berlin. He had made up his mind, he told them: anti-Semitism was clearly on the rise and he'd be moving on. He would go and live in France or England. Maybe in America or Canada, even though it remained to be seen if Jews that weren't rich and famous were really welcome in any of those places.

"You could stay here," she said to him. "You're a writer, you can work from anywhere."

Koren shook his head. No, he couldn't, he said. No more

than he could go back to Hungary. He looked at Erika and said, "We've been having talks about that."

Erika said nothing.

"You can't go back to your childhood," said Koren. "Too many unpleasant memories. I'd shrink as a person, never mind as a writer. And then, what if the Nazis do get in?"

They sat listening; she, Erika, and Mitzi. Albert had not been able to come. They were drinking coffee on a hotel terrace near the university. Mitzi wore her white cosmetician's coat because she was helping out that day in the hotel spa. She and Erika had their books with them because an exam was coming and their heads were swimming with Arthur Schopenhauer and Rainer Maria Rilke. With an exploration of his *Sonnets to Orpheus*. And for a history paper they were living in their minds not with desperate dictators, but with men of fabulous vision and strength of character, such as those of the Convention of 1787. They were reading *We the People*, the entire text of which they were expected to know point by point.

"Another reason I'll need to move is so I can finally write the truth," said Koren. "My story on the Austrian Nazis? I queried Ullstein, and a friend took me aside and warned me off. 'You're a Jew,' he said to me. 'What are you thinking?' So that's the reality now."

He went on about party thugs and criminal elements, and they listened. They nodded. They sipped coffee. The waiter in an old black suit with a white napkin on his sleeve shuffled up once in a while and set down fresh glasses of water from a silver tray.

"I'll have to go soon," she said.

"I can tell you're not worried, Clara," said Koren. "You're hardly listening."

"Oh, I am listening."

"We're no longer thinking of the Nazis or the Communists," said Erika. "If anything, maybe we'll vote for the Social Democrats."

"Vote. Did you say *vote*?"

"Yes. There'll have to be an election at some point. But we also think we need a new party altogether; maybe that's what will come of all this. More women at the top."

"You're dreaming," said Koren.

They had in fact been talking about that, over wine by candlelight: their own political party. Women who weren't simply waiting-and-hoping but who went out and took action. Women Who Did. Women without Prince Charming.

That afternoon at the café David Koren went on to predict that, should the Communists come to power in Austria, they would ruin what was left of any economy by their inherent corruption and lack of productivity. And if the Nazis came to power, the entire country would be swallowed up by Berlin and run as a colony.

In the end only Mitzi took David Koren seriously; she and Erika did not. Not then, anyway. At the very least it would have required taking a position, and they had no real idea what that position would have to be, especially since things kept changing. Apart from that, their heads were elsewhere.

"SO IS THEO A NAZI?" she had asked Albert that snowy Sunday night after the meeting. "I mean, is he active in the party? Not just going to those meetings?"

She'd tiptoed to his room long after dinner at the horse farm. His parents were still in Vienna. From the bed they could see the window, and in the pale light of snow everywhere they could see just the outlines of furniture in the room; the desk by the window, the dresser mirror, the screen with her clothes hung over it. They could hear the wind on the roof building drifts, hard snowflakes curling down against the window glass.

"Is he?" she said sleepily. She was lying on her side, with her head on the pillow and her hand on his chest. She stirred and stuck one hot leg out from under the duvet into the cooling air.

"Well, yes. You could tell at the meeting. They let us in because they knew him."

"Isn't that dangerous for him? I think Erika is right that we shouldn't go to those meetings any more. It's not worth the risk."

"I agree. Theo confessed to me that he was arrested in those first few days of the Emergency. He was actually proud of it."

"So he shouldn't go either. Or at least not be active."

She yawned heartily. "Excuse me. What a day. What I mean is, wouldn't he get a serious sentence if they caught him a second time?"

"He won't get caught again. We had a good talk about it and I think he's learned his lesson."

They were silent for a while. "That young woman at the meeting," she said then. "I have to admit I really did like her. So cool and in control. No doubt in her mind. So focused. How do you get that way?"

"You believe. That's how. You're falling asleep." He leaned over and kissed her goodnight.

SEVEN

ON FEBRUARY 12, 1934, she and Erika were at home studying when they heard gunshots. They opened the window and leaned out trying to see what was going on. It had rained the day before, then frozen and begun to snow. Ice and snow was covering streets and roofs, and in the early morning people had put sand and fireplace ashes on sidewalks. Now gusts of wind were raising clouds of dust, and flakes of burnt paper rose high in the air.

They heard shouting somewhere and truck engines racing, and with every harsh sound pigeons rose from roofs opposite and circled and landed again. ·

"I should go and see," said Erika.

"Don't. At least wait until we know what's going on."

They closed the window and tried to ignore the noises. There were more gunshots farther away, then near again.

In the afternoon Albert came pounding up the stairs.

He took off the motorcycle coat and hung it on a peg. He took a black pistol from the coat pocket and laid it on the table.

Nazi agents had infiltrated the security forces, he told them. They had arrested some Social Democrats, who were now fighting back, organized assaults from trucks with machine guns on the back.

During that day and the next he made quick forays into the streets. He always came back within a few hours and put the pistol back on the table. Once, he slipped out the magazine and put two new shells into it. From somewhere he brought milk and bread and cheese and apples. By the end of the second day the various militia had united against the government, and army units had been mobilized.

In the apartment the radio was on all the time; not because the official news was trustworthy, but because if the government needed mounted units, Albert's dragoons might be called up.

He made her and Erika practise pointing their index fingers. "The lamp," he would call. "The door! Do it more quickly. The radio! The window on the left! The kitchen door!"

"That is how you fire a handgun," he told them. "You don't aim. You straighten your arm and point. Again. The door lock! The picture above the bed!"

He took out the magazine and ejected the shell, and he made them point the empty gun and squeeze the trigger. "The kitchen sink! The window!"

Finally he taught them how to load the gun, and to pull back the slide and feed the first shell into the chamber.

"Keep it here," he said. He looked around. "Maybe in that drawer. Hidden but close by. Keep this box of shells with it."

The battle lasted three days. When it was over, the militia had been defeated by regular police and military units. Many were dead, especially in the crowded workers' districts. Some had been executed in the streets.

The government in Vienna declared a new constitution that swept away the last pretence of democracy and the mood in the country darkened further.

A few months later, on July 25, eight men climbed the sweeping stairs of the chancellery and walked quickly along the hallways to the chancellor's office. The newspaper later said that the two security men at the door had stood aside, but old Mrs. Kaltenböck, the chief secretary, had tried to stop the men. They pushed her aside and crowded into the inner office.

Chancellor Engelbert Dollfuss was sitting at this desk, and the men took out pistols and began shooting him in the face and chest. Twenty-four bullets, according to the newspaper.

SO BEGAN the Nazi putsch of 1934. Simultaneous with the assassination in Vienna, thousands of young men and women across the country stormed provincial and municipal offices. In the south and west large groups of them fought police and Home Front units. Some of the young Nazis had firearms, and so now they were no longer mere hothead students. The police had orders to shoot to kill. The military was called out and issued live ammunition. Gun battles took place in city streets and in country lanes and fields.

In the apartment the radio was again on continuously. The announcer became hoarse with excitement and he kept clearing his throat until another announcer, a woman, took over. She said that the eight assassins, among them two third-year medicine students, had already been arrested and executed.

Albert's 3rd Dragoons were ordered to stand by in full gear at their horses. He and his men were issued the long-barrelled pistols carried in saddle holsters and the heavy dragoon battle sabres. They slept and ate beside their horses, awaiting orders.

SHE RACED to the post office on her bicycle, standing in the pedals for extra power and speed.

"You should have come home," cried her mother on the telephone. "My God, why didn't you? It must be so dangerous in Vienna now."

"I was going to come home next week. Erika and I are studying. And Albert is here. Was here."

"*Albert*," said her mother.

"It's all right. He was keeping us safe. Now that he's gone his parents are sending a car and Erika and I can go to the estate."

"It's not safe anywhere with those Nazi fools and the police in the streets. Here, talk to your father. He's been so worried about you."

Back at the apartment she and Erika packed for a few days. They brought along Arthur Schopenhauer on *Will and Destiny*, the work that had influenced Nietzsche and Wagner, and they brought William Blake for a tricky paper to be written over the summer on Sensuality and Freedom.

When the chauffeur arrived she asked if Mitzi could come too, and the chauffeur in tunic, cap, and grey deerskin gloves said he did not know, but he supposed so.

He called them young misses. "If the young misses are ready," he said. "Hurry a bit. The army is blocking some of the streets."

In the Daimler the glass to the driver's compartment was slid shut but the windows in the back were open wide. They rode with warm air blowing in and out, stirring their hair and clothes. They saw a column of military trucks, and twice they saw a line of soldiers combing a field. Once, they were stopped but the chauffeur showed papers and they were waved on.

ON THE ESTATE grain stood high and golden in the sun. In the long sheds down by the river saws were ripping the first pine logs of the summer, and everywhere the air was warm and filled with the crackle of things drying and with the lazy buzz of bees and flies.

Servants in green aprons showed them to their rooms in the guest wing. Doors and windows stood wide open, and from across the yard they could hear a piano. The playing stopped abruptly and they heard Albert's mother, Cecilia, speaking to someone in her regal way, then a door slammed and a radio was turned on somewhere. They could hear that clearly because even though the yard was large, perhaps thirty metres across, the air lay heavy and still.

For lunch they were five at the table, with one more place set but the chair empty. They were served pan-fried trout and vegetables and small summer potatoes in a dill cream sauce. Servants passed bowls and platters, but no one ate much. In the kitchen the radio was on, and Cecilia told the maid to turn on the apparatus in the living room also.

The announcer was speaking excitedly about confrontations across the country. Police and army were winning everywhere.

Cecilia instructed the maid to keep Theodor's lunch warm. He might be home any time.

"Where is he?" said Mitzi. Cecilia glared at Maximilian, and Maximilian shook his head at Mitzi.

By mid-afternoon that day the parents had sent servants off in all directions to search for Theodor. Cecilia in her buttoned and laced city dress swept into Clara's room, where she sat studying at the desk by the window.

She slipped a pencil between the pages and stood up

from the chair. Cecilia stood by her side, looking at the book cover.

"Schopenhauer," she said. "*Almost all our sorrows come from our relations with other people.* So true. Motherhood and marriage would be good examples there. What else? Something about fleeing to solitude, away from the stings and flies in the marketplace. Meaning the sheer annoyance of other people, of course. But you probably know all that."

Clara stood looking at her. The last quotation had been Nietzsche, not Schopenhauer, but she said nothing. The woman had been crying but had worked at repairing the damage to her face. Cecilia stood proud and erect, her chin up, but her eyes red.

"How can I help?" she said.

"Albert likes you a great deal, Clara. He speaks of your sense of purpose, your pride. In a good way."

"Thank you for saying that."

"Come with us. With me. Max is getting the car."

There was no chauffeur. Maximilian himself was at the wheel, and when the car doors were closed he headed the Daimler out the main gate, along the estate road, and through fields and forests toward the village. Grain stood rich and golden to either side. Far ahead they saw dust rising from some vehicles driving away.

They did not speak one word in the car. She sat in the back, and Cecilia in the passenger seat, holding on with white fingers to the handle on the dash. Cecilia wore no jewellery other than her wedding ring and a small gold watch on a black strap. Her dark-brown hair with the first signs of grey in it was pinned up with tortoiseshell combs, and strands of it had fallen to the lace collar of the blouse. She looked back once over her shoulder at Clara, but she never spoke.

In a far field they saw people in a great patch of grain beaten down as if by hail, but there had not been any hail. Maximilian veered off the road and drove along the tractor lane into the field. There were men and women there, some of the women crying. More men and women stood farther out in the field.

Maximilian stopped the car and climbed out. The men took off their hats and one of them came up and said something to him. Maximilian turned to the open window. He said, "Wait here," and he walked away with the man.

The people gave them looks and turned away. Grain crackled in the heat and cicadas rasped.

"Excuse me. You, in the blue jacket!" called Cecilia out the window. "What is going on?"

The man came up and he turned and pointed. "The soldiers," he said. "They came with trucks and they . . ." He stopped when he saw Maximilian coming back.

She and Cecilia met him less than halfway and he took Cecilia's hand, and moments later they stood looking down at Theodor. He lay with his legs twisted and his arms flung out, as if he had fallen from some great height. His eyes were wide open and his lips pulled back. His front teeth were broken and bloody and bared in a grimace, a horror face that she could not look at but that she still must have seen, because it would later stare at her some nights and it would stare at her from Hemingway's writing, when he said that in battle men died like animals. That they plunged in an instant from peaks of intensity and vibrant aliveness down to wholly unexpected horror.

There was blood also on Theodor's shirt and trousers, and blood had pooled under him. Flies were on him already, and Cecilia reached out to shoo them away. She looked down at the boy, and she turned away and then looked at Clara with a helpless, a terrible plea. Finally she fell to her knees by his side and leaned over and held him.

At some point Maximilian left. He walked to the Daimler, started it up, and brought it close. He lifted Theodor up, held him in his arms, and carried him to the backseat.

Years later, but not so many years, Cecilia would say that her husband began dying the moment he had to carry his dead boy like this. Broad-shouldered and strong though he was, she could see it in his face. Those few staggering steps to the car and the grief and humiliations that followed were what killed him, she'd say, and not the heart attack listed in the document.

At the estate they put the body on a wooden trestle table in the hallway. They closed his eyes and lips. They washed his face and combed his hair with water, and they covered the rest of him with a white sheet. They put candles in stone niches in the walls, and staff came and went on tiptoes and bowed in silence to the parents sitting there.

The date was July 27, 1934, and that evening in her nightgown at the desk in her room she began to write.

IN HER FILES for the years leading up to the war she had the examiner's handwritten death certificate. It gave Theodor's age as seventeen, and it said he had died from three 9mm bullets through mouth, lung, and spine.

With the Nazi rebellion put down, police came to the estate in several cars, and there was much door-banging and shouting and noise of police boots in the wooden stairways of the building. They performed a search that lasted several hours. Simultaneously police also searched the apartment in Vienna and various other buildings that Maximilian as the managing director of the estate was in charge of.

They found nothing to connect him personally to the forbidden Nazis, but Theodor had been a minor and by law his father was held accountable for his actions. In a quick judgment by the travelling court he was sentenced to two years in prison; after his release he would be barred from practising his profession for two further years.

Albert, too, was held at least morally accountable. The judge in the black stole of his office said that as the older brother and as an officer Albert ought to have influenced Theodor and steered him onto a better path. Albert was handed a dishonourable discharge from the military and given a notation in his police file for moral wrongdoing bordering on the criminal.

That day in court as the entire family stood accused of having neglected the youngest son, Cecilia requested to be allowed to speak. She stood up and asked the judge if he had children.

"An inapproprium," said the judge, an old man in an Imperial beard not seen much any more. "But I will answer it. I do have two sons. And I provided them with much stricter discipline to their benefit than you appear to have done. Your son was a—" he glanced at the documents before him. "Your son was a mere boy, not even finished with his baccalaureate. Boys that age need the rod and a very short leash."

He frowned at her, and when she opened her mouth to speak again he waved a hand and looked away from her at the court gendarme.

"Next," he said.

Lawyers acting for the count in faraway America gave the family just three days to remove their personal belongings from the estate and to hand over all keys and records.

They loaded their things onto a truck. She had ridden out there that moving day with Albert on the motorcycle, and she stood by as Breck handed him his riding boots and hefted the English hunter saddle into the sidecar.

"A bad thing, Master Albert," said Breck, and he nodded at her and said, "Young miss."

———

FOR THE DAY of Theodor's funeral Maximilian was allowed out of prison. The family walked behind the two-wheeled horse cart that carried the coffin through the small Mariahilf cemetery in Vienna. From beyond the brick walls they could hear trains at the station. Cecilia's face was hidden behind a black veil, and Maximilian in a black suit and black tie supported her with one hand under her elbow. Albert walked by Cecilia's other side, and young Sissy, his sister, walked behind them. Sissy had on a sailor dress, black stockings, and new black patent leather shoes. She walked looking down at the path in order to avoid the horse droppings. Behind the family came Erika, and Mitzi, and Clara, followed by a handful of friends of the family and of Theodor.

A hole had been dug, and the diggers with fresh mud on their shoes stood back leaning on their shovels among some apple trees in fruit. A chair had been provided at graveside for Cecilia, and there she sat, with Maximilian behind her and his fingers on her shoulders.

The priest said something about there being no political parties in heaven, and forgiveness at hand for all who repented even in the last moments of their lives on this earth.

He took the censor from the ministrant and waved it at the coffin.

The diggers took this as their sign and they came forward and took hold of the ropes, and down went the coffin into the black hole. The ornamental lip caught at one corner, and they had to raise the coffin again and one digger passed his rope to someone else to hold while he chopped at grass and soil with the edge of his shovel and then levered the coffin away from the edge to help it on its way down.

EIGHT

✦

ON CHRISTMAS EVE she was in the kitchen, basting the goose, when she heard Mitzi in the hall. She opened the door and said, "Why don't you ever ring the bell? I'd have come down to help."

"Because I don't want help."

"But it's slippery around the house and I'd much prefer it if you rang so I can come down."

Mitzi shook her head. "You've put down sand, so there's no problem." She raised her nose. "Smells good."

Clara wiped her hands on a towel and said, "Come. I want to show you something."

In her study she pointed at the row of banker's boxes against one wall. "These are the ones they'll be picking up any day now. Mr. Heller at the archives knows about it and he'll be sending someone. But not those two with the red labels." She pointed. "See? They're marked *personal*.

They are staying here."

Mitzi gave her a look and said, "All right. And why are you telling me?"

"Because I want you to know. Someone besides me should know."

Back in the kitchen they made coffee and then sat drinking it. A grainmoth fluttered. They sat while the light outside dimmed.

She outlined the new novel she had been sent by a Frankfurt publisher to translate from English into German. It was good, she said. Good story, good writing. She was looking forward to the work. The London publisher was the same house that had distributed her own works in English translation.

They finished their coffee and then Mitzi passed the cups and she rinsed them and put them upside down on the drainboard. She checked on the goose once more and turned down the heat and looked up at the wall clock.

There was snow on the ground and on tree branches and as the taxi crossed the bridge, steam rose from the cold river into air even colder. Mallard ducks sat on islands of skim ice around rocks.

At the cemetery they bought candles and matches from one of the vendors at the gate. Inside it was already busy, shapes of people moving along paths, standing before graves, striking matches for candles.

High above, the icefield shone like silver and the mountain stood black against the sky. Small yellow lights glowed in houses along the mountain road and the Christmas fire burned on the Tölldner peak. The flames sawed in the wind and when they leaned west they shone onto the enormous cross of polished steel up there, and onto the trusses that anchored it to rock.

First they went to the family grave of the monarchists from her mother's first marriage, a corner plot with evergreens and Japanese maples, and with memorial tablets set into the wall. The monarchists were Count Torben and his family and her own two stepbrothers, Peter and Bernhard. Peter's wife, Daniela, was buried there too; utterly loyal Daniela, who had doted on Peter and loved Clara like a sister. How proud the monarchists had been of their history, of the title and the heraldic family emblem.

"But if you half-close your eyes," Daniela had once whispered to Clara. "If you squint a bit, then that thing might also be a plucked chicken with just a few feathers left. Rather than a plumed helmet."

They lit candles and put them into small wrought-iron lanterns by the list of names in black marble. After a few moments of silence they walked to the other grave, the one of her mother and father and her mother's side of the family. Albert would be resting here too, once his urn was installed and his name carved on the tablet. If the stonemason ever came back from his holiday. They lit candles at the foot of the angel with its wings chiselled in great detail and the face turned away and hidden behind the hands. In silence they stood close together in the dark for a minute, and left.

LATER EMMA AND TOMAS came to the house to exchange small gifts. They did not stay long. As he was buttoning his coat, Tom asked in a low voice if there was any news from the museum and she just shook her head. Then he asked if they might perhaps take Albert's wall clock. Emma would love to have it, he said.

Clara looked at Emma, who was already standing by the door, waiting for him.

"Emma?" she said. "Is that right? You want that clock?"

"I'd love it, Mom. It would look nice in the living room."

"Fine. It's yours."

The clock was the four-day Silverbell Napoleon that Cecilia had rescued from the bombed Vienna apartment. If Emma wanted it, she should have it. It would go to her anyway. Or to Willa. She wondered briefly if she should be more specific in her will as to who should get what.

They left with the clock wrapped in a blanket, the two of them bent over and stepping carefully while carrying it downstairs to the car. Emma called another Merry Christmas from around the corner in the stairway. The lights went out and Clara pushed the button for them.

She and Mitzi enjoyed the roast goose with potatoes and peas and a small green salad, and they shared a bottle of wine. There was no tree, just a small Advent wreath of evergreen on the table, with the four candles burning in it. By Mitzi's place setting, Clara had put a purple cashmere shawl in a paisley pattern, nicely wrapped, and Mitzi had given her a small plate of home-baked cookies including almond crescents and vanilla kisses covered in cellophane.

At eleven o'clock, when the bells rang at the stone church, they gave each other a hug. They were family to each other, now more than ever. Mitzi's own parents were long dead and buried some place she did not even know, maybe in what used to be East Prussia, maybe in Poland, but she thought of them often and now in her old age she met them in her dreams, two people in shtetl clothes sitting side by side on a wooden bench. Mitzi had never been to a shtetl, but it was one of the many Yiddish words that came to her lately. In her dreams her parents sat close together on that bench but far enough apart to also suggest a certain self-reliance so as not to lean too much on the other, as they would have said in the marriage vows of old. Behind them was the wall of a small clapboard house, a *heusele* with fine scrollsaw work around windows and eaves.

EARLY IN THE NEW YEAR, Mitzi had another appointment with Dr. Caroline Gottschalk about her hip. Clara came along.

"We'd better do it sooner than later," Dr. Gottschalk said to Mitzi. She looked much like her grandmother, slim and fine-featured like Cecilia had been, and those same black and steady eyes and resolute ways.

"Give me those canes and stand for me." She held out her hand and looked at Mitzi over her glasses. "No. Let go of the bed. Let me see you stand on your own."

Mitzi stood, or tried to.

"Now, take a step," said Dr. Gottschalk. "Mitzi-dear. Look at you. How much longer do you want to wait? And wait for what?"

NINE

❖

IN OCTOBER 1934, three months after Theodor's
funeral, Mitzi had finally asked Cecilia for the name of
the forger. She was washing Cecilia's hair at the time,
putting in a chestnut rinse because of all that grey
suddenly.

"What forger?" said Cecilia without opening her eyes.
They were in the bathroom of the Leonhardt apartment,
with Cecilia sitting on a chair and leaning back into the
handwash basin.

"Albert said you knew one. From the estate. Something
about customs documents that he could . . . you know."

"Albert said that?"

"He did. Lift up a bit and turn this way."

And so it began, Mitzi's quest for a safe personal history.
What she wanted was a new name, she said to Cecilia. And
an ID card and a driver's licence. Getting them might take

a while and she wanted to be ready, for the day that everyone was whispering about.

"Why?" said Cecilia. "This is not . . . what's your real name?"

Her name was Naomi Friedmann, she said. German Jews, her parents, both long dead. Raised by an aunt, she'd been; one Mitzi Schuster, from whom she'd learned her trade and taken over the business name. And David Koren had said that if the present government were to lose to the National Socialists and she wanted to stay here, she would need another identity.

"You're Jewish," said Cecilia. She wiped away foam and squinted up with one eye. "Child, half the gifted world is: musicians, writers, composers, you have no idea. That's why you're so good at what you're doing. You're an artist at this, with an eye for the three-dimensional."

"Thanks," said Mitzi. "Will you help me?"

Cecilia said of course she would, and later that day she and Mitzi took a taxi to call on the forger. He lived in an apartment in Hietzing, on a narrow street not far from the little church there and from the palm house and Schönbrunn zoo, where peacocks screeched and monkeys threw peanuts at children.

The forger took his time inspecting them through the spy lens in the door. He let them in, glanced past them down the stairway, then closed the door quickly behind them. He was a small red-haired man with unusual glasses that had layers of extra lenses attached. He led them into the living room, which was filled with shelves of papers and books, and tables with special lamps and presses and photographic equipment.

Cecilia came straight to the point and told him what Mitzi needed: a birth certificate, a certificate of baptism, an identity card, and a driver's licence.

"And all in a name that has a clear history," she said. "A pedigree, Mr. Binder." She spoke to him the way she had spoken to the staff at the estate, clearly and firmly. She sat forward on the wooden chair, her feet in high heels tucked back and close together, her shoulders straight, her chin up.

"But I don't do those, Madame Leonhardt," said the forger.

"Of course you do, Mr. Binder. What is your fee?"

"My fee," he said and looked at Mitzi with his pale eyes, with all those strange lenses trembling. "What Madame Leonhardt is asking is illegal," he said. "We would all be risking jail."

"Nonsense," said Cecilia. "Look at me, Mr. Binder. What is the fee?"

He sighed and moved and consulted a list in a folder that lay so conveniently close by on his desk that it was clear theirs was not an unusual request. He adjusted one of the lenses and read out a few names, looking up after each one.

They agreed on Anna Susanne Toplitz, the real one dead and buried in faraway Maria Zell eight years ago, but the name according to his research cleared to 1867.

"And the fee?" said Cecilia. "Considering our past business dealings."

"Ah," he said. "The fee is one thousand Swiss francs for each document. Half up front, the rest on delivery."

"Four thousand Swiss francs," said Cecilia. "A fortune. Perhaps she won't ever need those papers."

The forger looked at Mitzi and from Mitzi to Cecilia. He took off all his glasses and put them down. "Oh, she will," he said. "The way things are going."

And he wanted Swiss francs, he said, suddenly very businesslike. In cash. Definitely not schillings. He could take the photograph right now. He sat waiting. "Oh," he said. "One more thing." And he mentioned a currency smuggler in the sixth district who would sell them Swiss francs at a good rate.

Mitzi had savings and she could pay for nearly half of that; Cecilia said she would lend her the rest in good faith.

SINCE THEODOR'S DEATH and the arrest of Maximilian the trio of women – Clara, Erika, and Mitzi – had become friends with Cecilia. They respected her mourning and her anger. They admired her strength and courage to push on.

Cecilia was the sole breadwinner among the Leonhardts now, and she'd plunged into commitments, taking on students from the conservatory on top of her coaching. While Albert was out looking for work, she coached full-time and the apartment in Vienna was filled with music all day long, with singers male and female warming up in bedrooms and bathrooms, full-throated intonations of the scales up and down, and loud rasping throat-clearings in between. It was hard to take at times, even for Cecilia, but there was good money coming in.

For the first two months Theodor's photograph had been sitting on the piano, with a black ribbon across the top right-hand corner; then Cecilia moved it to the dresser in her bedroom.

"I hope you do understand what this has done to us," she said at one time to them over dinner. They were sitting around the table at the apartment, just the women. Albert was out of town; they were expecting him, but they did not know when.

"Theo dead and Max in jail," said Cecilia. "And I the only one who did not know what the boy was up to. Albert knew and Max knew. At least he suspected, and all of you, you knew too."

They avoided one another's guilty faces.

"Well say something."

"Of course we understand that," Clara said then. "And we have no excuses, only explanations. It seemed harmless. It really did. We would probably have said something to you otherwise. Or Albert would have. We thought it was just one of those student causes."

"Harmless. You've said that before and I can't hear that word any more. They had been outlawed, so it was not *harmless*. It was illegal."

"So are the Communists and even the Social Democrats

now. Lots of things are illegal and nobody cares. It's terrible, what happened, but be fair, Cecilia. No one could have guessed this outcome."

They ate in silence until they heard the door and Albert said hello from the hall.

Cecilia turned her head. "Any luck?" she called.

"Don't ask. When I have good news you'll be the first to know. All of you."

They heard him in the bathroom running water, and Clara put down fork and knife and rose. "Is his dinner in the warming oven?"

"Yes," said Cecilia. "Go and talk to him."

She found him standing in the bathroom, drying his face and hands. She sat down on the bathtub rim and he hung up the towel and sat down next to her.

ALBERT'S MILITARY CAREER in Austria was in ruins, but as a horse trainer he had much to offer. He travelled the country by train and on the Norton, applying at stud and horse farms. One of the first places he tried was his old equestrian college where he'd graduated summa cum laude, and when the rector told him there was no position available Albert had set off on long loops into the provinces: to the Eschenbach stud farm, to the Trauttenhoffs, the Wolframs, and to other breeders, stables, and farms. He was gone often for days, at times sleeping like a vagrant in off-road barns, twice stretched out in a church pew, he admitted to her.

He filled out a dozen applications and left his resumé, but the horse world was exclusive and intimate. News about the judgment against him had travelled fast, and breeders depended on the government for any number of permits and licences. She could see the effect of months of rejection in his face; around his lips stretched and dry, and in his eyes uncertain and quick to look away from her as they had never been.

In order to lend her support she came along on what would turn out to be the last of these trips. It was to a Lipizzaner feeder farm for the Spanish Riding School in a distant province. To get there they loaded the Norton onto trains and off-loaded it for connections. It was late afternoon on a day in November when they finally continued by road. The sidecar was still bolted to the frame of the motorcycle, but as usual she rode on the pillion seat with her hands in the pockets of his leather coat, holding him like this with her hands not quite meeting under the coat in front, and two fingers poking through a tear in the seam of the right pocket lining. She rode pressing the side of her face against his back, her leather helmet buckled under her chin. She wore brown lace-up boots, a lined jacket he'd bought for her at a motoring supply shop in Vienna, and she wore her dark-brown tweed outfit with the skirt tucked up under her knees so as not to get it caught in spokes or chain.

There was no snow yet, but the sky was grey everywhere and trees were bare and black. To the south once

in a while they could see clouds like vast sails and ship-
wrecks sliding down mountainsides to the valley floor.
Winter lightning trembled high above them where the
peaks might be.

To talk to each other they would shout, and he would
half turn his head to hear. When he shouted she could feel
his voice in her hands flat on his chest at the same time
as the wind tore the words from his mouth and whipped
them over his shoulder.

Under her, somewhere on the black machine something
metallic had begun to rattle and slap.

"What's that," she shouted. "That noise?"

"Chain needs tightening."

"Tightening?"

"The wheel gets moved back," he shouted. "There are
frame spacers both sides of the rear axle. I'll get around
to it."

She sat and burrowed her face into his coat again. She
could smell the leather, old as the thing was.

This ride, so far down their common path already. She
and Albert, now. So different from the early days in Vienna,
the laughter, the excitement, the faith come what may.

She squeezed her eyes shut against the icy wind.
Moments later they were nearly run off the road by a
lumber truck that came fast around a bend and veered
sideways when the driver saw them. The rear of the
truck and the harsh breath of exhaust and wheelspin
barely missed them and the Norton skidded and died.

She could just free her hands from his pockets when he climbed off and stomped over to where the truck had slowed and the driver was now grinding the gears in his hurry to get away.

Albert stood looking after him. He raised a fist, comical on this dark and winding road, a man in goggles and helmet cursing after a truck long gone.

"Albert!" she said. "Let's go! Let's find a place for the night. Get some food and rest. Come."

She felt a stab of pity for him then, for the first time. Or perhaps it was not actual pity but sorrow, empathy for a loved one who is trying so very hard. Helpless and hopeless he seemed to her at that moment, a man at a wholly unexpected lowpoint in his life.

"Albert." She walked there and reached for his arm. "Come. Let's go."

They spent that night in an inn where they cleaned up and ate dinner in a low-ceilinged room with wooden beams and wooden tables and a large green tile stove with iron rails for wet clothing above.

Out the window of their room they could see the white lines of paddock fences, and they saw the dark shapes of horses as they moved and drew together near the open stable gate. At some point that night she felt him leave the bed, and he sat on the bedside and put on his shoes. She pretended to be asleep, but she saw him put his coat over his pyjama shoulders and walk on tip-toes out of the room.

She heard him outside then, and she swung her legs out of the bed and stepped to the window. There he was ducking between paddock rails and then he stood, and the horses with slow steps and heads hanging came to him through the grass in the cold moonlit night, and steam rose from his mouth as he spoke to them and stroked their long necks. She watched as he bent down and tapped the foreleg of one, and it raised that leg and he bent to examine the underhoof and with his fingernail he pried out something, perhaps a small stone. He slipped it into his pocket out of the way.

In the morning after breakfast they drove the remaining twenty kilometres to the estate. It lay in the flat November light like a Kafkaesque castle, it seemed to her; elevated, walled, and self-important in this countryside, tile roofs and copper turrets, the enormous wooden gate shuttered.

"Monarchists!" he shouted over his shoulder. "Very condescending. They think they're God's gift to the horse world. But I have to try."

He stopped the motorcycle at the gate, knocked, and someone slid open the spy window. They saw a rolling eye and a nose.

Albert explained and a voice said, "All right. It's almost opening time anyway." There was the clacking of wooden drawbeams and the carriage gate swung open. He drove the Norton into the inner yard as wide as a marketplace and cobbled most of it in blocks of cedar as in the Middle Ages to save the horses' hooves. Administration buildings and stables surrounded the yard, all timbered structures painted ochre and forest green, the old imperial colours. Bare trees stood tall, and under them men in boots and linen stable jackets were walking horses, some snow white, others, the younger ones, no longer in their foal black but ash grey. Albert shut off the engine and asked a man leading a young horse in a rope halter for the manager.

"The Rittmeister," the man corrected him.

"If you say so. Where is he?"

The horse handler pointed at a group of men across the yard. "There," he said. "In the uniform."

That man was looking their way now. He waved his arms and shouted, "That's far enough on that motor-machine." He turned his back on the men with him and came crossing the yard.

He had on the two-cornered hat worn sideways in the old imperial fashion meant to make an officer's head look more impressive and also to protect his ears and neck from sabre cuts. He wore dark-blue breeches with leather seat and inner thighs, and a tight uniform tunic with gold buttons. The hat from corner to corner was nearly as wide as his shoulders. His riding boots gleamed, and they made hardly a sound on the wooden cobble blocks. With each step he slapped a braided quirt against his right leg.

"What?" he shouted. "Who are you?"

"Just look at him," said Albert under his breath to her. He stepped away from the Norton and began walking toward the Rittmeister. They met some twenty paces away and words were spoken that she could not make out. Behind them in the yard men stood staring, even the one who had been working with broom and stickpan sweeping up horse buns. As she waited by the motorcycle she smoothed out her skirt, then took off the leather helmet and shook out her hair. She smelled horses. She smelled the harsh aroma of fresh oat feed that a stablehand was shovelling from a circular bin nearby into a feed barrow.

The Rittmeister stood slapping the quirt into his left hand now, and the next she heard they were arguing, shouting. But it had been in the air all morning. It had been in the air since the truck incident last night, this bitterness.

"Even if your rank still existed it would at best be equal to mine," Albert shouted. "So I won't have you speak to me in this tone."

"Rank?" The Rittmeister laughed. "From what I under-stand you no longer have a rank." He looked over his shoulder at his men. "Get on with your work," he yelled at them. "Don't stand around."

In turning back he glanced at her. He stared for a moment, then he leaned close to Albert and said some-thing that she could not make out.

Off to the side she saw Albert's face white and tense. Next he raised his left hand and stood pointing curiously with his index finger and he moved that hand, still point-ing. Momentarily perplexed the Rittmeister watched the hand and seconds later he sat on the ground with blood on his face. Albert stood rubbing the knuckles of his right hand.

The man on the ground touched his nose and mouth, looked in disbelief at the blood on his glove. He rose to one knee, then to his feet. Behind him in the yard every man stood watching but none came forward.

"How dare you?" screamed the Rittmeister. "In front of my men. I will have you for this." He picked up his two-cornered hat, swept hair from his forehead with forked fingers, and clapped the hat back on, wild-eyed like some crazed Napoleonist.

She tossed the leather helmet into the sidecar and walked quickly up behind Albert.

"You insulted me," Albert was saying. "In front of your men. You challenged me." He took a step toward the Rittmeister, who backed away and held on to his hat, and with a wary eye on Albert ducked to pick up his quirt.

"You are quite mad," he said. He saw his men watching. "I said get on with your work!" He waved his arms. "Everybody! This is none of your affair. You, Emile! Go to the office and call the gendarme."

Behind Albert, Clara stood tugging on his coat. "We should leave," she said. "Albert. Now. While the gate's still open."

"Stay where you are!" The Rittmeister cleared his voice and spat blood. "You will wait for the police. I am arresting you."

"Now, Albert. Let's go." She tugged harder, and he came

away reluctantly. The Norton started at the first kick and they drove off with the Rittmeister gesturing behind them, screaming nasally at the keeper to close the gate, but by then they were almost upon it, already in second gear and the gatekeeper leapt out of their way.

Minutes later on the road she was first to laugh at it all.

"What?" shouted Albert over his shoulder.

"The whole thing. And that poor Rittmeister, he was so upset. What did he say? Why did you punch him?"

"He was asking for it, and I just suddenly had enough. All these patronizing idiots."

"But what did he say?"

Albert pretended not to hear and drove on. After a while he shouted, "I may have to look for work somewhere else. Until this blows over."

"Where?"

"Germany to begin with. Then perhaps France."

They drove on not saying anything.

"I want to finish my degree. The dissertation," she shouted over his shoulder then, a round high shoulder that these freighted words travelled across. "At least two more years."

"They'll go by quickly. We can visit."

"Visit."

The drivechain had begun slapping again, and it was getting worse. Eventually they pulled up behind a stand of trees off the road, in case the police were looking for them. They crouched by the rear wheel and she watched him work with two spanners moving the axle back along the frame slots and then setting the counter-nuts to secure the bolt. She could smell the hot engine and the sun on the leather seats of the Norton. There was black oil on the chain and the chain ran under a guard from a small sprocketwheel in the engine block to the larger one in the rear axle. He worked with bare hands so as not to get any oil on his gloves.

"Carbon grease," he said. "Very sticky."

She watched his fingers. She watched his face from the side, his concentration. She saw the curve of his lips, saw him breathe. She leaned quickly and kissed him on the cheek.

"I'm glad you punched him," she said. "I couldn't stand him from the moment he came strutting our way, yelling at us like some overlord. And that little whip and the hat."

"These people. So very arrogant and stuck in time. I could never work for them anyway. This was a good day, sweetheart. It made things clear." He wiped his fingers on tufts of grass. "I'll start in Germany. They know about horses," he said. "You don't mind?"

"What? You looking for work elsewhere?"

"I'm thinking of your family." He shook his head. "Actually, no. I'm thinking of you. Your career. Your future."

"I know you are. But there's no question I'll finish my degree. After that I'd rather we could stay here. But if we can't, we can't."

She sat down on the dry cold patch of grass, gathered her skirt, and cradled her knees in her hands.

"It could be interesting," she said. "Maybe Heidelberg. Heidelberg would be fantastic. Or Hamburg. Once I have my degree, my career will be quite portable. It's essentially up here. All of it." She tapped a finger to her forehead. Professor Roland Emmerich's words.

TEN

·❖·

TWO DAYS LATER a gendarme came to the Leonhardt
apartment in Vienna to take Albert's statement as to the
assault charges laid by the Rittmeister.

"You broke his nose," said the gendarme. "He claims
you attacked him unprovoked. What was it about?"

Albert shook his head. "Not unprovoked. He insulted
me and the woman I was with."

"How? What did he say?"

"I won't repeat it. He was being arrogant. It was an
unpardonable insult and just one too many."

The gendarme, an older man in piped grey trousers and
a grey tunic, sat studying him. "You should state your
reason," he said in a fatherly way. "In the report. What
did he say?"

"I'll repeat it in court, if it comes to that. If I absolutely
have to."

Cecilia, who had sent a student into the far bedroom to warm up, brought coffee and biscuits. She offered schnapps, and the gendarme raised his spectacles to look closely at the bottle label. In the end he accepted a drink. He leaned back and sipped it. Through walls and doors they could hear the student, a young woman, doing the scales. The gendarme cocked his head but said nothing. Not long thereafter he folded the signed statement and left.

"I'll have to look for work outside the country," Albert said to his mother eventually. "I'll start in Germany."

Cecilia said nothing. She rose and cleared the table. When she was back from the kitchen she said, "In case you are wondering. I am very angry. You see what this has done to us, this *harmless* thing? It is getting worse all the time. Theo dead, your father in jail, and you having to flee now, which is what this is. And punching a Rittmeister, a well-connected monarchist, what on earth were you thinking?"

"I wasn't. But I had no choice. Leave it, Mother. I'll never apologize for that."

"And Clara? Look at me, look at your mother!" She sat angry and upright, waiting. "I like that young woman very much, Albert. If you leave to work in another country, what will become of her? She is good for you, and she has spunk, that girl, and substance. Make sure you deserve her and treat her well."

"I am. Clara knows I'll have to leave. We spoke about it. She wants to get her degree first."

"Well, of course. I'd expect nothing less from her. No woman should ever have to depend on any man. God knows. Not even if he's a son of mine."

"Mother. None of this, none of it, could have been foreseen."

"So you say, but I disagree. It was foolish. Look at the consequences." She sat a moment longer, then she stood up. "I have work to do."

That same day he applied for a passport in order to be able to leave the country, and when he was denied one he went to the forger for documents in another name. Four weeks later he had just picked them up and surrendered his last money when he was approached by a man in a dark-blue winter coat and hat outside a tobacconist kiosk on Schubertring in Vienna.

"Captain Leonhardt. Wait!" the man said. He stood with his back to the driving snow and he reached into a coat pocket and produced a German military pass. It identified him as a major, and a second document certified that he was the military attaché at the German embassy in Vienna.

"Captain," he said. He had a lean face and watchful eyes. He was taking his time. "To us you are still a captain, even if your own military has no use for you at this moment."

Albert nodded at the coat pocket into which the major's passes had disappeared. "Are they real?" he said. "The documents."

"They are. I'll give you a number you can call."

"About what?"

The major shook his head. "Captain," he said. "Is that not enough now?"

"Enough what?"

"Enough rejection. Every one of them an injury to the spirit. Such insults. And from people you thought respected you. You have a name, a good reputation. We've heard of the incident with the Rittmeister."

Albert shielded his eyes against the driving snow and stared at the man. "What's this about?"

"The general must have seen you once on a horse," said the major. "And what the general wants, the general usually gets."

"What general?"

The major now reached into the inside coat pocket and handed Albert a letter in a sealed envelope.

"Read it," he said. "Think carefully and call back. Call this number on the envelope. I will take your call and tell you what to do next."

The meeting took less than two minutes and the man was gone again.

Albert stepped into the tobacconist's shop. He nodded to the woman behind the counter and turned his back to read.

The letter was typed under the official letterhead of the German Ministry of Defence; it said that his academic and military records had been carefully reviewed, and that on the strength of them he was being offered a commission and full pay at the rank of major. It said that if he accepted, he would be assigned to the Senior Officers' Academy outside Munich, and that, after completing the intensive training in tank warfare, he would graduate at the rank of lieutenant colonel. He would also be given a horse of his choice and asked to ride in military competitions for the school.

That evening he drove the Norton through a snowstorm to her flat. He showed her the letter. They sat at the small round table and she read by the light of the lamp her father had fashioned from a small Roman urn, some bronze fittings and a cloth shade.

When she had finished reading, she looked up at Albert, and she saw it in his face that he had already decided. All he wanted was her approval.

FOR HER, THE SEMESTERS of 1934 and 1935 were filled with hard work and academic challenge. The oral exams in English and Latin had to be prepared for, but they were easy compared to the papers she had to write in Philosophy. Professor Emmerich was as demanding as ever; now in his fourth year with them he had lost some students, but the remainder he drove as hard as ever. And he told them why. He said that this now was the time when they were putting in place the key elements of the intellectual structures they would be referring to for the rest of their lives.

"These are not just words and ideas," he said. "These

are principles of thought. Of attitude and morality. Principles."

He had moved on to Nietzsche and his idea of the Übermensch, not as the Nazis would corrupt it for their own notions of superiority but as real men and women who did not run with the herd but who took on the solitary struggle to overcome their own dark sides, and who in doing so found morality and strength right there, within themselves.

He gave them Kierkegaard again, and he advanced Kant and Hegel, and Husserl.

"To truly know a thing," he paraphrased Husserl. "To truly know anything, ask: what is its basic idea? What is its primary purpose? Never rush yourself. Make it one of your principles to be methodical and think things out for yourself. Ask, what is this thing in itself? Find the one perfect word to express it, and go from there."

He gave them *these barebones men,* as he called them, these uncompromising thinkers whose ideas were hard as granite, and he set their minds on fire all over again — hers and Erika's, and all those who would not miss a lecture of his, not even if they had to travel extra miles around police actions and demonstrations and sometimes around gunfire to get to it.

He made them write paper after paper, and he taught them how to think and he made them come alive to ideas even as the social world around them was disintegrating, as the government that had replaced the murdered Dollfuss was slipping deeper and deeper into economic failure, and as the forbidden Nazis and the Communists were gaining strength.

"This merely temporary world," Professor Emmerich reminded them. "A passing and insignificant one in its current confusions and contradictions. Pay only enough attention to it to get by, but don't take it seriously. Eventually we will deal with that too; with different ways of seeing it. For now, as always, trust only your own mind and be secure and calm within yourself. Nothing else matters. Nothing. Nothing."

ON NEW YEAR'S DAY 1935, they became engaged. They celebrated at the Leonhardt flat, with Erika, Mitzi, and Cecilia as the solemn witnesses to this happy deed.

There was wine and good bread and black-market ham, and Cecilia played American music on the piano for them. They danced and they sat on the big couch in the living room, she leaning against him as he held her. At one point her happiness overwhelmed her, and not just her happiness, but a sudden fear also, a dawning of perhaps some enormous consequence looming.

Always look closely at fear, Dr. Freud had said to them. Fear as a warning, an alert like pain to pay attention. Or fear as a yellow traffic light. The least one ought to do, he said, was slow down and look in both directions. A day later she understood what the fear was, and she packed and took the train to St. Töllden. There she admitted everything to her parents. Peter, who was visiting with Daniela, sat in.

She told of the shooting death of Theodor, of the incarceration of the father, and of Albert's dishonourable dismissal from the Austrian cavalry. She skipped his breaking the nose of the Rittmeister, but she did tell of his signing up with the German military and finally of their engagement.

Defiantly she said she fully intended to marry him, once she had her doctorate and her own career. But as she said so, her lips were quivering and her eyes filled with tears.

When she had finished, there was a terrible silence. Peter looked stunned. Her father looked heart-broken, and her mother had raised both hands to her mouth in disbelief. Only Daniela was secretly winking encouragement.

ELEVEN

✤

LATER SHE AND PETER sat in what used to be called
the study room; now, with all of them grown up and gone
from home, garden chairs were stacked in a corner, and
under a bedsheet a pile of unwanted items awaited the
Samaritans.

"After you were here with him, your father had the
family investigated," Peter said. "His brother, Theodor,
was picked up during the Emergency. Did you know that?
Look at me. I think you did. Mother called me and asked
my opinion, and I said let's wait and see. The man is an
officer."

"You could have told me. *Investigated?* Isn't that a bit . . .
what else do they know?" She watched him pacing back
and forth. "Peter. Would you please sit down? I know they
want you to talk some sense into me, so let's have this
conversation. But sit. You're making me dizzy."

He crossed the room and sat down in the ancient leather armchair. She was sitting on the matching couch. When she was small the boys had shown her how to use that couch as a trampoline, cheering her on to bounce as high as she was tall. Once her mother caught them, and the boys lost their pocket money for an entire month.

"What else do they know?" he said. "They know about that Rittmeister getting punched a few weeks ago. You conveniently forgot to mention that. Actually . . ." Peter was suddenly grinning. "I think that's rather funny. Maybe not wise, but funny."

"It was, in retrospect. The man was so shocked. You should have seen him. But I hate to see Mom and Dad so upset."

"They are worried. Can you blame them? The brother a dead Nazi, the father in jail, he a pugilist."

She laughed at that. "Peter, Albert's not a *pugilist*. He just had enough. If you'd seen that man, the little whip he had, his condescending way. The way he spoke to Albert, like to some serf. No, Albert did the right thing. He stood up and I support him fully in that."

Peter sat watching her.

"He did do the right thing," she said.

"If you say so. Why didn't you ever bring him around for dinner? Or at least introduce him."

"I called a few times but you were never there."

"Well. Too late now."

"Too late for what? I think everyone is overreacting.

We can work it out. Albert will go to Munich, on that course, and I will carry on with my studies. No change there. The Germans made him a major, Peter. And he'll be a lieutenant colonel when he gets out. He has a military career again."

"But not here. And once he leaves, he won't be able to come back. And if you marry him, neither will you." He shook his head at her. "His family, Clara. What are they? Managers of another man's property. And from one day to the next they were evicted. Not much substance, was there? Traditions and principles are important anchors in life. They give you a place in the world, but they also determine what you may do, and what you must never do. His brother, and I'm sorry he died so young and all that, but he was a fool and on the wrong side."

"I don't think he was a fool. On the wrong side, yes."

"Drop him, Clara. Cancel the engagement. Concentrate on what matters. Your studies. Nothing else does. Especially in these times. Get the best education you can. Have something to offer."

"My studies are going very well. If anything, Albert's a help. He is a good man and I love him." She paused and listened happily after those words. "I don't know that I've ever said that out loud. But I do. And his mother is nothing short of admirable. I'm not going to drop anybody."

"You'll regret it."

"I don't think so. But please let it go, Peter. Tell me about your father instead. The count. How did he die?"

He shook his head. "Drop Albert. It's my advice and it's what your father thinks too."

"I won't. I know different. I feel different."

He stood up and sat down again. "So pigheaded. You can still be so very pigheaded. How old were you that time when they grounded you and you jumped out the window into the lilacs and walked back inside through the front door."

"Maybe eleven. It wasn't that far down. In any case, you're wrong. He loves me, and he has lots of substance. And he's very good with horses."

"Horses. There are grooms for that. Hired hands."

"Oh? And what's this?" She turned and pointed at a picture on the wall, a photograph of Peter as a thin young man on an enormous horse; Peter in a First World War lieutenant's uniform – the cap, the braid, the sabre. Tall and straight, looking down his nose at the camera without a smile. But the horse made up for that, for it was curling its lips in a big toothy grin, as if it alone could see the vanity of uniforms and young men's big ideas. The picture was a family classic.

"Peter," she said. "Do you love Daniela?"

"Danni? Of course I do. With all my heart."

"Didn't Mama think she was beneath you? And Bernhard did too, I seem to remember. A dancer?"

"A former *ballet* dancer. You should have seen her on stage. Bernhard was only jealous. Daniela is wonderful."

"Of course she is. I like her too. But my point is—"

"There's no comparison here. Because of this Nazi thing your Albert has a criminal judgment against him that will follow him for years. And now he's putting on a German uniform. How can you defend that?"

"Defend what? There's nothing to defend. The Germans were our allies in the war, when you sat on that horse. You fought on their side and they on ours. And I would not have wanted Albert to wait around and be more and more humiliated. He has pride. You can feel that in him. The Germans must have, and they made him a senior officer. It's an honour. Their *military*, not their politics. He warned me that there'd be those who don't know the difference."

"Nonsense. The military goes where the politicians of the day send it. For example, we know that Hitler wants Alsace-Lorraine back. What do you think will happen? And *tanks*? What's he thinking, your Albert?"

"He says tanks are now what heavy cavalry used to be. In any case he has a horse there too."

Peter grinned at her. "How sweet. They gave him a pony to lure him across."

"Don't make fun of him. He loves horses and he wins all kinds of trophies. You big oaf." She kicked off her shoes and swung her legs up on the couch. It was of the smoothest leather, buffed and worn thin in places by generations of grown-ups' bottoms and children's sockfeet.

"And speaking of it," she said, "are *you* happy with the guilt clauses? What an insult! In a way you can't blame the Germans for getting off their knees. Billions of marks."

"Hundreds of billions, actually. But it's no excuse for provoking another war."

"But, Peter. It was bitter everlasting revenge, nothing more. On us too. Making sure we'll never stand up again. We should rebel against it too. Don't always be such a reasonable lawyer. For God's sake, be a wild man once in a while."

"Clara. That famous treaty . . . the worst thing about it is not the debt itself, it's that it enabled a man like Hitler to ride in like a white knight with promises to restore the nation's honour. And about your Albert, I'm only cautioning you. I want the best for you. We all do."

"I know that." She swung down her legs, reached out and patted his knee. "I know you mean well. Thank you. But enough of that. Trust me to work things out for myself." She took a deep breath. "Can we change the topic now? Count Torben, your father. How did he die? Mother has never really said."

"Probably because he died in a duel, which most women think is a ridiculous way to go."

"A duel? Really? With pistols?"

"Swords. He died in some forest clearing. He and a Hungarian captain ran swords through each other. In their full proud uniforms, with their seconds looking on."

"Both dead?"

He nodded. He sat in the chair, his knees nearly as high as the elbow rests. "I have his sword."

"You do? Can I see it?" She stood up.

"Drop him, Clara."

"What? No! Please stop it now. You're sweet and I thank you for caring. But let it go. Sometimes it's good to be wild, a bit reckless even. It makes life much more interesting."

He said nothing to that and she looked at him, sunk in the chair. "Peter," she said and crouched down in front of him. She took his hand. "Peter. You've always been so good to me and helped me and given me useful advice. But in this case, listen, I'm so very happy with him. I feel no need to try to explain him, let alone apologize for him. Look at me. I am so very happy altogether. Can't you tell? My studies, my career plans. And Albert. I'm happy, Peter." She waited. She patted his hand and let it go and stood up. "Now, where's that sword? Show me!"

"Why?"

"Because these things are interesting." She put a finger to her lips and whispered, "I think Mama still loves him."

"My father? She loves your dad. She adores him."

"I know that. But that doesn't mean she can't love the memory of her first husband too. Come on now. The sword, Count Peter."

He sighed and rose, and he crossed to the wall closet and reached behind the clothes there. His hand came back holding a long nickel scabbard. The handguard gleamed golden.

"Be careful. It's very sharp," he said. "Hold it there and pull. Don't touch any metal."

It came out of the sheath with a whisper of steel, and she held that lethal thing in her hand and turned it in the light.

"Good Lord," she said.

"Cut and thrust, double-edged with a stiff centre spine. The grip is sharkskin, the guard gold-plated."

"He killed the Hungarian with this?"

"Yes. And was killed at the same time, probably with a similar one."

"How? Where was he cut?"

"He was run through the chest. Both were. It was unusual but it did happen. There is a move called *pas d'honneur*. It's when a duellist fears he may lose and so he stops defending and he attacks and charges the blade and at the same time sinks his own."

"Sounds desperate."

"It's hard to relate to today. For an officer then it would have been unthinkable to lose a duel. Absolutely dishonourable. His life would not have been – it was unthinkable."

Peter took the sword from her, wiped it with a cloth he had hanging on the tie rack, and slipped it back into the sheath. "My father did not lose that duel."

She heard the note of pride in that, and it moved her strangely. "But he was dead, Peter. Was that better?"

"Than losing a duel? He would have said so. Yes."

"You mean that?"

"Absolutely."

"Did you see him? The body?"

"I did. I was nine years old, Bernhard four. The seconds brought him on a blanket and put him down in the entrance hall. Blood came though the blanket and the entire tunic was soaked. He had cuts on his arms and in his face too. I saw him first, then Mama came running from the parlour."

"And?"

"I don't really remember much after that. The noises. We were sent upstairs. We could hear her screaming. The doctor came in a carriage. We could see him from the upstairs window, getting down from the carriage and putting his hat back on. It was fall, I remember that. The linden trees. We could hear mother and the doctor downstairs, and other noises. Her crying. Out the window the coachman was putting a feedbag around the horse's neck. It was so normal. I remember that too."

AT THE END OF THAT DAY they all went for a walk. Where the path was wide enough, she walked between her parents, one arm each around their middles. There was snow on the ground and the air was crisp and clean. She could smell the ice-cold river.

Her father took them to the new Roman excavation site that he was in charge of. There was a temporary wooden roof over it all to keep off the snow while the digging went on. Now, over the holiday, the site was deserted. On large worktables within their drawn outlines lay surprisingly modest tools: small shovels, soup spoons, uniquely curved picks like large dentist tools, sieves, sable brushes, tooth-brushes, and paint scrapers.

The strata were clearly visible, layers of clay and lime-stone and gravel. Within the perimeter, the rooms were nearly all laid bare; the tile stove that had conducted heat along clay pipes to other rooms, the kitchen, the steam bath, and the lead pipes for bringing water down from the mountain.

Years earlier, on the shores of the lake not far from St. Töllden, other sites had been found. Dwellings from the Bronze Age and earlier, her father had said. Tools and cook-ing pots, and weapons. The shoulder blades of goats carved into combs. Bows with tendons and charred stems for fire-making. Shoes of salt-cured leather with fur on the inside, six thousand years old, seven thousand, and more.

All those artifacts were now on exhibition in the museum that her father was in charge of. His digs were funded in part by the provincial government and in part by an American museum. He said the Romans had found those sites too, and others from the Iron Age. They had searched them for metals and flint.

The Romans had also mined salt in the mountains nearby. They'd done it by boring deep holes and piping water into them, siphoning off the salt solution and then boiling away the water. Over time the boreholes became large underground caves with walls and ceilings of salt. Salt had been like money, her father said. It was currency. They had paid their soldiers with it, hence the term. The root word *sold* meant salt, he said, and the expression to be worth one's salt came from that time also.

That night in her childhood bed, snug under the duvet and with the curtains making the familiar rustling sound as cold air stirred them through the half-open window, she imagined the Romans, two thousand years ago. Perhaps men in togas, or men and women in fine purple silks and tooled and gold-embossed leathers, poking through the remains of that earlier primitive civilization of people who wore animal furs, but who had nevertheless known how to build homes on stilts, how to make fire and melt iron from rock in small furnaces to cast tools and weapons.

To think of their lives then flooded by rising waters, crushed and buried by rockslides. Gone, but unearthed again and again, and marvelled at.

That night also in some dream an image came to her of two men duelling far away, with the first light of morning skimming low through trees, flashing in drops of dew on tree branches and on their swords. The image stayed with her until she left the bed and in her flannel nightgown and bare feet padded to the bathroom. She sat on the toilet and drank water bending over the tap, and by the time she was back in bed, the image had left.

In the morning over breakfast would have been the right time to put their minds at ease, to say something about not rushing into anything, perhaps even about postponing commitments. But there was nothing to say. The best she could do was to let them see how confident and happy she was. At some point she said, "Dad. Mom. Peter and I had a good long talk yesterday. You can ask him. Please do."

SHE HAD PHOTOGRAPHS of herself as a baby, and then at one and two years, and older. Photographs of family outings. Sunday hikes to guesthouses in the country. In one picture the adults were sitting on plankboard benches around plankboard tables under trees. Food was on the table, farmer's bread and cold meats and jugs of cider. Her father sat holding her on his lap, and he was absolutely beaming at her, adjusting her knitted cap with one hand. So much love for her. Such warmth and safety. He would have been fifty then, but a youthful-looking man with an upturned moustache, short-cropped hair, and bold eyes. And her mother thirty-nine but looking older.

In another picture she was already a teenager. Her father now white-haired sat with her in a photographer's studio, in a prop like a small ship and they were both at the helm. And other pictures, she in her lyceum uniform looking overly serious, and one of herself and Erika and Mitzi on ice skates, the ones you fixed onto boots with a small crank. In the picture they were holding hands and practising skating in a chorus line with one leg up like in a French nightclub. Ski pants tucked into socks rolled over at the ankles, and those clumsy boots and skates, and woollen mitts and hats with stars on them, and dangling pompons. She remembered they were laughing so hard posing for that picture they kept falling down.

———

BACK IN VIENNA Albert was getting ready to leave. The German embassy sent a truck with diplomatic licence plates. He ran the Norton up a ramp onto the bed and lashed it down, then the truck left. He packed his suitcase over Christmas and she spent most of her time with him at the Leonhardt apartment.

On the day of Epiphany the truck came back and it stood in the street with its engine running and exhaust smoke rising white in the cold air. They looked down on it from the balcony, all of them: she, Albert and Cecilia, and Erika and Mitzi, who had come to say goodbye. He carried down the suitcases, then came back for the English hunter saddle. He set it down on the floor and they kissed while the women turned their backs. He did not want anyone to walk downstairs with him.

And so they stood watching from the balcony, the driver coming out and saluting Albert and helping with the saddle, and then Albert climbing up to the cab. For a moment he stood on the footrest and craned his neck and looked up. He waved. She waved back.

"Child," said Cecilia to her afterwards. "Go wash your face. Straighten up and get on with it."

TWELVE

※

WITH ALBERT AWAY she threw herself fully into her studies. 1935 would bring her sixth year at university. Dr. Freud had withdrawn to his medical practice and to write, but in the spring the increasing numbers of book burnings in Germany prompted her and Erika to initiate a petition asking him to come and examine the issue. Freud agreed.

He came and stood on the dais and held up his three most recent books: *The Ego and the Id*, *The Future of an Illusion*, and *Civilization and Its Discontents*.

"You want me to talk about the book burnings," he said. "In truth, they don't deserve talking about. Some forms of denial are so transparent as to be childish. Burning books to deny what's in them. Think about it. In time they may move on to burning the authors also, as they did in Spanish Inquisition, the witch hunts. We shall see."

He said it was possible Europe was entering another era much like those dark centuries, where power was given not to those who had earned it and would use it to the benefit of society, but to those ready to support the self-serving intentions of their masters.

"Will it come to its senses and end soon? Probably not. Will it come here too? Probably. We shall have to see. For now it does not deserve any kind of serious investigation. You might say we refuse to stoop to that." He put the books down on the desk. "Let's instead move on to something much more interesting."

He said the office had asked him to consider delivering one more set of lectures. He could do that, he said, but he would be practising his English on them and if theirs was better than his, they were welcome to help out; he said he would also be recording the lectures for his own purposes. Later it became clear that he had used the occasion to practise his ideas in English for the day when he would leave Vienna.

The series he began that day consisted of six lectures on what he called *Practical Psychology for Everyday Life*. There was the usual informality about them that worked well, and they were interesting. She filled three notebooks, one for each topic. After the first session, word of the event spread among students, and for the second lecture the auditorium was filled, seats and standing room. The doors were opened and students pressed in from the hallways to hear.

The lectures were on women's relationships with other women, then on men's relationships with other men, and finally on men's and women's relationships with each other. As usual, Freud spoke off the top of his head, without notes. He stopped frequently, turned away and coughed into his handkerchief. He took a few deep breaths and continued. On occasion he asked if there was a better English word or phrase for what he had just said, and if one was offered, he would look around for consensus and then write it on the blackboard.

Essentially he said that women's relationships with each other turned on common experience as the co-endurer, and on the intuitive feminine; on likeness and recognition, and on empathy rather than competition, at least as long as there was a common fate and there was not much at stake beyond a sharing of experience. But if women were in competition with each other for anything – the love of a man, for example, or interesting work and recognition – then it was tooth and nail, the fiercest struggle of all.

The relationships of men, he said, turned on competition and power. If a man smelled fear in another, or weakness, or an eagerness to be accepted, then that man was already as good as dead, or at least discounted. Respect and honour once lost could hardly ever be regained because a truth had been glimpsed, if only for a moment, like a door opening and closing. Trust and true friendship among men, because they were about admitting weaknesses, took a long time to develop. It was about strength. About dominance and submission, as among wild animals, he said. Throughout history, how many men had killed the competitor; how many fathers had killed the son, how many sons the father?

With men and women, he said, it was much more complicated. He challenged the class to define the words *liking* and *loving*, and to carve out the line between them. Then he added sex to the discussion, and asked them to define sexual love. He asked them to think about what it was women wanted from men, and men from women.

A sea of hands went up, and words flew out: *Love, Sex, Money, Children, Family.* He stood by the desk, never far from his microphone and bulky tape recorder, and he rocked back and forth on his Oxford brogues.

"Yes," he said, and, "Yes, yes. All of that. But what else? Let's do this the Socratic way. You will have studied Edmund Husserl. What does he say?"

"Ask what is the thing in itself," someone shouted.

"Ah," Dr. Freud said. "Close. And have you done that?"

He told them to look at his book, *The Interpretation of Dreams*, switched off the tape recorder, and left for that day.

For the sixth and final lecture, university staff placed a second microphone on his desk and ran wires to loudspeakers out in the halls.

Dr. Freud stood there as usual in suit and tie and fobbed watch chain, and he began by saying that one had to accept the fact that humans were in most ways no different from animals; in fact, they were animals enfeebled by morality and social influences.

But creatures of deep nature, humans were, he said, and nature cared only about one thing. And that thing was *More*. More trees and more flowers with a billion seeds drifting on the air and perhaps one of them falling on good soil; more monkeys, more whales, more human babies, even if they starved to death in desert lands, and drowned to death in flood zones, and were strangled by their parents because they kept on coming.

Nature was a blind multiplying machine, he said. And nowhere did the notion of human happiness let alone dignity enter into her gears. Nature's job was *quantity*, not *quality*, even though quality might once in a while be the accidental by-product of quantity. And so, as to the question what did men want from women, and women from men, and how could they live happily together, one might apply Husserl, he said; but one had better not. It would be too sobering.

"Sexual tension," he said. "The push for *more*, at all ages and in all situations. The added tension of the unavailable, the luring, the romance. But behind it all, the blind and ruthless and single-minded sex drive. A woman in her mature years looking on her flock of children, six, seven, eight of them, all forever with their beaks open. And she, wondering where her plans for her own person had gotten lost in all that procreating. I see them every week in my practice."

He looked at the class, gave a rare smile, and added, "However wonderful and exciting at your age you may feel sexual tension is. I don't wish to take that away from you."

There was not a stir in the auditorium, and none in the hallways. In his pauses one could hear the echo from the loudspeakers out there in marble corners and ceiling vaults of this ancient university.

"As to the basic question you have been pondering," he said. "All answers are fine, but not even the sum of them is adequate. Not adequate because of the X-factor. We'll come to that later."

In one way, what men wanted from women were kind breasts, he said. They wanted nurture and warmth, kindness, even sweetness and understanding. They wanted neither competition nor argument nor challenge, of which they had plenty from other men. They wanted sex.

And likewise in one way, what women wanted from men was security and containment; it was being desired and valued and understood. Beyond that of course it was about having a sexual mate who provided and protected, and on close inspection all of it, absolutely all of it, had to do with nature's *More*.

He put his hands together and said, "Well. So it is Husserl in essence, but that essence is enormously overshadowed by our complicated psyches."

He gave examples of sexual desires and sexual acts in direct contradiction to natural and moral laws, perversions always rooted in childhood, he said, which in turn set up great inner tensions and misdeeds and unhappiness later in life.

"So," he said. "Where does that leave us with our question of what men want from women and vice versa?" He stood and looked around at the class, from front row to doorway and standing room at the back.

"Where indeed?" he said. "I invite you to continue the exercise with your boyfriend and girlfriend. Ask her or him to put into words what it is he or she wants from you. If they think long enough and are honest, they will discover that what they want from you is a feeling that is in turn the result of something that is rather more difficult to define, but that stems directly from their own individual psyche, be it healthy or sick. Why are they with you? They are with you because being with you makes them *feel* a certain way. And why are they leaving you? They are leaving you because, be they psychologically healthy or sick, they are *not* feeling the way they want to feel. And that one phrase"—he paused and looked at his enormous class— "that one phrase, *psychologically healthy or sick*, is always the great unknown. It is the X-factor in the formula of human relations."

He bent over his tape machine and took his time searching for the right button. He punched it and picked up his cold cigar that had been lying on the desk. He coughed and wiped his lips.

"So," he said. "I refer you to my books *Three Essays on the Theory of Sexuality* and *On Narcissism*. If you can find them. Are there any questions?"

———

ONE DAY AROUND THAT TIME there came a knock on the door of the Leonhardt apartment in Vienna. Cecilia was about to go into a coaching session, but she opened and looked out the crack. When she told the story later to Clara she said that all she could see was the doorman standing there in his admiral's uniform and behind him a young man, a tall boy.

"He insisted," the doorman said to her, and he stepped aside.

A tenor was warming up in the bathroom, but she had a moment. The boy was carrying a brand-new leather briefcase. He was dressed in long trousers baggy at the knees and a suit jacket. In his lapel she saw the Red Cross button some of them were wearing now since the swastika was banned.

The boy stepped forward and said he had been a friend of Theodor's and he was bringing something for her. She unlatched the chain and let him in.

As soon as he was inside, he leaned and peered around the doorway to the living room. "What is that noise?"

"A singer. Carry on."

He said he was from Mr. Seyss-Inquart's office and he had come to present her with the Blood Order in recognition of Theodor's sacrifice for the cause.

She sat down on the bench in the hall, under the wall-mounted telephone box there.

"What order?"

"The *Blood* Order," the boy said proudly. "It's an award, like a medal." He unbuckled the briefcase and reached inside. "This," he said.

He took out a sheet of paper and held it for her to take. He stood in the light of the ceiling lamp with his keen boy-eyes glinting and the shadow of his nose cast down on his mouth and chin. He shook the paper at her.

She reached but then lowered her hand.

"Take it! That noise," he said irritably. "Can't you stop it?"

"No."

She could see black printing on that paper, some Gothic calligraphy, the prominent heading, *BLOOD ORDER*, *awarded to . . .*

She shook her head.

"Read it."

"I don't want to."

"Theodor gave his life for our cause. Take this in his honour. There is also an actual medal, but we don't have it yet."

"He didn't *give* his life," she said. She stood up and walked to the door and opened it. "What pompous nonsense. He was simply gunned down in some field."

"He was not the only one that day," said the boy. "Take it. Take it for Theodor. These first editions have been signed by the Führer's undersecretary in person."

In the end she took it, and the next time she visited Maximilian in jail she told him about it. *Whispered* it to him, she said to Clara; to him, a decorated war veteran himself.

"Romantic nonsense," he whispered back. He glanced at the guard who stood not far away leaning against a wall. This took place in the visiting room made of poured concrete. They were one of three couples, all on iron benches bolted down, at iron tables bolted down also.

"I'll burn it if you think I should," whispered Cecilia. "I took it only because I thought it might be useful one day."

"Well. Keep it. You never know."

"No whispering," said the guard.

Cecilia said that Maximilian had aged greatly. His hair was white and he looked dead tired. He was much thinner.

He was getting used to it, he had told her during an earlier visit. But eight people they were in the cell now, one whose feet had been crushed with iron bars by the police. They had a tin plate and a wooden spoon each for food, and a covered bucket for shitting, which he could no longer do now without bleeding. Steel beds cantilevered from the wall, roll-up mattresses on them and a blanket. He tried to make a joke of it. "Other than that, it's not bad," he said.

For a few weeks Cecilia kept the document on a shelf in the living room, and Clara and Erika and Mitzi all saw it there: the black ink, the Nazi seal. Then one day Cecilia took it away and put it out of sight.

———

IN MUNICH Albert had adjusted quickly to his new life. A tailor had come and measured him for his uniforms, with an assistant to take notes while the tailor snapped his tape and crouched and measured and called out numbers. The uniforms when they arrived were snug and sharp with excellent needlework; fully six sets for everything from the parade ground to panzer blacks, to horseback riding, to small dress and full dress. The shirts were fitted, even the track and field outfit was, and the pyjamas.

Albert was assigned a batman and an adjutant to be shared with two other officers. The plan was that in a seamless series of long days stretching over nearly two years, he would learn everything about tank warfare and strategy and leadership in battle the school could teach.

Field Marshal Paul von Kleist was in charge of building the tank army of the German military, and he listened closely to the ideas of General Heinz Guderian about lightning warfare. Guderian had been behind the school's program, and he often came there to observe exercises with the panzer models II and III, and the prototype of the new panzer IV that was in production now. Gunnery was practised with the 37mm turret guns, the 75mm howitzers, the 88mm, and the new 50mm. They also practised with 150mm armoured cannons that fired shells that on incoming roared like freight trains. They knew this, Albert said, because as part of their training they had to endure incoming live fire in a trench.

On several occasions General Guderian brought General Erwin Rommel along to observe exercises in landscape boxes the size of four and eight billiard tables, with artificial hills and rivers, and trees and houses and valleys to cross. To move their unit symbols, they used long rakes or they sent aides on stockingfeet into the toy landscape.

"Speed and absolute relentlessness," Guderian said. "Tanks are the iron fist to punch through defences and they never stop moving forward. Stuka dive bombers and Messerschmitts provide cover and support from above, and infantry on trucks and APCs follows closely and cleans up the conquered areas."

To make their cannons more effective, Krupp had produced a new armour-piercing projectile with an improved charge. If it struck a tank, it blasted just a small hole through the armour, but the compression and heat and the needle-thin steel fragments killed every living thing inside. Since the enemy was expected to have a similar charge, the Type IV panzers were equipped with a new kind of armour with air spaces between plates set at a greater degree of slope.

In addition chemists were developing a revolutionary type of gunpowder, Albert said. He explained to her that the only way to drive a projectile faster with a given charge was to have a propellant where every single grain fired at the very same instant. Unlike traditional powders, he said, some of which burned so slowly that grains still came out as sparks when the shot had already left the muzzle.

Apart from the tanks, new weaponry kept arriving at the school for the students to integrate and deploy. There were night exercises and brutal marches with full gear and mortar base plates just to show them what their men would have to endure, and to gain leadership experience he and his fellow officers were posted as seconds-in-command to ever larger units across the country. He spent weeks near Hamburg, near Cologne, near Berlin. Back on the base, days were filled with more classroom instruction on anything from new tank technology and refinements of existing materials and mechanisms to military history, strategy, and psychology.

"Men respect other men only if they see qualities in them that they want for themselves," the psychology instructor told them. "They'll respect you if they want to be like you in some way. Men respect moral and physical courage and strength. They want leadership, but leadership they can look up to. We are talking about things that are felt, not seen," he said. "We *see* people only for the first few seconds. Then we *feel* them. Even if we are looking at them, our eyes are really only probing them to inform our intuition. We *feel* things like courage, decisiveness, moral fibre, and honesty. And fear, absolutely. Never show fear. Never."

The weeks and months went by quickly, for him and for her. They spoke on the telephone, he from the school office or from other postings with his back to the clerks, and she from the post office or from the Leonhardt apartment, sitting on that bench in the hall staring at coats on the rack opposite.

He had also been issued a good horse, he told her, a strong and wilful mare. He was riding her most days.

"You love it," she said to him. "The whole experience."

"I do, absolutely. But I miss you."

"I miss you too."

She said Emmerich was working them as hard as ever, and so was Professor Ferdinand. But it was going well. She was also still doing the parks with Erika. Sometimes the depot was out of supplies and then all they could do was drive around and talk to people and bring drinking water. The other day they'd taken a girl and her mother to the hospital.

"Come and visit," she said.

"Come and visit. How?"

"What about the other passport?" she said. "You know. The one the forger made for you. You said it was good."

THIRTEEN

❖

IN VIENNA the murdered Chancellor Dollfuss had been
succeeded by Dr. Kurt von Schuschnigg, the former education minister. The newspapers praised his diplomatic
skills; they said he had been working to secure an alliance
with Italy and Hungary against Hitler, but then those
countries saw more advantage in siding with Berlin, and
they abandoned him.

She saw a picture of Mussolini and Hitler striding side
by side, Mussolini like an opera diva wearing a large-
brimmed hat with pheasant feathers in the band. *March
of the Fascists*, the caption said.

Soon after that the papers reported that Chancellor
Schuschnigg had signed his own peace agreement with
Hitler; in exchange for not being invaded by Germany, he'd
had to give the Austrian Nazi Party legal status and accept
Nazis into his cabinet.

"You realize what that means," said Peter. "It's the infamous thin edge of the wedge." He said it was not what the chancellor had wanted to do. He knew that for a fact.

One night in August she and Erika were helping some injured people in an underpass when the trucks came back. They could hear the engines in low gear and already it was too late to run and hide. From the truck beds handheld searchlights found them, then men jumped off the trucks swinging steel bars and wooden clubs.

They broke her left arm with one blow and nearly tore off Erika's ear with another. A young man stood there, lit from behind by the truck headlights with his face in darkness and his ears like a bat's sticking out pink.

"Next time we find you helping them we'll set fire to you and your car," he said. "We'll kill you."

"But we work for the Red Cross," Erika screamed. "This is what we do. We help, you idiot. Unlike you." She stood with her hand pressed to her ear. Blood was running between her fingers, down her wrist, and into her sleeve.

He stared at her. He raised his stick and poked her hard in the breast. "Don't help any one side. Don't interfere. Let the strongest win."

The men ran back to their truck, talking and laughing.

At the Red Cross station Erika's ear received eight stitches and Clara's arm was put in a cast. There was no X-ray machine, but the nurse said the arm looked straight and she did not think it needed resetting.

At first she did not tell her parents, so as not to worry

them. She hoped that by the time she saw them again the cast might be off. But she did tell Albert on the telephone, and they spoke for a long time that Sunday while she sat pale and subdued in Cecilia's hall.

"The entire arm?" he said on the telephone. "Sweetheart. How terrible."

"Just about," she said. She felt better talking to him. "From wrist to shoulder, bent at the elbow. It's in a sling but it's still heavy. Like carrying a suitcase around."

Eventually she told her parents too. They wanted her to come and see Dr. Mannheim, but she said the cast was fine and she was very busy right now. She stood and looked at herself in the mirror and resolved to get on with her life regardless of all the turmoil. To live above events and not be at their mercy, Professor Emmerich had said.

Peter was rarely in Vienna, but when he was, she tried to get information from him. One Sunday he told her he had been in Rome with a delegation from the League of Nations to protest once again against the Italian massacres in Ethiopia, but they had been sent home. A flunkey in a white suit had come to tell them everyone was busy with more important issues.

The League was not successful in creating true allian-ces, he admitted. There were too many conflicting inter-ests, and the League had no real power to enforce anything.

She made notes for later, for something she thought of as *Life in One Room, in One Mind*. She began it after the attack, which if anything after the first few days had made her more determined. It had driven her back into herself and forced her to examine what was important to her, and what was not.

She was no saint, this she knew. And no selfless battler against evil and stupidity. If she could ever contribute in any way, she decided, it would be through her studies, through what she was learning there. Things she could do with her mind.

She also began to plan her dissertation; it would be inspired by Rainer Maria Rilke, she thought. Something departing from his writings about inspiration. *Moments of Faith and Power*, perhaps, as a working title.

It resonated with her own view of philosophical structure as a house to inhabit, and to see the world through its windows. When Rilke spoke of faith, she did not think he was referring to religious faith but to faith in one's inner power and will to create meaning and purpose.

There was more, she felt, and it would have to do with the survival of soul and spirit in dark moments. The writers and poets she admired most were men and women who examined and observed and noticed, and thought for themselves. They might have wished they could simply believe, but that was not the same thing. And in any case, had their faith been blindly religious, their lives might have been easier but they would have been much less interesting as writers.

She spoke again to Professor Emmerich, and he sat and

listened. He nodded and said, Good, and that he wished her luck. From this point on she should not consult with him about her idea any more, he said. She should talk to her Ph.D. adviser.

He saw her disappointment. "What?" he said. "It's standard academic procedure, Miss Herzog. To avoid any conflict of interest and too narrow an approach."

She sat with the cast in her lap, taking this in. She would miss him, miss these informal talks. "But on other topics," she said. "Like on the new material now?"

"Of course. But not on your dissertation." He nodded at the cast. "It must get in the way. Does it make it hard to type? Or even sit at a desk properly?"

"It's impossible to type. Much too slow, and I can't type capital letters. I tried. So I'm writing everything by hand. You've seen my papers."

He smiled. "Miss Herzog, when you are ready for an adviser just tell the office."

AT THE APARTMENT Mitzi had looked at Erika's ear, at the stitches coarse as in some homemade soccer ball, and she had given her a new asymmetrical hairstyle that swung forward to her jawline on that side and covered much of the damage. Women stopped Erika in the street and asked who did her hair, and soon Mitzi had a half-dozen more clients who wanted a hairdo just like that. She'd picked up her new papers in the name of Anna Susanne Toplitz, and she kept them in a safe place in her apartment. The identity card and driver's licence had a surprisingly good photo of herself.

Mitzi always dressed well in clean white smocks over black blouses and knee-length skirts that showed her good legs in silk stockings. She was focused on her work, making house calls only in bright daylight and in good parts of town. The in-colour for youngish women who could afford it that year was jet-black, with bangs nearly to the eyebrows or no bangs at all but straight and parted in the middle. Rich older women, and Vienna had many of those, liked a perm and a little blonding or purpling, depending on their natural colour. Rich older women also had regular manicures and pedicures. They had hairs plucked from their chins, and vigorous facials with hot cloths and French salves to stimulate blood flow and make the skin look alive and pink. Rich older women could have anything they wanted; they never haggled over price and they tipped generously on top of that. Mitzi was doing well.

IN NOVEMBER 1936, the officers' academy granted its students one week's leave. Albert put on civilian clothes and with his forged passport crossed into Austria. He travelled by night train from Munich to Vienna, sitting in a corner seat by the window. The only other people in his compartment were a couple perhaps in their seventies who sat at times holding hands. They'd said good evening, and nodded and smiled, and that had been it. At the border near Salzburg the train stopped and whistles sounded. He let down the window on its leather strap and looked out, and saw teams of armed police boarding the train at either end. They had dogs, and that worried him.

He could hear the policemen sliding open compartment doors one by one, coming closer. Soon they were in this car; he could hear their voices. One German, one Austrian. Out the window the station lay in poor light from overhead lamps, and the engine stood not far away, puffing steam.

They yanked open the compartment door and one of them said, "Passport control" and held out his hand. The old man and the woman handed over their passports, and he too reached into his jacket pocket and took his out. The woman looked terrified, but the dog paid no attention to her. It was looking at him. Watching him closely.

Do not make eye contact with the dog, he told himself. Do not. A large, shaggy Alsatian. He nodded at the policemen and they appraised him: his suit, his military haircut. The Austrian one opened his passport to the picture page and passed it on to his colleague, who did the same and handed it back. The dog came closer. A male. He could smell its rankness. The German policeman lengthened the dog's leash and waited a moment. He said something to the dog and yanked it back, and they moved on to the next compartment.

He stood by the open window to calm himself. He looked out and eventually saw the policemen climbing down, four men and two dogs. The watering-funnel swung away from the engine and a whistle sounded. The train jerked and stopped, and moved off. Coal smoke and steam came in the window and he closed it.

AT CLARA'S BUILDING the concierge pulled the door-latch for him on her long string and then watched him from her spy window. She craned her neck at him.

"We're winning," she said.

He stopped and looked down the dark stairwell. "Who is?"

The concierge stared at him. She slapped shut her window.

On this leave, he and Clara went out only once, to visit his mother. He did not want to risk being seen, and so they spent the rest of the time at the apartment. Erika moved upstairs with Mitzi, and at lunch the first day they all came together and made bacon and tomato omelettes and they drank real coffee that Albert had brought from the school kitchen. They talked and laughed and the women pretended they were not afraid of developments out there; of the frequent sound of gunshots; of running footsteps in the street by night.

Her arm was still in the cast, but it no longer hurt as much. Erika's ear was healing, more or less, but the scar was thick and ragged because of the poor stitching. She showed it to Albert and pretended not to care, but in truth she did. She was teaching herself to get past it with personality, and most of the time she succeeded. The hairstyle helped.

At night, in her room, they talked for hours. She told him it was only now that she realized how much she'd missed him. Just being with him. Talking, listening. Being together.

School was going well, she said. She had a Ph.D. adviser now, another professor from the philosophy department. A younger man. Not as good as Emmerich, but all right. And you? she said.

He talked about his horse. About the generals. Rommel and Guderian. So bold, these men. So clear in what they wanted.

Nights at times, talking like this, they sat up tailor-fashion, facing each other on the bed, she resting her plaster cast on a pillow on her knee. She would reach out and touch his face in the dim light of the streetlamps. She would open his pyjama buttons and feel his chest with her eyes closed, his muscles and ribs there, feel his words as he spoke. She lay in his arms with her cast sticking up like strange and massive rigging on some ghostship sailing through the night.

When it was time to leave, he knew he would not take the risk to cross with a forged passport a second time. He had other plans, and he discussed them with her. And on the morning of that day they said goodbye and kissed, and she went downstairs with him to the taxi and saw him off.

He told the driver to take him to the German embassy, and there he walked up the wide stone steps under the Nazi flags and the black eagles, past the armed guards. At reception he gave the woman his name and asked for the military attaché. Within minutes then he sat in the major's office and confessed his situation.

SHE SPENT THE FOUR DAYS of Christmas at home with her parents and brothers, and with Daniela. There was snow on the ground and snow all the way down the mountains. Ski slopes were busy, and hotels and restaurants were filled with English and American tourists.

Dr. Mannheim, the family doctor, said the cast should come off. He wanted to see the arm under it and he wanted an X-ray picture taken. The picture showed that the humerus had knitted at a slight offset.

"You have a choice," said Dr. Mannheim. "You can leave it, or we can break it again and reset it. I'd leave it and start exercising the arm."

The arm was noticeably thinner than the other, but it looked straight enough to her. She left it, and Peter showed her how to exercise the biceps by curling a bucket filled with an increasing volume of water, and the triceps by doing push-ups first against a wall and eventually on the floor.

Her mother suggested a visit to the church, and they agreed as they did every year at Christmas. They walked nave, transept and aisles, all empty between services, the stones cold, and the woodwork soaked in incense these hundreds of years; the carved and gilded altars, the Romanesque art, the Gothic windows.

At the base of the tower they watched the sexton in his black robe and hobnailed boots standing among the bell ropes, sorting them. He wrapped a thin one around his left wrist and a thicker one around his right. He closed his eyes and dropped nearly to his knees and rose again, and he began pulling the ropes, standing there solidly now with his arms going up and down and up and down.

On the way home her mother slowed to walk by her side behind the others. Clara knew what was coming.

"It's been two days now and you haven't mentioned Albert," her mother said. "We were concerned about your arm, but now I need to ask you what your plans are. Have they changed?"

"No, they haven't. And I don't think they will, Mama. At the moment Albert is busy with his courses and I am busy getting ready for the finals and for my dissertation."

"I see. Do you remember the letter I wrote to you after you brought him here?"

"Of course. I wrote back to you. Thanking you."

They walked in uneasy silence and she waited for her mother to say more, but she did not.

FOURTEEN

⬩⬩⬩

DURING READING WEEK she travelled to Munich to
see him ride a military cross-country tournament. A reckless undertaking, it turned out to be, on horses rough-shod
for frozen ground and with natural barriers nearly as high
as a man; with snow on fields deeply chewed up by tank
tracks, and half-frozen rivers to be forded. She watched
him at the starting line, in military cap and tunic, as he
kept leaning forward to talk to his horse, a nervous high-
stepping thing with its head up high and eyes wild at the
sound of his voice.

At the viewing area Clara stood with his adjutant,
Lieutenant Bahr, and other observers, some generals with
red lapels and braided shoulder boards. They could see much
of the course except for stretches through trees and across
low marshland and down into a gully. On a steep incline the
horn sounded for the first accident, but the race went on.

They watched the riders now far away, black against the snow, flying past tank targets on tow rigs, but she could not make him out at this distance. Minutes later they passed in front of the stand in a cloud of snow and pounding hooves, the field already stretched out. He was two horses behind the leader. The riders were lying nearly flat on their horses' necks for the long jump across a frozen river, and down they plunged into the gully and immediately after that came a steep climb through trees and bushes for a flat-out run at a high fieldstone fence. The horn sounded for another accident, but the race went on for seven more laps. Ice and mud coated the horses' flanks and ice from their breath clung to their manes.

Albert won silver for the school; gold went to a tank unit in Berlin. He had a gash on his forehead and his horse stood mad-eyed and shaking and covered in frost from its breath. Three riders were in hospital and one horse had to be shot.

"Crazy," she told him, and she did not much care who else heard her. "What for? I am actually very angry. This was so needlessly dangerous." Some officers nearby turned to look at her, but all she could think of was her mother's Torben dead in the hall and Mother running from the living room to see what the commotion was.

"How can I be trusting you?" she said, and Lieutenant Bahr raised his eyebrows and said, "Shh." He moved to block the view of her toward the generals.

"How? Albert? You tell me that."

"But it was nothing. I had a good horse. Didn't you see?" Albert stood crestfallen. "And I won silver. It's good! I don't understand."

"You won silver but at what price? You might be dead now, or crippled for life. And for what? For silver? How much silver? And I thought you loved horses."

"I do. But not as pets to be coddled. Once in a while they need to be stretched close to their limits. It builds their confidence."

"And if it had been you that crashed into that stone wall? And you in hospital now? Maybe crippled."

"Well, it isn't. And it couldn't be. Stop it, Clara. What is the matter with you?"

She stomped away angrily to where mess orderlies in white jackets were serving mulled wine and rum toddies, while a medic cleaned Albert's wound and put in four stitches right there and then without freezing.

She asked for two toddies and took them back to where the medic was finishing up with a last knot and gauze taped over the cut. "Done," said the medic.

Albert turned to her, still looking crestfallen and puzzled. But she had forgiven him already, and thinking back years later she would come to see that it was at the moment when he turned to her with that white thing on his forehead and his brown eyes so worried that she finally knew she would marry this man.

She stayed there for three days, in the visiting officers' apartment the school had provided. They played house and talked, and they went out for dinners at restaurants. They heard Bach performed at the cathedral, and they snuggled up in bed and made love and walked arm in arm through the old town and kissed in dark doorways.

At the school dinner to celebrate the silver medal, both generals were at the table and she sat not far from them, close enough to be able to watch them eat and talk, and to be able to study them and think her thoughts. At one point General Rommel stood and pronounced the first toast to horses and humans because of the ancient and noble bond between them.

They drank to that, they drank to Albert, and then all the men rose and stood and drank to her as his fiancée, and they wished them well.

She watched the generals converse and sip wine and eat their meal and touch napkins to their lips, and some years later when Albert told her what Hitler had ordered Rommel to do, she remembered this very dinner and the man's good face, his unhurried glances of appraisal of her to decide whether Albert had chosen well and whether this union would strengthen or weaken him as a man and as a soldier.

IN FEBRUARY OF THAT YEAR, after extensive manoeuvres with tanks, dive bombers, and live ammunition on the plains of Lüneburg, Albert graduated. She took the train out to witness the ceremony, and she stayed with him at the same officers' temporary apartment. They had just two days, then she returned to Vienna.

Field Marshal von Kleist put General Guderian in charge of one of the tank corps, and Albert was assigned to that corps and given command of the newly formed 14th Armoured Battalion Landshut Black. It consisted of nearly a thousand men and seventy-seven Type IV and Type III panzers, of armoured personnel carriers and trucks and motorized 88mm and 150mm field guns. Landshut Black was classified as an independent battle unit operating in support of the 7th Panzer Division under the command of General Erwin Rommel, and it was stationed not far from the town of Landshut, near the highway to Munich.

IN VIENNA Professor Emmerich in his workingman's clothes and bicycle clips was delivering his concluding lectures to her graduating class. He picked up on Nietzsche's Übermensch, and with clear references to the Nazis began to delineate the opposite notion, that of the Untermensch: a person who had deliberately chosen not the morally high road but the low.

He asked them to consider that if Nietzsche's ideal in the absence of God had been the light within, might not in the absence of God the temptation be irresistible for some to develop the darkness within? Just as liberating, he said.

"Liberating, especially if there are no consequences to worry about. Liberating. Consider that word *liberating*. *Setting free* from what? Well, from shame, fear, failure, of course. From self-loathing."

Liberating from constraints of conventional morality and society, he said. And an embrace of violence instead, to act out the darker emotions. One could see examples of this happening now.

"You understand," Professor Emmerich said with a thin smile, "that these are merely philosophical exercises. Philosophy empowers us to examine ideas, to pause and examine life. To ask clarifying questions that go to the root of things."

He had taken to sitting tailor-fashion on the desk, resting his elbows on his knees and leaning forward as he spoke. She would watch him from her usual place in the second row, and she'd realize that it was because of people like Mrs. Allmeier so long ago in high school and Professor Emmerich now that she wanted to be a person living by her mind; this brilliant man sitting cross-legged like a friend on the desk, pulling knowledge and fantastic ways of seeing things from the corners of his mind and offering them up like this, so casually, as if they were nothing.

"Is it also possible, then," he said, "that this preferred choice to pursue the light is not within all of us? Or to different degrees? Is it possible that nature on average gives birth to monsters as often as it does to saints? The selfless and the selfish? The givers and the takers? Those with morality and those without? The nurturous and the murderous?"

"But we have laws for that," she called out.

"Ah! Again?" He pointed at her.

"Laws, to govern behaviour."

He climbed off the desk and picked up a piece of chalk. *LAWS*, he wrote on the blackboard.

"Think about it. To govern behaviour means ruling on what is permissible and what is not. If monstrous behaviour is suddenly permissible by law, encouraged and rewarded even, then what do you think will happen? Which will it encourage, light or darkness? All this in the absence of God and with morality resting in the eye of the beholder.

"We have that already in Plato," he said. "Where he talks about surmounting oneself. But it requires work, does it not? And it requires the will to perform that work and live in the light, which is Nietzsche." He picked up the chalk again and drew a fast-ascending curve.

"If you take away just one thing from our time together, then let it be this," he said. "Well, *two* things. One: always, always, always trust your own mind and think things through for yourself. And two, go up. Up and up. Especially in the absence of God. Always strive to go up, never down."

BY THE TIME SHE BEGAN WRITING her dissertation on *Moments of Faith and Power*, she had already spoken to the rector about teaching as an unpaid lecturer, and so working her way into an assistant-professorship and eventually perhaps into a full one. Professors Roland Emmerich and Anton Ferdinand in Vienna, and Ludwig Wittgenstein writing from England, had put in a word for her, and based on these three references the rector agreed to consider her, depending on the rating of her final work.

The heart of her thesis was to be the attempt, the decision, and the action to seize the bright moment and to carry it through darkness the way Stone Age man carried fire in his hands, had sheltered and fed the precious embers from a lightning strike so as to have fire again another day. She knew that principles of morality and attitude had to do with it. But principles were only the hands, not the fire.

Since she could find few direct references to her core idea in literature, she plowed ahead and built it from her own insights, and for background and structure she referred to hints of approaches in the works of western philosophy and in writers such as Hemingway, Steinbeck, Woolf, Tolstoy, Dostoyevsky, and Zweig. She referred to Rilke and to Yeats, his famous scene of inspiration flaring up and dying in a London tea shop.

She sat at her desk at the apartment, and she wrote for weeks and weeks; nine, ten pages a day. She wrote outlines and drafts by hand, she edited and rewrote; she typed them clean. For breaks she did housework and shopped, and she bicycled to the post office to call Albert and her parents. Often, if it was in the early evening, Erika would come along and call Koren, who had by then moved to Stockholm.

Before those calls Erika would change into one of the blouses Koren had liked so much on her, the light blue one or the green one, because they went so well with her black hair and eyes. She would dress as if for a date, even put on a touch of lipstick. And then at the post office, which smelled of the oiled floor and of stale bread somehow, Clara would watch her through the windows in the booth, and Erika would be sitting on the round stool in there and lean forward and hold her forehead and Clara could hear her even through the glass, saying, No, she could not just pack up and leave and would he please stop saying that. She was developing a career, Erika said. The Red Cross, and she liked being needed. You come when this is over, Erika said, and how much longer can it last?

For some of that time Erika's ear was under a bandage again. She had found a plastic surgeon who said he could remove the welted scar, and since neither of the women had the money he was asking for, Mitzi had struck a contra deal with the surgeon's wife for one year of free hair, nails, and face.

MOMENTS BECAME A WORK of 285 typed pages, fully referenced and annotated. She submitted it in June 1937 and on September 15 that year she received her Ph.D. She was twenty-six years old. The certificate was handwritten in Latin. It began, *Nos rector universitatis litterarum vindobonensis* – and it listed the faculty, and went on – *promotor rite constitutus, in dominam clarissimam Clara Eugenie Herzog e St. Töllden in Austria, postquam et dissertatione cui inscribur . . .*

On the day of the award ceremony there was gunfire in the streets in some of the districts, and so the convocation took place not in the great hall with its street-facing windows but in the inner courtyard of the university. Just five doctorates that year in Philology, the recipients being called one by one to the stones around the sundial, and the rector himself in the flowing velvet gown and the black hat of his office presenting the scrolls.

Her parents were there for the occasion, as were Erika and Mitzi, and Cecilia and Maximilian just released from prison. Peter was there with his Daniela, who beamed at her across the courtyard.

Only Albert was not there. In a deal struck with the school office, his penalty for crossing a foreign border illegally had been postponed until after the horse race and his graduation. But now it was in force. At the time, he had been summoned to the office of the general's aide, Colonel von Heintzman, and the colonel had spoken of principles and of the Officers' Code of Ethical Conduct. The colonel had confiscated the forged passport and pronounced the cancellation of all leave for one full month.

BY DECEMBER OF THAT YEAR, *Moments* as a work on applied Existentialism had become something of a hit among university publications in German. The rector's office agreed to count it as her first academic work for distribution, and to register the points and pay her the usual copyright honorarium once legalities had been worked out.

FIFTEEN

❖

DR. GOTTSCHALK had booked Mitzi into the hospital for tests and X-rays before the operation, and they'd marked the day on the calendar in Clara's kitchen. She and Mitzi were aware of it even if they never spoke of it. But it was on the weekend before the trip to the hospital that Mitzi mentioned the churchbells.

"I hear them all the time," she said. "I hear them but I've never seen them."

"We should have done that years ago."

"Well, I didn't think of it years ago. I'd like to see them."

"It's up steep and narrow stairs," she said. "And you can hardly walk on level ground."

"Can hardly walk? I beg your pardon. Look at me. I can walk very well with canes. It'll just take a bit longer."

She agreed to go with Mitzi to speak to the priest, and Father Hofstätter looked at Mitzi standing there on the stone floor in the church annex, trying not to lean on her canes.

"Mrs. Friedmann," he said. He shook his round head. "The problem is the length of time it would take you to climb the stairs. Even just half-way up the tower the bells are very loud." He brought up his hands and made them tremble close to his ears. "As you know they ring every fifteen minutes. It's automatic these days, for years now, actually. A radio signal triggers an electric mechanism." He pointed up. "From space. Imagine."

"How long would it take me?" Mitzi asked.

"I don't know. But longer than fifteen minutes. Even I can hardly go up and down within fifteen minutes now. The serviceman from the satellite company can do it, but he is young and fit and he's used to it."

"My friend Doctor Herzog here," said Mitzi. "She saw them when she was young."

The priest smiled. "So let her tell you about them. Nothing has changed. The beams and the bells are the same, but instead of ropes we have the satellite signal now."

They walked back to the house. Halfway there the bells rang eleven o'clock. "The first one," she said. "This one is no bigger than your hat. The vesper bell is even smaller."

They stood on the sidewalk and a group of kindergarten children led by a young woman swirled around them like a river.

"And this one," she said. She held up a finger. "Just listen. It's very big. Bigger than my desk."

Mitzi stood listening. Her lips moved with the number of bell strikes. "That big," she said then. "Imagine."

THE NEXT DAY she was back in Father Hofstätter's rectory. He stood up from the chair by the desk and folded his hands in front of his stomach.

"Doctor Herzog," he said. In St. Töllden everyone had always called her by her maiden name. "So soon again."

"Father, I realize what I am going to ask for may be inconvenient. It may even cost money for the technician, but I am prepared to pay for the service call."

He stood waiting. Behind him they were both reflected in the new climate-controlled glass case along the wall that held the leather-bound books with the history of the parish since the early Middle Ages.

"What I am asking," she said, and she reached into her coat pocket and took out a one-hundred-euro bill and unfolded it for him to see. Father Hofstätter looked at the bill. He looked back up at her.

"I'm wondering," she said. "Father, would you mind calling the technician and asking him to shut down the bells for as long as it takes Mrs. Friedmann to climb the stairs and come down again? Is that possible?" She offered the bill. "For the service call."

The priest hesitated. He took the money and slipped it under the flap of his jacket pocket.

"Well," he said. "It's an unusual request, but I think it may be possible."

And so, a few days before the appointment with Dr. Gottschalk, she and Mitzi, accompanied by a young girl ministrant in a red surplice, climbed the stairs to the bell tower. The ministrant had blond locks and a button speaker to her cellphone in one ear. She was quick as a squirrel. She clicked light switches and she held a flashlight for them to see the oaken treads worn thin over time. On the way up she kept stopping and observing them bright-eyed over her shoulder.

"Take your time," Clara said over and over to Mitzi. "Always one hand for the railing and the other for the cane. One step at a time."

"Sorry to be so slow, dear," Mitzi said to the girl. "It's very good of you to do this for us."

"No worries," said the girl. She took her cellphone from her pocket and looked at the display. This while Mitzi stood resting, leaning against the handrail and the stone wall nearly as old as Christendom itself.

Eventually they did reach the top, and here was the bell chamber exactly as she remembered it. Except that on the south wall, lugged into the stone, was a dish to receive the radio signal for the bell timer. Mitzi stood breathing deeply, taking in the room, the enormous timbers and joinery; the ironwork and the bells in their bell tree, arranged not by size but by pitch.

"My," said Mitzi. "Imagine."

They looked out the small arched windows over the town, the warren of tile roofs edged in copper for snow to melt from eaves; the tower at the end of the once-gated market square; the ten-foot sundial high on the south wall of that tower.

The building that had once been her father's museum was now being used for social housing. Its contents had been moved years ago to the site where the dig had been, and the Roman villa there formed the centrepiece of a new museum and of the town archives. In those archives the key contents of her files would have their own display wall behind glass, the archivist had promised. Her father's name was engraved on a plaque near the door.

"And what's that out there?" said Mitzi. "Are those the new suburbs?"

"Yes," she said. "And subsidized housing."

The ministrant stood thumbing her cellphone. "Whenever you're ready," she said without looking up.

"Are you ready to go?" she said to Mitzi.

Mitzi nodded, and they began the slow descent. The girl first, then Mitzi, then Clara.

SHE KNEW it was from her mother that she had her love of churches. But churches as works of art: no priests, no sermons, no people to distract from just these great vaulted spaces full of peace and art and timeless yearning.

"*Chambers*," her mother had once quoted Rilke more or less accurately in the Benedictine Abbey Church at Lambach, "*in mimicry of the human heart and, like it, forever waiting to be filled.*"

The fabulous Benedictine Abbey at Lambach was one place where young Wolfgang Amadeus Mozart had walked, as had schoolboy Hitler, when his name was still Schicklgruber and he was just another village lout looking for trouble. And while Mozart had been inspired there to compose his bright Lambach Symphony in G-Dur, young Schicklgruber it was said had seen there for the first time the ancient sun rune set in stone; the crooked cross. The firewheel obliterating all in its path to make room for a new order.

ALBERT'S ASHES had come from the crematorium in a small brass urn with his name on it. *Albert Bertolt Leonhardt*, and the dates of his birth and death.

At the grave Father Hofstätter uttered a few words in Latin and swung his censor over the frozen ground while the stonemason placed the urn in the wall niche and cemented the glass window shut. She, Mitzi, and Emma in dark clothes and hats stood by the grave. Albert's name was on the marble tablet now too.

She slipped Father Hofstätter a twenty-euro tip and the stone mason a ten, and then she and Mitzi and Emma went for a coffee at the new restaurant by the post office.

"Have you heard from Willa?" said Emma. "I rarely do."

"Yes. By email. She's fine. That trip to Nairobi probably won't happen."

"So we won't see her until — whenever." Emma sat sipping her latte, her eyes on her mother's face. Clara reached across the table and Emma set down the cup and took her hand. She gave a squeeze and let go.

Light came in soft and even through the half-curtains, and in the background the espresso machine chortled. A little girl with black hair in braids said something in Turkish and a woman answered patiently in that language.

IN THE MORNING of the day before the appointment, Mitzi came to visit. While Clara cleared her desk and shut down the computer, Mitzi made coffee. Clara was roughly one-third into the translation of the English novel. She'd been working on it steadily, a certain number of pages each day.

They sat on the old elbowchairs in the study and Mitzi said, "None of your girls wants the salon, am I right? Or even one of Emma's kids. They'll think it's beneath them."

"Your hair salon? What brought that on?"

Mitzi took her time. "The hair salon, yes," she said then.

"Maybe. Have you asked Josephine? She's the younger one of Tom's kids."

"Josephine, yes. I did, last fall. She told me she wanted to be a fashion model."

"She worked in an office for a while. Emma says she's on some kind of social assistance now, some government program. Maybe ask her again."

"Once they're on that . . ." Mitzi waved a hand.

"You could still ask her. Or Emma. Or Tomas. Well, no. And Emma likes teaching."

They were sitting in the corner away from the desk with the computer. The sun was on the other side of the house, and pale blue light came down from the sky in the window. It fell on Mitzi's shoulder and on her cheek, and in this light Mitzi's dear old cheek looked like a wrinkled peach. Her hair was snow-white with just a faint blue cast.

"What's this about?" she said. "That question about the shop. They do these operations all the time now. Doctor Gottschalk says the risk is negligible."

"I know. So listen: Magdalena, the woman who's running the salon for me, has been loyal since day one. She works hard and she's a single mother. The clients like her and she's good with the stylists. She runs the place and I'm never even there."

"I know. You've said so."

"Do you want it?"

"What? Your salon? Mitzi-dear. I'm speechless."

"Do you want it?"

"I'm not a hairdresser, I'm not even a businesswoman."

"You could just run it. Own it."

"No, I couldn't. I like what I do and I plan to do it for as long as I possibly can. This." She waved at the desk. "For what it's worth."

Mitzi sat looking at her. "I know," she said. "I'm asking because this afternoon I'm seeing the lawyer."

"Ah. The lawyer. I see."

There was a long pause. Cars passed in the street below

and not far away the ten-o'clock bus honked its horn at the blind corner with the traffic mirror.

Eventually she said, "Do you want me to walk there with you? To the lawyer?"

"If you could. I'd like that. If you can take the time."

SIXTEEN

❖

THERE WAS A PHOTOGRAPH of her graduation in the box on family and social history before the war. In the picture she stood in cap and gown displaying the scroll, with all her family and friends around her. Her parents were standing as far away as possible from Cecilia and Maximilian, whose face even in this black-and-white picture looked yellow and his collar two sizes too big. They had been introduced, but after that had pointedly ignored one another.

The university was giving a reception in the cafeteria, and it was there, in the corner by the display case of school trophies, that she told them she'd talked it over with Albert. She wanted them to know that she would soon be making preparations to marry him.

"I know you don't agree," she said as gently as she could. "But I hope you'll change your mind. I really do

hope so. I can't explain it to you. And I won't try to jus-
tify anything. I said that to Peter too. It's how I feel, and
I am asking you to give him a chance."

A difficult time followed; her parents would not speak
to her, and Peter said it was astonishing that one could be
both so smart and so stupid at the same time. He said she
was making a mistake that could not be undone. He had
travelled in Germany recently and he had seen the steel
towns from the train. Essen, the entire Ruhr district. The
sky red by night and black by day. And fields and fields
of brand-new weaponry, tanks and artillery, all in defiance
of Versailles.

"If it's just the sex," he said. "Get it over with and come
back to your senses."

She almost slapped him for that, but he apologized
quickly. "Sorry," he said. "I'll take that back. But it doesn't
mean that I don't think you're mad."

Only Daniela was still openly supportive, and for a
while Daniela became part of their group. In the winter
of 1937–8, the women would meet regularly on Sunday
afternoons at the Leonhardt apartment for coffee and
conversation. But then Peter found out, and he asked
Daniela not to go there any more.

He said that this was about family, and on family matters there could at times be disagreement, but in the end
the family must always, always stand together.

Clara kept the Vienna flat she was sharing with Erika,
and over the weekends she travelled by train to Munich

and on to Landshut near the base, and stayed at the hotel there. Albert as the battalion commander had a small house on the base, but it would have been unseemly for her to stay there with him, unmarried. Twice a week in Vienna she was allowed to assist Professor Roland Emmerich in Philosophy and Professor Ferdinand in English. At times, after they had seen and approved her lesson plan, they would even allow her to lecture first-year students herself, while they sat in the very last upper row making notes.

Christmas that year was difficult. Albert could not go home, and she wanted to be with him. She stayed again at the hotel, and at Christmas Eve she was there with him in the officers' mess at a long table covered in white linen, with silver and crystal and many candles. The men wore the full dress uniform, the women evening gowns. Sommeliers poured wine and champagne, and waiters in white jackets served the meal, the main course of which was poached carp under copper domes, as was traditional. A candle-lit tree stood in the corner, and on the Gramophone Lale Anderson sang "Stille Nacht" and "Lili Marleen," and Hans Albers sang "La Paloma."

That winter semester she taught American Literature to Professor Ferdinand's class, and in her first lesson plan after Christmas she wrote, *The importance of detail: example: F. Scott Fitzgerald. And conflict as the lifeblood in all writing, perhaps best in Am. Lit.*

Back at the podium after the break she was nervous at first, but as she spoke, her nerves settled.

"In *The Great Gatsby*," she told the class, "look at the way the narrator describes Tom Buchanan when he meets him again at Daisy's house. Feel the darkness gathering. He shows us Tom's muscles shifting under his thin coat. He shows us the memorable detail of his powerful calves straining the laces of his gleaming boots. The potential violence contained in this body. In fact, what he thinks is, *it's a cruel body*. It puts him on guard and there you have the seed of conflict planted like a promise to the reader that, yes, there will be blood."

THE GOOD THING about that Christmas away from home had been that her parents realized she was serious: she meant to stay with Albert. One day in January, while she was in Vienna, she received a telegram from them that said, *We love you and we miss you. Do as your heart desires. We wish you much love and happiness.*

The wedding took place in February at the municipal office in a small town just across the border in Germany so that no one needed to travel very far. Afterwards they sat down to a meal at the local inn. Out the windows they could see the mountains not far away and granite cliffs blackened with melted water and a swath of trees between cliffs broken and uprooted from some slide, earth or snow, and the lumber yet to be harvested. Clouds had moved in and already it was snowing heavily above the tree line.

At one point her father stood up and said it was a fine day. A day of great happiness for both their families. He was seventy-two by then. He had to pause and look away from her face because he was so moved.

Most of the people she loved were there that day, except for Peter. Daniela explained that he'd been asked as a representative of the League of Nations to accompany the chancellor on a mission to Hitler's residence in Berchtesgaden. It was not a request he'd been able to refuse.

SEVENTEEN

✦

AFTERWARDS PETER SAID the whole thing had been
terrible. He said they'd been travelling in the chancellor's
private railroad car, a lavish affair, but the mood had been
tense. For much of the journey the chancellor had sat in
a chair in the far corner and read briefs that his secretary,
Mrs. Helwig, passed him from a black leather case. She sat
taking notes.

Shortly before they arrived, Dr. Richard Bachmann, the
chancellor's senior adviser and diplomat, sat down next to
Peter and reminded him that Hitler had signed an agreement not to invade Austria, an agreement that was not
renegotiable. The chancellor would be reminding Hitler
of that, and Peter would be the international witness.

At the station they were met by SS guards and drivers
in two Mercedes cars and whisked away to Hitler's elabor-
ate mountain residence. There was no formal reception,

no one to greet them other than more SS in black uniforms who took them into a long ante-hall and told them to wait.

They waited for more than half an hour and eventually a door at the end of the hall opened and an SS major came their way and asked if they were ready.

They all stood up. Mrs. Helwig dropped some papers and Peter crouched to pick them up for her.

Just the chancellor, said the SS major.

They watched them walk away, their blond earnest chancellor and the major, through the door that then closed and only minutes later the shouting began. It was at least two rooms away but it was so loud, Peter said, they could understand every word, every humiliating threat of invasion and devastation and of levelling Austria, country of the man's own birth, down to burnt soil, down to nothing, nothing, nothing, they heard him shout. To nothing for a thousand years.

Mrs. Helwig in her nice dark-blue secretary's suit with the white lace collar sat round-eyed and shocked, and Richard Bachmann would not look up from his lap, he was so embarrassed.

They sat, the three of them, on wooden chairs in the hall hearing the shower of abuse while the SS men stood unmoving in their blacks and in their shined boots and gun holsters. They stood like statues with their hands clasped behind their backs, and never once did they unclasp their hands or turn their heads or pay the least attention to the foreign visitors.

Eventually the door opened and their chancellor came out white-faced with the SS major at his side.

Through that same door, Peter said, he saw Hitler just turning away. Peter was strangely detailed and troubled about it when he told her. He said he kept seeing that five-second image for days after, like some never-ending coiling motion in dim light, and he caught a glance from those black eyes and he saw the moustache and the strand of black hair across the pale forehead, and he saw the shoulder and then the man had turned away and the doors were closing.

On the journey home the chancellor told them the threat had been that unless he signed the agreement on the table right there the invasion would begin within the hour. He believed it, the chancellor said. The agreement committed him among other things to appoint the leader of Austria's Nazi Party as minister of security. In charge of police, the chancellor said.

Peter asked if he had considered refusing.

Of course he had, the chancellor said. But then he had looked into the man's eyes and he had absolutely believed the threats of burning things to the ground, to nothing.

A FEW DAYS LATER at the apartment Clara heard Hitler's unmistakeable voice on the radio. It was ten o'clock in the morning, and he was making a speech, saying that he was no longer willing to tolerate the suppression of millions of fellow countrymen across the border. He now wanted a full union with Austria. For our combined strength, he shouted. Our prosperity.

She packed a lunch of two nice ham sandwiches with mustard and sliced pickles and on her bicycle rode to see Peter at his office.

"A full union," he said to her. "I have no idea where that is suddenly coming from."

She sat in a chair by his desk with her feet on the lower rail of the other chair, unwrapping their lunch. She pushed his across. In the office, doors stood open and telephones were ringing. He told her she could stay, but he was expecting someone and had no time to eat. But he took one big bite of his sandwich, chewed, and took another bite.

"Not bad," he said. "Where do you find real ham these days?"

"In the officers' kitchen at the Landshut base."

"Of course. Where else." He kept eating. When he was finished he wiped his mouth with his handkerchief. He balled up the sandwich wrapper and tossed it into the wastepaper basket. He grinned at her.

The telephone on his desk rang and he picked it up and spoke into it. He hung up. "That's him. He's at the reception. If you put all that away and wipe your hands and sit like a lady, I'll introduce you, sister-dear. You never know when you might need a friend in Switzerland. Especially you."

The receptionist showed him in, a man Peter's age in a good dark suit and rimless glasses with a trenchcoat over his arm. Peter shook hands with him while she swept breadcrumbs off her skirt.

"My sister, Doctor Herzog," said Peter. "Doctor Hufnagel is the chief diplomat at our office in Geneva. My sister is a lecturer and a writer."

Hufnagel said it was a pleasure. While he searched his pockets for a business card he said, "A writer. Indeed! Interesting times, are they not? But what is it the Chinese say about interesting times?"

"They say may you not be living in them."

"Ha! And yet." He handed her a card and smiled at her. To Peter he said, "Washington is thinking about it, by the way."

"Are they?" said Peter. "And London?"

"Well," said Dr. Hufnagel. "They haven't said no. But it's the Americans who are now beginning to say that the Versailles Treaty was perhaps flawed. The first journalists are saying that, not the politicians."

She was about to open her mouth, but Peter looked at her and shook his head ever so slightly. He said, "Let's stop blaming the treaty. It's a distraction. Hitler did not need any excuse."

When she left, Dr. Hufnagel said again that it had been a pleasure and he hoped to see her again. Peter showed her out. At the office entrance he said he was glad she'd kept her mouth shut about Versailles. None of that sort of talk was helpful now, he said. Urgent appeals had gone out to the other members of the League of Nations to come to

Austria's help, and the issue was tabled for the next Assembly in Geneva, but that was months away.

"So frustrating," he said. "Always so slow. This need for consensus among so many."

At the elevator she pushed the bell and then leaned and gave him a peck on the cheek. "Thanks for the beautiful crystal bowl," she said. "Danni brought it and we unpacked it. It's on the sideboard. Maybe in the summer I'll put fruit in it. I'm living in the house on the base now. It's a bit small but I think I can make it nice."

He stood looking pale and worried.

"Dear Peter," she said and patted his cheek. "Go back inside to Mr. Hufnagel. Sort out this crisis. I'm in Vienna all week and maybe we can have coffee. Give my love to Danni. And if this elevator takes much longer I think I'll walk."

She waited until the door was closed and then walked down the stairs, her heels loud on the stone steps. There was something else she was thinking about. She felt she knew, but she'd wait another week or so and then take the train to St. Töllden and see Dr. Mannheim.

NEXT DAY Chancellor Schuschnigg in his own speech on the radio said that Austria did not want a union with Germany. No *Anschluss*, he said. He proposed a plebiscite to make certain.

Hitler angrily forbade a plebiscite, threatening invasion again, within the hour.

Schuschnigg backed down once more, and this time

Hitler went over his head and demanded from the Austrian president that the chancellor who had suddenly, so unexpectedly, stood up to him be fired and the new minister of security, the Nazi Seyss-Inquart, be appointed in his place.

On March 11 Schuschnigg resigned his post. In the name of peace, he said, and the president, Dr. Wilhelm Miklas, accepted the resignation.

Hitler promptly broke his promises not to invade, and German troops poured into Austria. At many points along their route they were met by jubilant crowds.

She was not in Vienna that day, but Peter said they could see much of it from the office windows. The office had a staff of six and they all crowded the windows overlooking Mariahilferstrasse and parts of the Ring, and they all knew they'd soon be out of work. The motorcade rolled past with Hitler standing like royalty in his fine yellow-and-chrome Mercedes convertible, holding on with one hand to a handrail there and saluting with the other.

Later he posed in front of the parliament building. By his side stood Mr. Seyss-Inquart in a long black coat, slicked-back hair, and round glasses. The newspaper had a picture of them shaking hands.

Schuschnigg was placed under house arrest and then kept in solitary confinement in the cellars at Gestapo headquarters. A year later she learned that he'd been taken to the concentration camp at Dachau and then to Sachsenhausen.

EIGHTEEN

※

THE NEXT TIME she arrived at the university administration building she was not allowed through the police line. The policemen looked different somehow and their uniforms seemed to fit in a new way, more filled out from within, as from some new important office that had swelled their collective breast.

She walked through the inner city, and it looked different too. Libraries and bookstores closed, Nazi flags on public buildings. Strangers with swastika party pins everywhere. New arrivals from Germany, Erika said at the apartment. They had come for the jobs because so many teachers and civil servants and elected officials were being fired and replaced by Nazis.

Next day she returned to the university, and this time she was allowed in. Men with party pins in their lapels were everywhere. In the libraries they were going through the stacks, pulling books and tossing them into carts. In the rector's office and in the department offices men unknown to her were sitting behind desks, going through papers and interviewing professors.

One of the pin-men asked her to sit down. He wore black shiny sleeve protectors fixed with elastics between wrist and elbow. He searched the files and found her name.

"A teaching assistant," he said. "I don't think so. But come back in a few days if you like."

It was astonishing. She walked the halls as smoke drifted in from the fires in the courtyard; she thought of Professor Roland Emmerich sitting cross-legged on the desk, talking about the deep irrelevance of passing social phenomena. She thought of Professor Ferdinand reciting E. C. Dowson's "Vitae Summa Brevis":

> They are not long, the days of wine and roses
> Out of a misty dream
> Our path emerges for a while, then closes
> Within a dream

The pin-men would not see her for three days. By then her professors and most of the faculty had been sacked and replaced. Word was that, were they to apply for party membership, they might be able to come back, but that was by no means certain because party membership now had to be earned, and the department chairs and teaching positions were taken by people who had been quicker to join the new order.

Much of the material that had been taught in Vienna was now suspect and in need of review. Many books in the library had been thrown out the courtyard windows, and down there they smouldered in fires from which dense smoke and ashes rose to the roof. Erika had heard that early on even Nietzsche had been questionable, until someone in Berlin decided that thanks to his Superman idea his works might have merit after all.

She did not see Professors Ferdinand and Emmerich again, and she hoped they'd be all right. Emmerich had been her very favourite; it was impossible to imagine him with a Nazi pin in his lapel, and so she knew he would not be back. He would withdraw from the current madness, she thought. Define it for himself, step back and wait it out. He, a man who could probably spend the rest of his life sitting in one chair while the light in the room changed from day to night and to day again, and he could survive on his inner resources that would forever be renewing themselves with thoughts as yet unexplored.

This was the fabulous thing about good and disciplined thinking; it was something he had tried to hammer into them, that good thinking was always fresh and progressive and one insight would lead to another.

Good thinking, he had told them, was what got you through life in an interesting way. Good thinking helped you live, and it would help you die.

In the end her pin-man with the sleeve protectors informed her that her services would not be required. He said the mark next to her name was a problem, but if she applied for party membership, she might eventually be able to work as a secretary.

"A secretary," she said. "I have no interest in working as a secretary. And what mark? For what?"

He ignored that. "Mind you," he said. "Party membership is a privilege and a fairly exclusive one. You may not qualify."

"A mark for what?" she said. "And given by whom? Surely not by the university. Is it political?"

He closed her file. As to teaching at university levels, he said, few women were able to get that far. Perhaps as assistants. Off the top of his head he could not think of one.

"But what about the new roles for women?" she said. "The promises in your election platform? Rewarding work beyond home and family. Recognition, emancipation."

"What election? There was no election."

"But there were promises that gained you supporters."

He shrugged. He raised his fingers off the desk and let them tap down thickly one by one. He looked over her shoulder and nodded at the next person in line.

AT THE LEONHARDT APARTMENT, Maximilian and Cecilia sat at the table under the yellow lamp in the dining room. "These," Cecilia said to him. "And these." She picked up some papers and squared the edges. "That would be a great help. Thank you so much, Maxi."

He took them and stood up. He smiled at Clara and headed for the other room. His face was grey, his hair white, his shoulders thin and rounded now. He seemed to have difficulties opening the door. Clara rose to help but Cecilia reached and held her back and gave a quick shake of her head. They watched Max changing his hands on the papers and then holding them with his chin against his chest and using both hands on the doorhandle. The door closed.

"He's not well," said Clara. "What is it?"

"The doctor says he doesn't know. But I do. It's since the jail, since Theo's death. And he's getting worse. He is helping me copy music notations, and his handwriting is still good. Never mind. It's lovely to see you. Tell me about your new life. And Albert, how is he?"

She talked for long minutes. She talked about the house, which needed paint and a woman's touch, about life on the base and the small town nearby. About her parents having finally come to terms with her choice. Things were much better now, since the wedding.

Max came back and Cecilia gave him more papers and he shuffled off again. Cecilia poured tea and at some point she said, "Child, you look happy. I'm so glad for you. You look . . . I won't say it. You would tell me, would you not?"

"Tell you what?"

Cecilia put a hand on hers and smiled. "It's in your eyes, my dear. Have you seen your doctor?"

She blushed deeply. "I'm planning to."

"Good. You'll let me know, won't you."

Clara helped with the tea things, and in the kitchen described her encounter with the pin-man at university. Cecilia listened. Her business was changing too, she said. At the opera and the conservatory coaches had been enlisted from the ranks of Nazis, and it was only because of her reputation among Italian and Scandinavian and American performers that she had any operatic work at all.

"There's something you might want to think about," she said. "With Albert away and Theo dead it's just Max and I in the apartment. Two full-sized bedrooms and the smaller one aren't being used. I was thinking that you and Erika and Mitzi could use those rooms. For a fraction of the money you must be paying now. It would help us all."

"You mean live here with you?"

"Well, yes. The place is big enough. Then again, from what you just told me, you may not want to bother with an apartment in Vienna at all. It'd be a shame, but I'd understand that."

"Oh no. I'll always want to keep a place here. Things will change again."

That evening she mentioned it to Erika and Mitzi. They had seen the rooms, old-fashioned with high ceilings and tall windows and built-in bookshelves. They discussed the money and by the end of the next day an agreement was reached with Cecilia. They gave notice at their flats on Beatrixgasse.

IN ST. TÖLLDEN Dr. Mannheim examined her and asked questions about dates and symptoms such as nausea. Some mornings, she told him. Yes. She got dressed and then sat at his desk while he was making notes in her file. Two months, he said. Two and a half. Based on what he could see and the dates she'd given him. All seemed well. But he wanted her to come more often now.

"This is good news, I hope."

"Very good news." She smiled. "The best in days."

She called Albert, not from her parents' house but from the post office on the town square. She waited while someone at the base went to find him, sat in the familiar telephone booth, so very happy, holding the receiver and leaning back against the panelling. The booth still smelled of newly sharpened pencils, that odd smell it had always had. The postmistress was new. She wore a Nazi pin and gave her suspicious looks through the window. Clara smiled at her because she felt like being generous.

She knew what he would say. They had talked about the possibility and he'd been so very pleased. At the other end she heard footsteps and someone picked up the receiver and said the colonel could not be contacted right now. He was in Munich, and was there a message or could she call back? She said, Never mind, and two hours later she was on the train to Landshut to tell him in person and to see his expression when she did so.

IN JUNE she and Erika and Mitzi moved in with the Leonhardts. As they lugged things in and out, neither the concierge at the old building nor the doorman at the new stirred a finger to help. Whereas once they had flung open doors and greeted tenants, even carried shopping bags and held umbrellas, they just stared now. The doorman too was growing a small Hitler moustache and he had taken to wearing a party pin among the golden frogs on his jacket.

SINCE ALBERT WAS BUSY with manoeuvres and frequent trips to Berlin, she spent most of that summer in St. Töllden. She put on a smock and helped out at the Roman excavation site, soaking and brushing dirt off fragments. In the evenings she translated the archaeologists' reports into English for the American museum that had bought co-publication rights for the dig.

Earlier that year her father had discovered caves in the mountain that showed signs of having been used as Christian hiding places and as places of secret worship. Existing caves with animals drawn on walls had been enlarged, and worship niches had been hewn with hand tools. On cave walls the fish symbol and the cross were drawn with paints of metal oxides, mingling with images of horses and stags and beasts with enormous tusks drawn in clay and vegetable paint ten thousand years earlier. Her father was told to apply for party membership and when he declined he nearly lost the museum. To qualify for continued funds for the dig he had to fill out many applications with eagles and swastikas on them in triplicate and take them to the municipal office where the clerks behind the wickets now wore pins too. They took his forms and whereas once they would have smiled at him and chatted, they now raised their eyebrows and asked questions before stamping the papers with more eagles and swastikas and tossing them into the tray.

In August two men and one woman from the American museum came to visit the site. The men wore bow ties and linen suits with knickerbockers and knee socks, the woman a long skirt, linen jacket, and brown hiking shoes. She was tall and friendly. She carried peanut butter-and-jelly sandwiches with the crusts cut away in a linen shoulder bag of many pockets, and most days she offered some to Clara. For the baby, she would say. She had lively eyes and freckles and she wore her hair up, the way Cecilia did.

In what appeared to have been the children's room at the Roman villa, archaeologists had found figures or dolls seven inches tall, cast hollow from native copper, with fine detailing of faces and hands, the dolls wearing clothing of fur, and one doll holding a broken spear in one raised hand. With all dolls the sprues had been nicely filed off and the cast lines dressed.

Roman, her father had said; a fantastic find. Teaching-toys for children, based on finds from much earlier ages, connecting children across millennia.

The Americans were refreshingly outgoing and appreciative. In their explorers' linen clothes and on hands and buttocks they clambered over rocks and down strata cuts. They held out helping hands to each other and talked excitedly, and they called one another Doctor Small and Doctor Henry and Doctor Isling, the woman. They took many photographs. In the end they renewed the contract with the museum for three years with the option to renew it further. The day the Americans left, Dr. Isling patted Clara's stomach and hugged her, and then she gave her a jar of peanut butter still half full and the linen bag of many pockets as a present.

AND SO WILLA was born in St. Töllden, at the small hospital there. Albert arrived in time; he came on the night train, wearing basic field grey. Before the delivery he sat by her bedside as long as the nurses would allow, then he waited in the lounge. Willa took her time. Late at night a nurse woke Albert where he was asleep in a chair and told him to go home. There was no telling how much longer it would take. But he stayed. Willa was born at four o'clock that morning.

Clara was allowed to have visitors only at the end of that first day, and only one person at a time. The baby could be viewed through the picture window of the maternity ward, one of a half-dozen wicker baskets with a small white bundle in it, and in Willa's case a bundle with a full head of black hair that had been rinsed and dried and now stood straight up. At that window like at a peephole to the future stood her father and mother, stood waving and smiling like changed people now in the presence of this grandchild. At other times Peter or Albert stood looking in. Her other brother Bernhard had sent a telegram from Salzburg.

The first time she held Willa in her arms and nursed her, looking down on the tiny perfect person taking nourishment from her breast she began to weep, whether tears of joy or sorrow she could not decide, but tears of a profound experience that none of her studies had prepared her for.

Later Albert sat with her, then her parents, and finally Peter.

"You be nice to Albert," she told him. "Will you? No arguments, no manly jousting over nothing?"

"I promise," said Peter.

"Have you spoken to him? Try him."

"We're fine. We spoke in the waiting room. About horses. I might actually get to like him. His uniform impresses people, but it scares me."

She said nothing to that.

"I told him I hoped he brought his marching boots. He'll be needing them soon."

"Marching boots?"

"Yes."

"If he does, so will you, don't you think? They'd draft you, wouldn't they?"

"Before I go to war for the corporal, I'd rather—" He leaned forward, made a gun with his hand, and put it to his temple. He sat back in the chair.

"No you wouldn't, Peter," she said. "Because there's Danni. And Mom and I. I haven't seen much of you. Where have you been?"

"In Geneva, mostly. We had to close the Vienna office and they wanted us to destroy all the files. Now we're allowed to send them to Switzerland. We sent them to Doctor Hufnagel. You remember him."

"I do. They let you send all the files?"

"All except the ones on minority rights. They took those away." He paused. "And you?"

"I spent a lot of time on trains. The base, Vienna, here. They fired the old faculty, you'll have heard. And I'm not there any more."

"That's too bad." He sat there on the wooden chair against the wall. He managed a smile.

"And how is Danni?"

"She is fine. She could have gone to Switzerland, but she didn't want to go without me. They took my passport."

"They did?"

"Yes. I am not allowed to leave. And I really do think there's a war coming, Clara. There's talk of closing the border. I mean, from the inside. By our new colonial masters."

She was leaning against the pillow, half-sitting and uncomfortably so because of the pad for the stitches and the bleeding. She was not keen to hear dark predictions.

He was watching her. "Are you in pain?"

"*Am I in pain.* Brother-dear."

"Want me to call the nurse?"

"God, no. She'd stop all the visiting right away. It's really the nurses who run this place." She paused. "What's that about war, Peter?"

"Things I hear. I asked your Albert, but even if he knew he wouldn't say anything. I think he knows."

A FEW DAYS LATER Neville Chamberlain met Hitler, and for a promise of peace Great Britain agreed not to interfere in the German invasion of Sudetenland. She sat listening to the news on the radio in the dayroom with just two other patients in the room, one of them asleep in his chair. Later that day the radio said Mr. Chamberlain had flown home to a hero's welcome at the airport.

"*Peace for our time*," the British prime minister called out on the crackling radio. People could be heard cheering. The date was September 30, 1938.

Next day there was a picture of him in the newspaper: smiling, a likeable and distinguished-looking gentleman waving a piece of paper.

"Where is your Albert?" said Peter to her that afternoon. They were sitting in the dayroom, just he and she, with the radio on. He had brought her a thermos of coffee made by her mother just the way she liked it, with milk and sugar.

"He went to Vienna to see his parents. He'll be back in a few days."

The radio was talking about the invasion of Sudetenland. It had begun that morning and was already completed.

"There goes your Treaty of Versailles," said Peter. "Guilt clauses and all. Torn up, tossed out. Remember? How did you put it? Standing up for ourselves, being wild for once? Not exactly what you had in mind, is it?"

"You know it isn't." She sat on the couch in her own worn terrycloth robe and bedroom slippers. "I want to get out of here," she said.

"You will. Isn't it just a few more days?" He crossed to the radio, raised his hand to the knob, and looked at her over his shoulder. "Enough of that?"

She nodded.

That evening Peter took the train back to Vienna. She never saw him again.

WHEN ALBERT WAS BACK, the head nurse made an exception and allowed him to be in the room with mother and baby. He had to be far away, on a chair by the window, and he sat on that chair in the windowlight like a moody painting of war coming. She looked at him, and she looked away. It was in his face and in his uniform. It was in that quality of late light with the sun down and the light above the rooftops orange at first, then silver. Now shades of grey filled the room. Grey walls, grey floor, grey uniform. He looked tired and he needed a shave. He had become thinner, leaner, and nearly hard-looking in the face, and there was something else that was new around his mouth and eyes, a bitterness, she thought.

"What is it?" she said. "You must be tired."

He looked at her and she knew his mind had been somewhere else altogether.

"Albert? Is everything all right?"

"Sweetheart, everything is all right. I'm sorry. I was just . . . I am very happy."

"Are you? You were travelling all day. Ask Mama to give you my room at the house. The bed in it is very good."

She saw him take a deep breath and let it out. "I'll have to leave again in a few hours, Clara. My driver is standing by."

"In a few hours? But you only just came back. Where do you have to go?"

"To the base. We may be moving out."

"Moving out? We're leaving the house? To go where?"

"Not you. Please don't . . . I don't have the transport order yet. Just the readiness. I'll call you here, or I can call your parents."

"Albert. Look at me, Albert. What is happening?"

"You won't have to leave," he said. "The unit may be ordered east. It *may* be. Temporarily."

She looked away from him down at tiny Willa and she told herself to be calm and that she had everything a reasonable woman could wish for: her health and a loving husband, the promise of her own career when all this was over, and this perfect child now. And yet at nearly the same moment, like a curtain drawn to reveal the stage for the next act, it felt to her like some enormous truth coming, the truth that all light and warmth and all safety had been illusions and that the reality was horror.

Albert saw her face and instantly he was at her side. He touched her cheek, then leaned and reached and opened the door, and he called for the nurse. He stood in the open doorway in his uniform and boots and gunbelt, waving his arms and shouting into the hallway, and two nurses came running.

NINETEEN

◈

SHE SPENT the next few weeks at home, not only because
her mother's help with the baby was a comfort, but also
because she did not like the idea of the empty house on
the base. The terrors came back several more times, especially in the early hours of the morning. Dr. Mannheim
spoke of post-partum phenomena as yet poorly understood; he was prepared to give her a low dose of bromides
to calm her, but she was breastfeeding and did not want
to take medication of any kind.

Instead she pumped and bottled breast milk, and the
next day she left baby and milk with her mother, and she
boarded the train to Zürich. There in the university library
she looked up Dr. Freud and found his notes on panic
attacks from an address he had given in 1936 in Sweden.

Premonitions of Death, he had called them. Essentially they
had to do with loss of control over one's life, not the actual

loss, but a fear of it so real it became a kind of foretelling.

He said the attacks appeared to be coming out of nowhere, but they were always triggered by associations made in the unconscious; often they came in daydreams and in the small hours of the morning. The low threshold hours, the psychiatric profession called them, when in shallow sleep or in daydreams the intellectual defence mechanism was weak and fears washed like effluent over the depressed threshold into the safe-room of the psyche.

The bad news was, Dr. Freud said, that the fears were usually correct, and the panic attacks justified. The unconscious saw the signs of a darkness coming; it added them up, and emotional terror was the result.

Reading him in the profound stillness of the library, she could see Freud stepping about on the dais, waving his cold cigar and using his free hand for motions to indicate the heart, the stomach, the forehead. *Angstzustände*, she heard him say. Rapid pulse, difficulty breathing, heat rising, a faintness like a profound emptying-out. She could see his lips nearly blue within the precisely carved beard pronouncing the diagnosis of justified premonitions of death not necessarily of the body but certainly of the soul. He would pause, listen for the trailing-out of that sentence as if he might want to reel it back in and edit it. But he let it stand, and the cigar would stab the air for emphasis and a period.

By the time she sat reading his Stockholm transcript in Zürich, in the nearest university where his publications had not been destroyed, Dr. Freud had already turned his back on Vienna, had rejected what it had become and was safe in England.

THE *KRISTALLNACHT* POGROM at the end of November changed everything. It made it impossible to go on hoping and pretending. She was back on the Landshut military base by then, and the base was much quieter with half the battalion moved east to an undisclosed location. She was alone in the house with baby Willa, struggling to make a home of the place with curtains and fresh paint. A home for how long she had no idea.

When she heard of the pogrom she put the baby in the carriage and walked into town. There had been no incidents in Landshut, but at the grocers people were whispering about Munich, the broken shopwindows there and at least three people killed.

She hurried back home, and there on the radio the announcer was blaming the attacks on the murder of a German diplomat by a Jew. The news kept coming in all day, and by the end of it countless shop windows had been smashed, ninety people murdered, unknown numbers arrested and taken away. *Disappeared in night and fog*, the newspaper said the next day. As if they'd lost their way and fallen off a cliff through some inattention of their own.

She put paint and sewing machine aside and with her fountain pen kept track of daily events. Pen and typewriter were her weapons. Her means of sorting and defining. She decided that in the *Kristallnacht* phenomenon one could see clearly all the signs of mob hysteria and its shrewd channelling by those in charge. It was fear and hatred of life itself. It was the scapegoat phenomenon already mentioned in the Bible. Heap your sins and fears and your own inadequacies upon the chosen goat and banish it. Chase it far out into the desert to be forgotten. Better still: kill it, so it can't come back. It's all the goat's fault, ergo kill the goat.

She wrote while baby Willa was asleep in her tiny room with the half-hung wallpaper of balloons and clouds, and she wrote while Willa lay in the crib nearby and played with fingers and toes.

Albert's unit came back from the east. She cooked dinners and sat with him, lay with him at night, wanted to feel close to him. She wanted him to volunteer information she could understand, that would help her make sense of developments. He said he knew almost nothing of the longer goals, and so nothing he could tell her would add up to a true picture of what was coming.

There were whisperings, he said. About further invasions. About Hitler. About what the SS and Gestapo were up to. Things he could not talk to her about without risking their lives.

By day the tanks rolled like thunder, and out the windows men marched one-two-three on the parade ground, and in torn and muddy fields motorized guns roared back and forth firing 50mm cannons. The noises were harsh and abrupt. They vibrated windows and dishes in the cupboards. At first they made Willa cry.

She held her on her lap and talked to her. At times she found herself writing notes not to herself, but to her child. It was much the same process, a recording of events and insights so that they might be available for later. *Dear Willa, on this day the radio reported . . . and then you and I looked out the window and we saw . . .* Long-distance messages for the child and for the woman the child would one day be. A girl and then a young woman growing older and perhaps wanting to know and understand.

She spent a week at home in St. Töllden and learned that on the day after the pogrom, the mayor had written an open letter in the daily paper condemning the attacks as cowardly and completely unacceptable. The culprits would be brought to justice, he had promised, and within days he and his wife and their two children had disappeared. A new mayor was appointed by the directorate, a pin-man and his family from some other province sleeping in the vanished people's beds, and with their knives and forks eating the food in their larder from their plates.

Mrs. Dorfer, the milkwoman, whispered that the new mayor's children had been seen wearing the vanished children's clothes to school. She shook her head and climbed on her bicycle that was hitched via a curved shaft to her milk cart.

Kristallnacht, she wrote in a letter to Erika, left no doubt as to how the game would be played, and absolutely so, with spying and reporting on thy neighbour to save thy own cherished hide, and with terror and disappearances, and with no hope of justice whatsoever.

"So write about it," Erika wrote back. "You're good at that, and I don't think anyone on the outside really knows what is going on here. Send it to a newspaper. In France and England. In Switzerland. Tell the world."

Fired on like this she worked on it for days, collecting reports and writing and rewriting. Relating what the newspapers and the radio were saying to what was in fact happening. What people like Mrs. Dorfer were whispering. Perhaps Erika was right, and she could publish it somewhere. In America ideally, perhaps through the people at the museum.

When she mentioned it to Albert over dinner a change came over his face and he stopped eating. He put down knife and fork and he wiped his lips with the napkin. He sat very still with his hands on the table.

"What is it?" she said.

"Clara, did you mention this to anybody? For example to any of the other wives, or to someone in town?"

"No. Not yet."

"To anybody at all? A newspaper? Have you written a letter to anybody about it? Does *anybody* know about this idea of yours?"

"No. I wanted to talk to you about it first."

"I'm glad. Let me show you something." He reached into a side pocket and took out an envelope. "I opened it, but

look at this, this tear in the flap, the way the edges over-
lap." He held it out for her to take. "What do you think
caused that?"

She turned over the envelope. It was a letter from his
father in Vienna.

"What do you think, Clara?"

She studied the flap edges, the fine creases.

"It's been steamed open and resealed," he said. "I think
they are watching him for fear he may agitate against them
now; after Theo's death, after the jail. As if he had the
energy. You saw him. I'll have to tell him not to write to us
any more. They can read our mail, they can listen in on
telephones. Some of the people in town are certainly inform-
ants, and you know that SS Obersturmführer Bönninghaus
is the official political observer. Every unit has one of those.
Don't ever trust him with anything."

He paused. "What is it?"

She shook her head. "Nothing. No, wait. I wrote to
Erika and she wrote back. Not in detail."

"Did you mail it on the base or in town?"

"In St. Töllden. When I was home."

"Were you alone? Did anyone follow you?"

"Follow me? I can't say. I didn't look."

"And she wrote back to you in St. Töllden?"

"No. Here."

"Show me the letter. The envelope."

She brought it and he held it close to the light, studied
the glueline along the flap edges. He handed it back to her.

"Clara," he said. "Please. You can write whatever you want, and I know it's important for you to keep notes and journals. But."

"But what? This is the one thing I *can* do. I mean *do*, rather than just sit and watch."

"I know. But for now please don't let anyone read it and don't ever put it in the mail. Just keep your thoughts to yourself. For now."

EARLY IN 1939 she received a letter from the party directorate in Vienna. In it they said that the office had become aware of the fact that the family had been awarded the Blood Order for the death of Theodor. In light of that, they said, her application for party membership was being granted, and the university would be looking favourably on her application as assistant professor. Signed and stamped *Heil Hitler*, with several eagles clutching swastikas.

That night she showed the letter to Albert.

"I never applied," she said when he looked up. "For party membership. You know that. I only asked about a teaching job."

"When you had the interview, could they have misunderstood?"

"I don't see how. I remember him saying that even if I were accepted, I might at best get a secretarial job. I told you all that. And he said there was a mark next to my name, and you said not to worry, there were marks next to everyone's name."

"I know. The question is, do you want to teach there? Under the new administration? This is as good as a solid job offer."

She rose and stepped to the window. Darkness out there, just her own reflection in the glass. "I was trying to imagine Professor Emmerich with a Nazi pin," she said without turning around. "You know how much I admired him. He taught us about intellectual honesty. Integrity. About trusting ourselves. I was trying to imagine him limiting his lectures to what they would allow him to say, and I couldn't."

She lowered the blinds and turned to him. He looked tired to her in the lamplight and she told him so.

"What is happening to us, Albert? I am close to weeping half the time. I can't talk to people. I can't write to my friends. I can't work. We can't be truthful about anything. It wasn't supposed to be like that. We are a young family just starting out."

"We are. This was not . . . things will change. They'll get better when we can see more clearly."

"Will we ever? And does this mean they have a file on me now?"

"Yes. They have a file on every one of us. You, me, your parents. All the senior officers. One of the jobs of the SS is to keep the regular army generals in line."

"I could take a few days and go to Vienna. I don't want to just sit and wait and hide like a rabbit. I could talk to the new rector, meet the faculty, see what the new rules actually are. We could hire that nurse again."

She walked toward the kitchen for a glass of water and on the way passed behind him and touched his cheek.

"We could," he said. He rose and followed her. "But they think they're honouring you with this. So be careful."

"*Careful.* You see, that's what I mean. Careful really means fearful."

"No. It means understand and respect reality."

She stood at the sink, ran water, and filled two glasses.

They stood in the dark kitchen, sipping water. Somewhere a truck engine fired. They heard voices and the truck driving off. The challenge at the gate, sharp and loud in the night. A dog somewhere.

"I hate this," she said.

Later, looking back and trying to define the moment her problems with the party and the Gestapo began, she would always come back to this moment in the dark kitchen and to the letter out there in the lamplight on the table.

TWENTY

⁂

IN VIENNA she sat waiting in the rector's front office.
The secretary was no longer Mrs. Holbenstern but a pale
young man who wore not only the party pin but, in case
someone missed that, he wore the swastika sleeve band as
well. Behind the rector's door she heard laughter, then the
sound of a telephone receiver being replaced. The buzzer
on the secretary's desk sounded, and the young man rose
and stepped into the inner office. On the wall above the
door the picture of the grandfatherly president of the
republic had been replaced by one of Hitler, a frontal shot
so that his black eyes followed you around the room.

The secretary came back, shaking his head. He waved
a pale hand at the door.

"Wouldn't even see me," she told her friends at the
apartment. "But I'll go back tomorrow and I'll sit there
all day if I have to."

They were in the kitchen, since in the living room a Swedish soprano was warming up for a session with Cecilia.

"You seem surprised," said Mitzi. "But David Koren kept talking about little else. And here it is." She turned off the tap and tipped her combs and brushes head-first into a glass jar full of green germicidal solution. She turned to face them.

"Here is what?" said Erika.

"The Nazis, doing whatever they want. Like Koren said. For example that day on the café terrace, think back. You weren't listening because you thought you had nothing to fear, be honest. And you had your heads in your books. You might as well admit it."

Mitzi picked up a towel and stood drying her hands. It was one of her business towels, with *Mitzi* embroidered on it in large letters. "Right?" she said.

"We were listening," said Clara.

"Not as closely as I. I knew what he was talking about."

"I think Clara and I did too," said Erika.

They heard the living-room door and Cecilia came into the kitchen. "We're starting," she said. She was dressed for work in a long black skirt and a white blouse with a high lace collar, and she already wore that focused, no-nonsense expression they knew well by now.

"Remember the rules," she said. "Stay in here, or go out that door to the servants' hallway. Don't be seen through the connecting door, and no noise whatsoever. She's doing Richard Strauss and she's nervous enough as is."

Cecilia turned the back of her head to Mitzi, and Mitzi reached and took out the combs one by one, caught a few errant strands, and slipped the combs back in.

When Cecilia had left, Mitzi said, "What I meant was not that you had *nothing* to worry about. Just not *that*. You're not Jewish." She took the brushes and combs from the jar and rinsed them and put them on another towel on the counter. She dried her hands again.

"You're right," said Clara. She looked at Erika and said, "She's right."

"Of course she is."

In the living room Cecilia struck a note repeatedly and said, "In the centre, in the centre, not off to the side and then sliding. Just this note now." The singer tried to hit the note dead-centre. She tried several times and finally made it.

"I almost quit," said Erika after a silence. "The dissertation. But then I decided to continue. I have to play by their rules, but they're not going to deny me my degree."

"Is Professor Emmerich back, or Ferdinand?"

Erika shook her head. "Oh no. I hear Emmerich moved to America. Freud is in England. Ferdinand, I don't know."

IN THE MORNING she was back at the university with a more aggressive plan. She strode to the secretary's desk and put the letter from the directorate in front of him. "I was here yesterday," she said firmly. "You show him this letter."

The secretary scanned the letter and sat up straight. "Well," he said. "Doctor Herzog. Why didn't you say so?"

"Just show him this."

"Of course. Please wait just a moment." He entered the director's office and was quickly back. He waved her in.

And so she saw how things worked. It was astonishing.

"The Blood Order," said the new rector. "Congratulations. You have a hero in your family. Someone who gave his life for the cause. Please, by all means. Sit down." He half rose and pointed at the chair in front of his desk; a man with a square face and reddish hair parted on the side, wearing a jacket with the pin in the brown cloth of the lapel.

"A hero," he said with admiration. "Well." He reached into a drawer and pushed a sheet of paper and a pencil across the desk. "Write down what you would like to teach, Doctor Herzog. English or philosophy. I'll speak to the department heads."

"What I would like to teach? As an assistant?"

"Well," he said. "Just write down where you think your competence lies. Perhaps a professorship. We shall see."

She wrote, and while she wrote she heard him crack his knuckles. She heard his stomach. Nothing about him fit the surroundings. The fine panelling, the tall curved windows. In the ante-room the secretary spoke and laughed on the telephone.

She pushed her list across the desk. The rector read and as he did so he blindly reached to his right and picked up a red pen. He began crossing out names and topics, and in the room the mood changed. He looked up.

"I am surprised," he said. "Disappointed. For someone from a family with the Blood Order you don't seem to be aware of the new guidelines."

"The new guidelines?"

He stared at her. "Perhaps you think you're above them."

"I don't know what the new guidelines are. Feel free to tell me."

He shook his head. "I'll keep this paper for your file," he said.

On the train back to Albert and Willa, her thoughts kept returning to Professor Emmerich. Who, too, had packed his bags. She remembered him speaking of the Up-way, never the Down; of being calm inside and judging issues for oneself. As he had done by leaving. Would he be wearing bicycle clips in America? In the land of moral courage and of *We the People*. Of large and comfortable cars. Probably not. In the land of Hemingway and Steinbeck and Fitzgerald and Cather and Eliot. In the land of peanut butter and drive-in cinemas and affordable lipstick and nylon stockings? Would Emmerich be sitting on the desk during lectures? Probably, and spin out his ideas and insights with full confidence, with his hard and generous brilliance that lifted you up and showed you things in a new light so bright and clear you forgot to breathe.

The train home travelled across rivers as the sun went down and it travelled through mountains and through forests of evergreens still covered in snow. It travelled from day to night, and at times she could see the engine up front, its yellow light probing the rails ahead but never reaching very far into the darkness.

IN AUGUST that year Albert's tank battalion was ordered to relocate to Burgenland in Austria, near the border with Hungary. Clara packed up the house and packed up little Willa, who was by then nearly one year old. She put her typewriter and her files and notes into separate boxes and insisted they be placed in her own compartment. Corporal Fuchs came and fetched the Norton.

The tanks, motorized cannon, and support vehicles were entrained and covered with camouflage tarpaulin, flatcar after flatcar, dozens of them, on two long trains with a steam locomotive each in front to pull and one at the rear to push.

The trains travelled the long way south and east, along the Danube, past vineyards and past fields in tall grain once more, and without stopping through industrial cities where tall chimneys smoked and cranes in factory yards lifted enormous rolls of shining steel.

Several times Albert came from the staff compartment next to hers and sat with her and Willa, but every few minutes then one of his lieutenants would knock on the door and bring papers for him to read.

"Not now," he said sharply at one time. "Put it on my desk. I'll be back there in a few minutes."

"You are very quiet," he said to her when the door was

closed. "I think I know why, and I can understand how you feel."

"It's this," she said. "Coming back to this." She pointed out the window, which was open just then and warm air came in, and the smell of coalsmoke and steam mixed with that of grain and grass warm in the sun. Along the way people in fields and meadows lowered scythes and rakes and unshouldered panniers, and they turned to stare at the trains full of heavy weaponry under tarpaulin but plain to see. She'd waved once or twice the way she'd done as a child, but now no one waved back. Most stared in silence but some craned their necks and shouted to each other. War was coming.

He said nothing, and what could he have said to help her with this? With the fact that she was riding back to her home country on this conquering train full of weaponry, tanks and field pieces, and large-calibre barrels like brutal noses poking from cover.

"You'll like the house," he said. "You'll have peace there. You can write and read. Write for later. One day this will all be over, Clara. There is a garden and the train station is close by. Your friends can visit, and you and Willa can travel home and to Vienna."

She closed her eyes and nodded and said nothing.

When he was next door in conferences she could hear the men through the thin wall talking. She could hear their boots on the wood floor and hear chairs being shifted. Someone laughed.

She closed the window and pulled down the blinds. She raised the blinds and opened the window again, and changed seats to be out of the draft.

She sat in silence against the seatback and she wiped angrily at her tears. Willa sat on her knees looking earnestly up at her face.

"Oh sweetheart," she said thickly.

The land became dry and flat, and soon she saw that the storks were back from Africa. Young storks were getting flying lessons, taking off from chimney roosts. On the wide and shallow Lake Neusiedel birds had built nests by the tens of thousands among reeds in the shallows, and the air was filled with a high chirring sound and it was stirred by countless small wings.

She went with Willa to the toilet and held her as the little girl sat on the wooden rim. Someone knocked repeatedly on the door and sharply over her shoulder she told them to stop knocking and go away. She washed her own and Willa's hands at the basin and returned to the compartment.

Willa fell asleep on the seat next to her, and for a while she held on to Clara's finger in her sleep, then she let go.

THE BATALLION COMMANDER's house was a neat cottage with thick white walls and a thatched roof. It stood on a dusty street of other houses just like it in the village next to the base. Tomatoes grew in the kitchen garden, and cucumbers and peas grew on small trellises and on string nets between sticks poked into the soil. There was a maid called Anna, an old woman on swollen and unsteady feet, who looked after house and garden and slept in the lean-to, off the kitchen.

The land was flat in all directions. Small white and blue flowers bloomed in the dry grass and were stirred by the constant warm wind that also stirred up the dust in the road and drove spinning dust devils up and down. Every morning for the remainder of that August, enormous clouds in black and grey layers formed towering structures in the distance. Lighting flashed among the clouds, and far to the east she could see grey curtains of rain falling, but never here.

The provincial capital was not far away, and it was at the railroad station there that on the last Friday in August she met Erika, Mitzi, and Cecilia, and she brought them home for the weekend. The two days that followed were wonderful and carefree. They took baby Willa on picnics and on boatrides in a flat-bottomed rowpunt on the lake, and around them the warm air was filled with bird sounds. The last of milkweed drifted low across the lake, and the air was fragrant with drying hay and with the scent of roses from the perfume factory on the south shore. Storks and herons stalked the reeds in search of frogs and small fish, and they clattered their long beaks.

On Sunday noon the women like a gypsy bridal party in bright dresses and ribboned hats rowed among the willows and pulled the boat ashore, and they spread out two blankets and a tablecloth for their picnic. They unpacked hampers of sandwiches and containers of cider and milk and cereal for the baby, and on a fine day like this and united as friends they could laugh and joke about their lives, none of which was turning out as planned.

"But literature is full of that," said Erika. "Isn't it, Clara?"

"Full of what?"

They were sitting on the blankets holding blades of grass between their thumbs, trying to see who could make the loudest honking noise.

"Full of the illusion of control. Best-laid plans going nowhere. In fact it seems to me that's where most good stories begin."

"Some," she said.

Cecilia put her lips to her thumbs and produced a loud wailing honk, the best so far. Willa laughed and clapped her hands. Cecilia tickled her, then leaned over the grass to find a fresh blade.

"The wide ones are best," she said to Willa. "Like this one." She plucked a blade and smoothed it. She blew into it fiercely but it only squeaked and frayed. They were on hands and knees chatting and searching for good grasses.

They lay on their backs and looked up through the cracks between their fingers at the sky, and they saw young storks practising what they'd learned and circling above the warm fields with no discernible wing movement whatsoever.

On the way back in the boat, Mitzi sat rowing next to Clara, and she mentioned for the first time that the forger was blackmailing her now with her real identity. So far she had been able to pay what he was asking, she said. She hoped he would never ask for more than she could give.

They tied up the boat and picked up baby and baskets. As they came closer to the cottage they could see the Mercedes with the 14th Armoured Battalion sign on its fender, and they saw Albert standing in the yard, looking at his wristwatch. He saw them and waved. He was standing next to the tomatoes red and ripe on the vines and the peapods filled to bursting. Behind him the cottage lay in the evening sun, and the sun shone warmly on its roof of golden straw and on the green shutters thrown open against white walls.

But the image of home and safety was all wrong because he was dressed for war in full combat uniform: pistol belt, boots, and the leather coat and dust goggles around his neck. Clara's heart was beating fiercely. She could see his driver and one of his lieutenants waiting in the staff car with the top down. Albert's batman came out of the cottage, carrying his field kit. Down the street, neighbours stood in doorways to watch.

Albert called to her. He waved urgently and he turned and spoke to the driver. In the house he waited until she had put Willa on the couch. She turned to him. She was shaking.

He held her and explained that his unit was entraining. By nightfall he had left, and by midnight his battalion was already rolling north and east toward the Polish border.

The date was August 28, 1939.

TWENTY-ONE

✦

LATER HE NEVER talked about the war because the
war changed him, but right after Poland he still did. He
described to her how they could see nothing but fire at
either side to the horizon, fire and explosions as the tanks
roared forward, firing 50mm and heavy machine guns on
the run. They stopped only to aim and fire the main turret
gun. The Polish tanks were no match, he said. And most
Polish field cannons were still mounted on horse-drawn
limbers and slow to move. Polish soldiers in proud uniforms rode the wheel horses and stood in the stirrups to
fire cavalry pistols at tanks. Horses reared and flailed and
tried to crawl away on shattered legs. Horses everywhere
screaming, with blue coils of intestines trailing, other
horses tripping over them. He had never imagined they'd
still be relying so heavily on horses.

It was terrible, he said, and she sat listening with her

eyes wide and her hands clamped over her mouth, sat in the darkened living room at the cottage because for a week or more afterwards he never wanted to turn on the lights and by daytime he told Anna to close the curtains and keep out the sun.

From above, he said, they could hear Stukas howling and diving and dropping bombs a hundred metres in front of the tanks, they could hear the Messerschmitt fighters. A fearsome push forward with maximum fire power, he said. They drove the Polish forces relentlessly on a wide front toward Russia, which by then was invading from the east to occupy the rest of the country. Pens of barbwire full of prisoners dotted their route.

Two days into the attack, on September 3, France and Britain had kept their pledge to Poland and declared war. It had come to her world on the radio and in the newspapers. "WAR!" the headlines shouted, and in the village it was the one word on everyone's lips.

In her notes for the Poland file she later added that war then had been not about bodycount but about territorial gain. This might be hard to grasp now, fifty or more years on, she wrote, but at the time the colonial spirit was not completely dead, and essentially that was what colonialism had been: the theft of entire countries simply by invading them and planting flags.

ONE MONTH INTO THE Polish campaign, SS Obersturmführer Bönninghaus, the political officer attached to

Landshut Black, came to the cottage and knocked on the door. Anna was on her knees in the kitchen garden, harvesting peas, and she turned and looked at him between the vines over her shoulder. Even without his armband she knew who he was; everyone did. She watched him knock and wait. She watched his broad back, his cap at a rakish angle. She could tell him that Clara had gone to the store, but she did not. Only when he simply pushed open the door and walked in did she get up heavily off her knees and come after him.

"They're not in," she said.

"Where are they?" He had progressed as far as the living room already, was standing by the radio listening. He clicked it off and turned around. He was a heavy man with a strong face and a scar through one of his eyebrows. He was dressed in tunic, breeches, and boots, and in the dim light from the window half covered by ivy he stood with one hand still on the radio knob and with the other slapping his grey deerskin gloves idly against his thigh.

"Shopping," Anna said.

"In town, on the bicycle?"

"Yes."

"So they'll be back soon," he said. "I'll wait. Go back outside. Go!" He waved her away.

When Clara returned with Willa, Anna was sitting on a low stool by the front door shelling peas. She looked up at Clara and put her finger to her lips. She beckoned. "The obersturmführer is inside waiting for you," she whispered.

"What does he want? Did you let him in?"

Anna shook her head.

She entered with Willa in one arm and the shopping bag in the other. He was not in the kitchen and not in the living room. He was in the bedroom, standing well inside the open door. He turned when she said, "What are you doing? Who said you could just walk in?"

"I thought I'd wait for you. You weren't gone very long." He took another look at the bedroom, turned, and came her way through the hallway. "Let me help you with this." He reached for Willa.

"No, don't. I don't need help." She put the shopping bag on the floor and carried Willa to the playpen in the living room.

"Obersturmführer, I don't want you just walking in here," she said. "You could have come back. What do you want?"

"I have something for you." He followed her into the kitchen, where she stood setting groceries on the table. "This," he said and held out his hand in a loose fist.

"What is it?"

"Take it."

"Put it on the counter."

"Take it." He laughed. "It's not a frog or anything."

She held out her hand and he dropped a shiny metallic ornament into it. She turned it in the light. "I don't want it," she said without thinking. She held it out again for him to take back.

He did not move. "The Gold Party Pin," he said. "You have been awarded a high honour, and you refuse it?"

"It's nothing personal. I never applied. It's a misunderstanding."

She put the pin on the counter, gold-rimmed in a wreath of oak leaves, the words *National-Sozialistische DAP* around the swastika in a white field.

"I never applied," she said again. "I'm honoured, but it's a mistake. Tell them I don't deserve it."

"And you may not," he said. "But it can't be taken back. You must have applied, and because of the Blood Order in your family you were found worthy."

"Worthy. Obersturmführer, I am not political. I'm honoured but I'm so unworthy." She listened to the sound of that and found it nearly funny. She tried a smile. "Take it away, please."

A strange light came into his eyes then. A sense of triumph, she would realize later. A victory. "This will go into your file," he said. "I advise you to accept it and to say no more and be thankful."

"I am thankful. But it must be a mistake."

He reached into his tunic pocket and took out a folded piece of paper. "Here is the document to go with it," he said. He put the paper on the counter next to the pin. He reached and unfolded it, glanced at it and put it back. "We have you as Doctor Phil. Clara Herzog Leonhardt, is that correct? Two last names?"

"Yes."

"You *are* married, are you not?"

"I am. We are. For academic reasons I like using my maiden name as well. Please take those things away. Someone made a mistake."

He stepped back. "Mrs. Leonhardt," he said. "You would be wise to consult with your husband first. With the lieutenant colonel when he comes back. If he comes back. Heil Hitler."

His boot heels echoed in the hall. He stopped, and she heard him call, "Mrs. Leonhardt! You have a great deal of room here, for one small family."

She held her breath, listening.

"Did you hear me?"

"I did."

"And something else. Your radio is tuned to an illegal station. The radio itself is illegal."

"I did not know that."

"You did not know that. Get a *Volksempfänger*. It receives only the approved station."

The floorboards in the hall squeaked. But he said nothing more, and after a few seconds she heard his footsteps moving away. The door opened and fell closed.

She hid the party pin and document in a kitchen drawer, left Anna in charge of the house, packed up Willa, and took the train to Vienna.

What she did on the train was to reason with her fears, try to look at them calmly and to stop her mind from racing. She sat with her eyes closed and with Willa on her lap, and she searched for solace in what she had learned and what she believed; she imagined herself being calm and in control inside the house that was the structure of her mind. In control, even as the outside world was breaking more than her windows. This was the real test, she knew, and it was so much more than words and ideas.

THAT AFTERNOON, Mitzi and Cecilia had gone to the forger once again. He had moved to a garage-type workshop, they said when they described the encounter. A place with a bed-sitting room behind a curtain at the rear. They sat primly on metal chairs next to a small printing press. The room was dirty, with various kinds of equipment and desks, and with lightshades hanging from patched wiring.

"It is finished," the forger said to Mitzi. He wore a pilled sweater that day and old corduroy trousers. His fingers were stained and on his forehead he wore a green shade. "It's done. Come and look," he said. He switched on a desklamp and stood back.

There it was, the document Mitzi would need under the new rules to be able to apply for a Trade Pass, and anyone practising a trade now needed such a pass. They were closing in, closing the loopholes at all levels and all walks of life; every week there were more regulations and forms required.

But here was her salvation now, in her new name; the short Aryan Certificate of Racial Origin, the *Kleine Ahnenpass*; patronizing, demeaning.

Printed front and back on the proper green-and-white document stock, six fields with lines for names and detailed vital statistics going back to the grandparents on both sides. Six fields, forty-eight lines, and every one an insult.

Result of Examination, it said about her, about Anna Susanne Toplitz: ARYAN. There, halfway across the watermark of the eagle's talons.

The forger stood close, watching her, judging her hunger. "You can have it as soon as you bring me the money," he said.

"But so much," said Mitzi. "Ten thousand. Can't you make an exception? And all the money I've been giving you. I need this. I'll give you free haircuts for as long as you live."

He thought she was joking, and he cracked a smile. He said he did not have enough hair left for that. What hair he had, he could snip off himself, in a mirror.

He waved a hand at Cecilia, who had not spoken one word, had sat upright with her hand folded in her lap, touching as little as possible in this filthy place.

"Perhaps Madame can help out," he said. "If she does, then perhaps I'll give her back the document we created for the estate. Horses, I think. Certain customs forms. Yes?"

"It happened only twice," said Cecilia. "And only because the government was inventing a new tax every day. In any case, we no longer have anything to do with the estate."

"Oh, but the authorities," he said. "They'll use any excuse for revenge against the privileged."

"You little man," said Cecilia. She stood up.

"And I seem to remember something else," said the forger. "Your son. I still have the file. A military man who needed a neutral passport. How is he? I might give you back his file too."

AT THE APARTMENT that evening it was the only topic of conversation. Mitzi was so upset by it she had heart flutters. She was lying on the couch, pale, with a cold compress on her forehead. The other women sat nearby in the living room, with Willa propped in a corner of the stuffed chair. Maximilian was shuffling back and forth serving glasses of cold tea.

"But why would he go to the Gestapo?" said Clara. "Think about it. He'd lose the income from the people he is blackmailing and I'm sure Mitzi is not the only one. So why would he do it?"

"For immunity," said Erika. "Or maybe he is getting scared and wants to stop. He can probably offer them the files of a few hundred people."

"Let's hope he won't do it as long as there's a chance to get money from anyone," she said. "What did you tell him?"

"I said, I'd try," said Mitzi from the couch. "But I need that piece of paper, and I need a Trade Pass. If anybody checks and I don't have them, I'll never work again. If I'm lucky."

They sat contemplating this in silence.

"How much can we raise if we all chip in?" Clara said then. "Even just a few thousand may be enough for him to wait and hope for the rest."

They took a count and came up with enough money between them to buy three thousand, five hundred Swiss francs. Two days later all four of them, Cecilia, Erika, Mitzi, and Clara with Willa in her lap, drove there in Mitzi's little car. They gave the forger the money and promised there would be more.

In the half-light in his garage he stood sucking his teeth. He looked from one to the other, not sure what to make of this united front. He looked at the child.

They wanted the document, they said, but the forger shook his head. He said he needed the rest of the money first.

"How long can you wait?" said Cecilia.

"I don't know," he said. "Bring me the money."

TWENTY-TWO

✦

LATE IN OCTOBER, before Albert was back from Poland, she knew she was pregnant again. Because she did not like the army doctor at the base, she packed up little Willa and took the train west into the mountains to St. Töllden. Dr. Mannheim examined her. She was worried, she told him, because she had been spotting.

Anxiety could do that, he said. He told her to rest as much as possible, to keep calm and to take no medication and no alcohol whatsoever.

"How about . . ." she said and blushed. "My husband may be coming home soon. I hope he will."

"Ah," said Dr. Mannheim. "Gentle sexual intercourse should be no problem. Unless the situation gets worse."

She stayed at home for several days and relished her parents' loving attention and their help with Willa while she slept and rested and enjoyed her mother's cooking. She had forgotten what it was like to feel safe. The bleeding did not recur.

By then both her brothers had been drafted and sent east. All within four days, her mother said. Called up and dispatched; Peter as an infantry lieutenant, and Bernhard as a mere rifleman with the support company attached to an artillery unit.

"Peter said he'd never go to war for the corporal. In those words," she said. "He suggested he'd rather shoot himself."

Her mother waved a hand. "They closed the League of Nations office and took his passport, but you knew that. He said he might have a hard time finding work. Go and talk to Daniela sometime. She is going to be lonely. And Mitzi and Erika, how are they?"

"Fine. Erika is still working on her degree. Mitzi is having problems getting gasoline, even on the black market. Albert thought he might be able to help out with requisition slips, but he can't. Maybe she can work from the apartment, but she'll lose clients."

They had this conversation in her bedroom, she in a flannel nightgown sitting up against the pillows, her mother in her quilted housecoat in the chair next to the bed. Willa was asleep in the white crib that had once been hers. Only the small lamp on the night table was on. Its light came yellow through the straw shade and fell weakly on everything; on the bookshelves and the bed, and on her mother with her hair in curlers under a silk scarf.

"Clara," said her mother. "Forgive me, but I need to ask. Are you happy in your marriage? Do you really love Albert?"

"With all my heart," she said without hesitation. "All my heart. It swells when I think of him. Do you know the feeling?"

Her mother looked startled for a moment. "Oh yes," she said. "I'm glad for you."

"Most of the time I am very happy."

"Even though he is away so much?"

"Yes. And he won't always be. Someday this war will be over. Until then I can take care of things."

"Good."

"Mama, I fell in love with him more than any other time on that trip when he was looking for work. Something happened that day, I saw something that – I won't try to describe it. But I did, and I haven't doubted him since. Not really. I love Willa, and I'll love the new baby too. And someday, when all this is over, I will have an interesting career, teaching and writing. I look forward to that. I'll have a profession, Mama."

"A profession!"

"Yes. I'm sure of it."

For a while they sat in silence, then her mother said, "But your Albert. Him, they didn't even need to draft. He volunteered for this."

"No. Not for *this*. You know he didn't. But he took the job, yes. It was exactly what he wanted to do. He saw it as an honour. You're going to ask me how I feel about that now."

"How do you?"

"Unsure. But it's only hindsight that makes it complicated. It obviously makes no difference any more. Look at Peter and Bernhard."

Her mother sat back in the dim light with her eyes red and tired. "Well," she said. "You can't help but wonder. If we'd all refused, if we'd all stood up and refused, we wouldn't be in this mess."

"If we'd all refused. The entire nation?"

"Something like that."

Nothing was said for a while. They heard Willa stirring in the crib that would soon be too small for her.

"It helps me to think of it as some sort of natural disaster," she said then. "An earthquake, and all you can do is hold on until it's over."

In the hall they heard her father's footsteps.

"They cleared out the museum and it's some kind of party office now," her mother whispered. "Your father is very unhappy. They loaded everything on trucks, the Roman artifacts. The breastplates, remember? They took them all away. The bronze horse harness."

"Where to?"

Her mother shrugged. The door opened and he stood looking in. "There you are," he said. "Let the girls sleep now, Mama. Come to bed."

Her mother stood up and moved the chair back

against the wall. Her father stood holding out his hand
to her.

SHE RETURNED to the cottage at the base, and it was
just three weeks after that Albert came back from Poland.
He cried out in the night and she woke him from night-
mares. Willa woke and called for her. Anna woke and padded
through the kitchen. Those were the days of the drawn
curtains and darkened rooms in daytime when he began to
talk about the Polish campaign and the screaming horses.

"It's not that horses are more important than people,"
he said at one time. "I am trying to understand this. It's not
that they deserve more sympathy. But it makes . . . something. An immorality," he said. "No. A baseness all the more
obvious. Drawing them into this. Noble animals."

Sometime later he said he must not allow himself to
think that way. He was struggling to work something out.

Work out what? she said. And could she help?

She was helping already, he told her. Just being with
him. Listening.

Anna brought them food and drink. Anna looked after
Willa, and through their door they could hear the two of
them, could hear Anna's felt slippers on the wooden floor.

When she told him she was pregnant, he was so moved
he turned away and sat like this until she came and touched
his shoulder.

As the days went by, he became his old self again. He
slept better and she heard him laughing as he played

with Willa. On the morning of the day he went back to the base he stood at the kitchen counter in full uniform with the ribbon of the new Iron Cross II in his tunic, and it was not until then that she mentioned the visit of SS Obersturmführer Bönninghaus.

His face changed. He set down his coffee cup with great care, and he opened the drawer with the Gold Party Pin slowly as though the thing might explode. He read the document and put it back, and he pulled out the chair and sat down at the table. He sat with his eyes closed for a few seconds, then he stood up.

"That man will never set foot in this house again," he said to her. "If this is causing you anxiety, please don't let it. I will settle this and we'll never have to speak of it again."

Next day she heard from his adjutant, Lieutenant Neumann, what had taken place. Albert had called the obersturmführer to his office, and through the padded double doors the lieutenant and the chief of staff, Major von Rhenold, could hear Albert shouting at the SS man.

He said that if the obersturmführer ever again dared to just walk into the house and bother his wife, then Albert would see to it that he was court-martialled for insubordination. *No! Shut your mouth*, he shouted. *You have nothing to say to me.*

Lieutenant Neumann told her this, talking sideways to her while keeping an eye on the cottage door, waiting for Albert by the car. He gave her a quick look. "If I were Bönninghaus I'd put in for a transfer."

And that was only the beginning.

Much later she realized that she could have chosen a better time to tell him about the forger. But by then it was too late. She mentioned it over dinner the next evening, and a nice dinner it was, of venison because it was the season, and with vegetables from their own garden. He listened, and only when she was finished did he ask questions.

"He is threatening me and Mother, and he has been blackmailing Mitzi all along?"

"Yes."

"And she never said anything?"

"She mentioned it once, but it had been manageable amounts, and she wanted to keep the peace. Now he wants ten thousand Swiss francs. We scraped together three and a half, but he wants the rest before he'll give her the paper. She can't continue working like this. If anyone asked to see her Trade Pass, it would all unravel for her."

For a while they ate in silence, then he put down knife and fork and said, "Do you know where he lives?"

"Not exactly. Mitzi and your mother would know. I went along just once."

He called the apartment from the telephone on the wall in the kitchen while she sat staring at her uneaten food. She heard him speak to his mother and to Mitzi. When he came back he said, "I'll go and talk to him."

He went to the bedroom and minutes later came back wearing his panzer fatigues, the black-holstered pistol, and lace-up boots.

"Now? You are going *now*?"

"Yes. I'll be back before morning." He pulled out the chair next to her and sat down. "The pistol I left with you and Erika in Vienna that day. Where is it?"

"Why?"

"I want to see it."

She had to think. "In the bedroom," she said. "Probably still in the same drawer."

"Bring it. Please."

She brought it and put it on the table, on the white table cloth between dishes and candles. He sat looking at it. He picked it up. "Was it ever fired?"

"God no."

He dropped the magazine into his palm, jacked out the shell in the chamber, and quickly within seconds took the gun apart. It lay in pieces on the table and he examined those one by one and clicked them back together. The shell went into the magazine and the magazine into the grip. He worked the slide and watched through the port as the shell slid into the chamber. He put the pistol back on the table and looked up at Clara standing there.

"Keep the safety on," he said. "We'll have to replace the hammer spring once in a while but the armourer can do that in a minute. With this model the lever has to be down. And keep it loaded like this. If you ever have to use it, just move the safety catch. Up, like this."

"You are scaring me."

"I am saying if. *If.* Most likely that will never happen."

He left soon after that, in his old leather army coat on the Norton, wearing goggles and helmet. She said to him that he'd not ridden it for some time, but he said nothing to that. He adjusted the goggles and nodded to her and kicked in the gear.

Eventually she went to bed, but she could not sleep and so stood up again and haunted the house. Anna came in robe and slippers from the lean-to and asked if she needed anything.

"Dear Anna. No. Go back to bed."

"A hot chocolate. It'll calm you."

"No thanks. Oh wait, yes. Thank you."

She sat in the living room, sat sideways with her sock-feet on the wooden bench around the ceramic stove and held the mug with both hands. She leaned against the warm tiles.

"Anything else?" said Anna.

"No. Thank you, Anna. Go to bed."

Gradually the stove cooled and she added more wood. She was careful not to make noise. The clock on the wall ticked. It was a cuckoo clock but the sound was broken and so the bird came out silently and went back in and closed the little door with just the clicking of small cogs and hinges.

Albert came back at four in the morning. She was asleep on the couch with the blanket on her. She heard the motor-cycle in some dream and woke when she heard the door. She sat up and her heart was pounding.

He was at the dining-room table, taking off the big coat. His hands were blackened and he smelled of something. Smoke. There was a mark on his cheek, a scrape with the blood wiped off. On the table lay a small stack of papers.

"Albert," she said. "What happened?"

He raised a hand. "Don't come near. Not now. I need a bath."

"What did you do?"

He pointed at the papers. "I brought the documents."

"How did you get them? What did you do?"

He shook his head. "Don't ask. I brought the papers and none of us needs to worry about him any more." From another pocket he took a wad of Swiss francs. "Three thousand. It was all I could find. Give it back to Mitzi."

"All you *could find*? What did you do to him? Albert!"

"Shh. You'll wake Willa. These are not normal times, Clara." He turned toward the hall. "I'll run a bath. Please don't follow me. Look at the documents. There's a Trade Pass for Mitzi too."

"He made it while you were waiting? How did you get him to do that?"

"He had no choice. And I asked you not to follow me." Albert stood in the bathroom, unbuttoning the fatigue jacket. Behind him the tub was filling, and holster and gunbelt lay coiled on the toilet lid. "I'm closing this door now, Clara," he said. "There is nothing to worry about. Go look at the documents."

"What is that smell, Albert? What did you do to that man?"

"What man? What smell?"

"That!" She sniffed.

"Dear Clara. Please go. We will not be talking about this again." He closed the door.

But she stood there, listening. She could hear water running, and behind the steady sound of it she heard the harsh metallic clicks as he was taking apart his gun and putting it back together and reloading it. She would not have recognized the sounds had she not heard them only hours ago in the dining room.

She stood and leaned and listened. Emotions flooded her, horror and relief and hope, and in none of her feelings did she recognize the woman she had become in so short a time.

In her bedroom Willa woke and began to cry. It gave her an excuse to step away from the door.

TWENTY·THREE

✦

ALL THOSE DOCUMENTS were in her files now, in the boxes for the archives, and they weren't the only horrific pieces of paper there. At first she had kept them as reminders for history, then for her children. At some point she almost sent them to Geneva along with some research assignments by Dr. Hufnagel for the United Nations; then the offer had come from the provincial archives for her own display section. She thought of them as useful for anyone who cared to find out how small fires ignored became infernos.

On the morning of the appointment she picked up Mitzi in a taxi and took her to the hospital. It was a new and private hospital in the outskirts of St. Töllden, founded by several specialists who had opted out of Medicare. Here they were providing treatment much more quickly and expensively than the government system, and they were letting rooms and facilities to other specialists such as Dr. Gottschalk and the cardiologist in town.

Mitzi's room was ready. It was a private room with one large window that overlooked not the new suburbs but the river and its northern floodplain; it overlooked the meadows rising to the mountains, and the mountains themselves. Bleak and harsh, snow everywhere; snowfields like mirrors in the sun, and snow and ice clinging to fault lines cold and blue on the shadowface of the mountain. Deep snow on meadows, and covered feeding stations stocked with hay and chestnuts for deer and for the stags that came down from the Italian saddle into the valley this hungry time of year.

Dr. Gottschalk examined Mitzi: heart, lungs, blood pressure, reflexes. She wrote prescriptions for the intravenous, and requested two X-rays. Clara walked alongside the orderly who was dressed in pristine whites from shoes to cap, and Mitzi already in her back-split hospital gown in the wheelchair. The corridor gleamed with light coming off vinyl tiles as off a frozen lake.

Later she sat in the chair by Mitzi's bedside. Mitzi had the intravenous in the back of her hand. The veins there were dark in her pale skin, and the one with the needle in it was thicker than the others. Mitzi was smiling. She was getting drowsy. "Dear," she said. "It's good of you to be here."

"After this," Clara said. "When they discharge you, and that'll be in just a few days, maybe a week, I want you to come and stay with me. I'll get Mrs. Sokol to make up the other room. You've seen it. There's a good bed in it and good light. I want you to come there."

"Well," said Mitzi. "Maybe."

"Not maybe. For sure. It'll be waiting for you."

Dr. Gottschalk came by once more. "We just got an OR and we'll do the procedure tomorrow morning at eleven o'clock. The nurses will get you ready, Mitzi. No more solids, please. Just fluids between now and then. Jell-O tonight. How are you feeling?"

Mitzi smiled up at her. "Fine. Thank you, Caroline."

"Good. Tomorrow, then." Dr. Gottschalk patted her on the arm and left.

The sun was behind the mountain now, the sky pink. In the valley trees stood black and solemn against the snow. Deer at one of the feeding stations. She could just make them out: three, four.

She stayed while Mitzi ate her dinner of green and red Jell-O. She watched her old friend from the side having difficulty spearing small cubes of Jell-O with a plastic fork but eating with grim determination as though it could change anything, as though it mattered.

Her eyes filled and she turned away. Tears rolled down her cheeks, so many, coming from where she did not know. She dabbed at them fiercely, hoping Mitzi was not looking. *God. Lord. Remember. Teach us to care and not to care; Teach us to sit still . . .*

She stood up and put her forehead to the cold window

glass. Out there lights were coming on, yellow in the blue of evening. No leaves on the trees, none on the fields.

Behind her, Mitzi said, "What can you see out there?"

"Not much, dear. Evening. It's getting dark." She turned back into the room. Mitzi lay against her pillow. The small bowl of Jell-O was empty.

"I'll be going soon," she said. "You rest. I'll be back in the morning." She leaned and kissed Mitzi on the forehead. Mitzi found her hand and patted it.

"Tomorrow," she said.

THAT NIGHT, AT HOME, she worked some more on the boxes. They were organized along national and regional topics, with chronological and subject dividers. St. Töllden during the war and during the aftermath figured prominently. Her personal files, her journals and notes to herself over the years, were organized in the two banker's boxes with the red labels that she'd keep at the house. She had yet to decide what to do about them.

She found the journal for 1939 and leafed to November. There it was, in ink, in longhand: *A. back late at night with the documents. What happened? How to deal with this?* And above those words, in pencil, in shorthand: *I know the smell of gunpowder. In Landshut it came in the open window from the firing range.* Then in the margin, something else in shorthand that had been erased.

She was about to climb into bed when Willa called: the conference had been moved to Frankfurt, and she could come after all. "Do you want me to? You aren't too busy with the book right now?"

"No. And yes, of course I want you to come."

"All right then. In a few days. Is everything all right?"

"Everything is fine. Mitzi is in the hospital. They're doing her hip. Tomorrow."

"Give her my love. Tell her a hip is nothing. We are experimenting with doing them on expensive breeders."

"On camels?"

"Yes. It's a congenital thing with some of them. If we can get a few more calves out of her, why not. Camels, people. It's all much the same bones and connective tissue. Even similar muscles."

"Well, I'll mention it."

In the morning she was back at the hospital, equipped with several pages of manuscript, writing pad and pen, prepared for a long wait. There was still time to sit with Mitzi before they came with the gurney and lifted her onto it to take her to the prep room.

Clara walked alongside as far as the sliding milk-glass door. "I'll be here," she said, and Mitzi craned her neck to see her until the door slid shut.

She waited at one of the white round tables in the coffee shop. Doctors and nurses came and went. She waited. She had completed five pages of manuscript in draft translation when Caroline Gottschalk came into the coffee shop and stood at the table.

"Everything's gone well," she said. She looked tired. She

stepped out of one of her white hospital clogs and briefly set her stockingfoot on the tiles. "She's in recovery now. We'll keep her for a few days, and then she can go into home-care. By then she can put some very light weight on it."

"She'll be fine?"

"Good as new. Eventually."

Four days later Willa arrived at the Innsbruck airport, just in time to help bring Mitzi to the house. Her plane had descended into the valley through a snowstorm and it was still snowing when they took a taxi to the hospital. They came back with Mitzi in an ambulance. Two strong orderlies helped her up the stairs, and helped put her to bed. There was a walker, and they left it standing by the bedside.

"My," said Mitzi and studied the walker. "Who would have thought."

Willa, decisive and capable, sat at Mitzi's bedside and took her pulse. It was weak and irregular. She said so in the living room to Clara. "She'll need lots of rest and good food. A bit of protein for healing. Soft scrambled eggs, vegetables, salads, a bit of beef stew. An open window once in a while and a bit of weight-bearing. More and more each day."

"She can have all that."

"What happens, Mom," said Willa. "Healing and aging, the whole thing about cell renewal is like making copies of copies of copies. Cells forget what they looked like when they started out. The original is long gone, and so the information gets less and less distinct. Eventually it's nearly illegible. And when on top of that some tiny code misfires, that's how we die, Mom. Like Dad. Doctor Kessler did the best he could."

"I always thought so."

Emma came over for dinner, and Willa entertained them with events on the camel farm. They were closer to a solution for the fetal necrosis syndrome; it might have to do with rare beetle larvae going around the world now, ingested by the mother with certain kinds of feed. Good news was also that there was success with a new crossbreed with pure Mongolians that thrived in the harshest conditions.

"Much better than four-wheel drive cars," she said. It was a joke, but nobody got it.

Emma said, "I'm teaching again, Willa. Part-time at the college. History. Sixteenth Century, right now. The English Reformation."

"Oh good. I'm glad for you. Speaking of history. I'm sorry, but I need to ask. Which of them took the Knight's Cross, Mom? I want to know."

"I asked you not to do that, Willa. Let it go."

"What's that?" said Emma.

"Nothing," she said. "Ignore her."

After Emma had left and they had gotten ready for bed, they met by the bathroom door in their long nightgowns like two ghosts in shrouds, and Willa said, "I'm sorry. I didn't know you hadn't told her."

"It doesn't matter."

"But it does."

"Then pick a better time. Right now there are problems with one of Tom's kids. The older one. He was arrested a few weeks ago."

"Arrested. For what?"

"Don't ask. I shouldn't say anything. You can ask her, but be gentle. You know what I mean, and maybe while you're here, spend some more time with her. Just the two of you."

"We're planning to."

On the day before she had to fly back, Willa said she wanted to put a candle on her father's grave.

They walked to the cemetery, she and her daughters, bought a candle at a stand, and put it in the lantern by the stone. Vandals had been in the cemetery and spray-painted looping graffiti on headstones and Roman burial tablets set into crypt walls two thousand years old, day-glo symbols or words in a foreign language no one understood. The stone angel had black paint on her wings and hands. At some headstones old people were rubbing at the graffiti with brushes.

"Turpentine doesn't work," called one man from a few graves down. "At least yours is not over inscriptions."

"No, but it's white stone and it's porous," said Willa. "Just look at this. How could anyone."

"Try the stonemason," said the man. "Maybe he can do something."

Back at the house Clara opened a drawer and took some-thing out. "There," she said. "One for each of you. Both the same. You and your dad."

"The one from your night table," said Willa. "In the silver frame."

"My favourite picture of the three of you, yes. I had it copied."

After Willa had left for the airport and Emma had gone home, she sat in Mitzi's room. She brought a floor lamp and sat in the chair with her reading glasses on and manu-script pages in her lap.

"Siblings," said Mitzi. "Old jealousies, I'd say."

"Maybe."

"It's good Emma's teaching again. Keeps her busy."

"It's more than that. She's good at it. She's substituting at the college where she was when she found that French pilot."

"The pilot. Yes. What was that about the Knight's Cross?"

Clara waved a hand. "One of the kids took it. Don't ask. Willa wants it back, but they can work that out."

She shifted the papers in her lap and began to read. For a while there were no sounds at all in the room. She looked up.

"I'm glad you're here, Mitzi-dear," she said. "Stay as long as you want. Even when you're all better. Stay here."

TWENTY-FOUR

THE POLISH CAMPAIGN had taken less than five weeks.
At the end of combat operations, Waffen-SS and regular
SS took over from the military. They began to organize
the occupation of Poland and the construction of labour
and concentration camps. To make their job easier, they
built walls and created the Warsaw ghetto. And the
Russians in their part of Poland, as the world would discover years later, murdered twenty thousand Polish officers and academics and scientists and leading politicians in
a forest place called Katyn.

But long before then Albert had returned. The curtains
at the cottage had been thrown back and the lights turned
on again, and on the rare evenings when Albert was home
before dark they played with Willa on the swing next to
the house. He whittled the first of many willow flutes and
worked with spanners and rags on the Norton.

He had made an inner decision, he said to her. In time he would tell her about it. He wanted her to know that.

Then her parents received news that Bernhard was dead. The letter stamped with eagle and swastika said he had died a hero for his country and that the Führer appreciated his sacrifice. No personal effects could be sent.

Albert made inquiries and learned that Bernhard had been assigned to a team of sappers, and while they were disarming a Stuka fragmentation bomb, it detonated. Of the three soldiers just the feet in boots were found. The dog tags were gone, but one of the men, his commanding officer said, would have been Bernhard von Waldstein.

There was a memorial service at the Benedictine chapel in St. Töllden, and because it coincided with Christmas it was doubly sad. She was home for part of the holidays, and Albert came along. He brought the full dress uniform. He stood in it tall and straight, and in the church the few men among the mourners looked at him and they nodded and said Colonel.

Near the end of the service, her mother and father stood before the congregation; he stone-faced, all in black; she all in black from shoes to veil, in her formal coat of black gabardine, heavy and long as had been the fashion in her day, with wide lapels and black velvet cuffs. When the priest spoke the words about the honourable death for cause and country she straightened, and when she reached out and laid a bare hand on the steel helmet they put on the bible stand for these services, everyone in the chapel could see the candlelight reflected on her streaming cheeks behind the veil.

There were twenty-nine people present and every one of them loved her, and they loved her all the more that day because they understood the unspoken and unspeakable lie that underlay all this.

SHE AND ALBERT spent New Year's Eve and the first day of 1940 at the apartment in Vienna. There was a great deal of snow in the streets and avalanches slid from the roofs of houses. Albert's young sister, Sissy, was there, and Daniela. Peter was in Norway, or maybe Finland, Daniela said. Sissy had finished boarding school and had received her teacher's certificate. Clara had hardly seen her since Theo's funeral.

At midnight they set off firecrackers on the balcony that sailed out and exploded in a shower of blue and orange wheels that sizzled and died on their way to the ground. They danced to the traditional *Blue Danube Waltz* that played on the radio at midnight, and they worked at being lively at least, if not cheerful. She felt well, and the baby was beginning to show. Cecilia came up once and winked and said, "When?" and she smiled and told her.

On the balcony, looking out over the sea of lights and other people's firecrackers, Erika told her that more and more reports were coming into the Red Cross office now about people suddenly missing. Abandoned businesses. Empty apartments and houses with everything left behind, but never empty for long before someone else moved in.

In a way Sissy was the one bright note that New Year's Eve; she who was young and lovely, and she still looked out at the world from trusting eyes. Eyes so black the pupil could not easily be seen within the iris, like in belladonna eyes two generations or more before. At some point Cecilia whispered to Clara and to Mitzi that one reason why Sissy was so happy was that she had recently met someone, a young doctor just finished with his internship, and that she was very much in love.

Cecilia sighed, saying this, and she looked sideways at young Sissy laughing with Erika and sipping champagne, this young woman who was carrying the light and the promise for all of them at the apartment that night.

THREE MONTHS LATER, Sissy's young doctor, whose name was Oskar Gottschalk, was ordered to report for his military duties. There were hurried preparations for the wedding, not the least of which was the short Ahnenpass certifying three generations of pure Aryan blood on both sides. Only then could they apply for the marriage licence.

The wedding took place at the municipal office in their district, and they signed their names in the large black book that lay on a table there, under the photograph of Hitler staring at them and at everyone in the room.

The new and rosy-faced husband, Dr. Oskar Gottschalk,

received cursory basic training, was sent to Norway as a field surgeon, and within two weeks he was dead; machine-gunned through chest and abdomen, the death certificate said. It arrived at the apartment in the same envelope as the official death notice from his company commander. By then Sissy knew already that she was expecting, and so by the end of April 1940 she was a pregnant widow not twenty years old.

There was a modest memorial service in a side chapel at St. Stephen's Cathedral, and as incense swirled and singing voices came from another part of the church, Sissy stood small and lost with her hand on yet another steel helmet. Maximilian and Cecilia and the dead doctor's parents stood behind her.

"Act as though thou hast faith," said the priest. "And faith shall be given onto you."

One month and two more willow flutes later, the last one quite ambitious with three fingerholes that actually worked, Albert received orders to entrain his battalion for the marshalling grounds near Cologne and there to report to the command of General Erwin Rommel.

She saw him off, crouching next to Willa under an umbrella as they stood in the rain among other wives and girlfriends and parents as the brass band played and the tanks rolled out the gates. Armageddon machines they were with heads in leather helmets like soft knobs poking out of hatches, loud and clumsy machines on the wet street; the very notion of them ridiculous, she wrote in notes to herself that night, if you allowed yourself to think about them well and clearly.

Armoured field pieces followed, and then came truck after truck, helmeted soldiers under the tarpaulins with their pale faces and anxious eyes searching for their loved ones while being carted away to a place and fate they could not imagine.

Albert stood in the command car as they headed out, in his field uniform, boots, and gunbelt, and the greatcoat over it, all wet in the rain, rain jumping off the cap visor and off his bare hand there saluting his officers as they went by.

She caught one last glance from him, a smile for her, before he spoke to his major, who in turn spoke to the driver. Albert sat down and the engine started and the car drove off.

In the crowd also stood SS Obersturmführer Bönninghaus. From Albert she knew that the man had in fact at the time asked for a transfer. He had been called to Berlin to make a report, and then had been sent straight back to Burgenland with new powers and responsibilities as the political district commander.

She did not notice him until the crowd began to thin, but there he stood in his black raincoat streaming wet, watching her.

THE OBERSTURMFÜHRER came to her house the very next morning. He knocked, and knocked again. When she opened, there he stood in his silver-accented blacks, with his driver waiting by the car. The rain had stopped, and he stood among the rich fragrance of spring and earth, with the garden greening behind him.

"Mrs. Leonhardt," he said. "This house has a full basement with an exterior entrance, does it not? Most houses in the area do."

"Yes. Why?"

"May I see it?"

She walked around the house with him, to the other side where the basement door lay hinged on two stone sills and steps led down into the cellar, stone-walled all around, with bins on the dirt floor for potatoes and root vegetables for the winter. She turned the switch and two bare light bulbs came on.

"Good," he said. "I've come to inform you that we've assigned twenty prisoners of war to this house. They will be working in the local agriculture. You are to house them but not to feed them. They will be picked up in the morning and brought back at night." He turned and looked at the open cellar door. "They'll enter here and they'll leave here. They are not to have access to the upstairs or to tools or matches. Straw pallets will be provided. Is that understood?"

"Do you have Colonel Leonhardt's permission for that?"

"We do not need your husband's permission for anything, Mrs. Leonhardt. This has nothing to do with his command."

That night in bed she began bleeding massively, and she crawled to the bathroom and on the way there she lost the baby. She lay on the wood floor in the hall, crouched on the boards as in supreme supplication before this cramping horror her body was committing, and the baby came out, nearly fully formed, too large already for one hand.

Anna heard the screams and she came to find her sitting in blood holding this baby and with her finger wiping blood and mucus from the tiny, tiny monkey face, a creature dead and alien as if fallen from some distant star.

Anna turned and left, and she came back quickly with a basin of hot water from the stove and with the sharp paring knife and bedsheets fresh and clean from the linen shelf.

SHE WROTE TO HIM, but the letters never arrived. So ferocious was the assault in the west that Holland, Belgium, and France all fell within weeks. At Dunkirk the tanks and the Stukas turned away from the retreating British and French forces and kept moving south with such speed and relentlessness that Berlin became worried and issued orders for them to slow down.

Near the end of the campaign he was injured by a bullet. He was standing next to the heavy machine gun in the tracked command car in dust goggles and helmet, speaking into the microphone to his driver, waving his arms and pointing, he said, when the bullet struck high in his left side and knocked him down.

At the rolling field hospital the surgeon stitched him up and they taped his arm in place so that he could carry on while the injury healed.

TWENTY-FIVE

❖

WHEN ALBERT CAME HOME on leave from France he arrived unannounced by train, he and one of his lieutenants. From the station he came home in a taxi, and he climbed out and stood paying the driver through the open window. The taxi with the lieutenant in the back moved off, and Albert turned. She saw him from the living-room window and did not recognize him until he had walked most of the garden path to the front door.

They sat on the couch holding hands and holding each other for long minutes without speaking. She stroked his cheek. His forehead. The powderburns and scars around the outlines of the dust goggles worn for weeks. She touched his arm.

"It'll be fine," he said to her. "They just fixed it in place. It doesn't hurt much any more."

Willa came tottering in from the kitchen, watching

him shyly. Behind her in the doorway stood Anna. She bent and whispered to Willa and then let go of the toddler's hand and gave her a small push in Albert's direction. He slipped off the couch to his knees and held out his good arm.

They had five days. There was so much to talk about it had to be done in considered sessions, in topics, small strokes leading up to the full picture.

She had yet to see a doctor, she admitted. There was none at the base, and in the village Anna was as good a midwife and doula as any. Clara insisted she was fine. She was so much in need of love and kindness she never left his side all those days he was home. Anna like a den mother looked after them again with food and drink and whatever else they wanted. Anna also did the basement work during the day, sweeping and carrying the latrine buckets to the pit in the field behind the house.

In the early mornings two grey trucks with tarpaulin covers would drive around the house to the basement entrance, and SS men in field grey would unlock the hatch from outside and watch the prisoners climb on board. Some would guard them while one with a submachine gun stepped down into the basement and made sure it was empty. After sundown the prisoners would be brought back, fed from a container on the back of the trucks, and locked up again.

She and Albert could hear them at night under the floor planks, talking, murmuring, stirring on their strawbeds.

In the far corner of the house, by the fire place in the living room, they could hear at times the sound of a harmonica. Once in a while, before they were herded below at the end of the day, one of the SS men would turn on the hose at the back and the men would be allowed to strip and wash with a block of lye soap under the stream of water from the well pump. The Polish prisoners were white and gaunt and bearded. Two had grey hair, and one of them wore horn-rimmed glasses that he took off and set carefully on the stone sill before lining up for the hose.

Albert had asked her if she minded, and she'd said, No, she did not, even if it was a clear attempt by the obersturmführer to get back at her and Albert.

Not only did she not mind, she said, but the men were company for her, a human presence she was sheltering. They were an opportunity to make good for something that she did not quite understand, and they were certainly safer in her basement than in a POW camp.

On the sixth day the lieutenant came to pick up Albert in a taxi. She left Willa with Anna while she came along to the railroad station, holding hands with Albert all the way there. The car sped along the gravel road through fields long and wide to either side; vanishing lines, row after row, of potatoes and cabbage, and of mountains of sugar beets to be chopped up and boiled down in enormous vats for their sweetness. In the fields hundreds of prisoners of war were doing labour for the farmers while armed guards watched from raised platforms like hunters in the fall with the buttplates of their rifles resting on their thighs.

Back at the cottage the radio in the living room reported that on the previous day Hitler had made the French sign the articles of surrender in the very railroad car where Germany had been forced to sign the treaty terms of 1919. Immediately following the ceremony, the German army razed the area around the railroad car. The only thing left standing was the statue of the French Marshal Foch, the announcer said, so that the marshal from up high might witness the final outcome of his act of humiliation.

LATE IN JULY Albert's father suffered a heart attack in the bathroom of the Vienna apartment. He fell down shaving and by the time Cecilia found him he lay dead on the tile floor.

There was a funeral that Clara could not attend because on orders from the SS District Office she had to care for two prisoners who had fallen ill. The guards had notified the office and Obersturmführer Bönninghaus had come to the house to see for himself. He inspected the back door and he strode into the kitchen to see the door leading down to the basement from there. He found the light switch and clicked it on, and walked down the creaking stairs. She followed.

The two men lay weak and white as candlewax on their strawbeds. One was young, and the other was the older one with the glasses. Sweat beaded on his forehead and she reached out to feel his temperature, but Bönninghaus told her sharply not to.

"There is no need to touch them," he said. "They have a fever and in most cases it passes in a week. Give them water and once or twice during the day simple food such as a broth."

"Why not get them a doctor?"

"We will, if they are not better in a week. Until then just give them liquids several times a day."

Back upstairs in the kitchen he studied the lock on the basement door. It was old and heavy of hammered iron with a large key in the hole.

"Good," he said. "Leave it locked at all times, unless you or the maid are down there cleaning up during the day. Do not talk to them, do not ask questions. Any kind of fraternization is strictly prohibited. Do you understand?"

She nodded her head, and he stood looking her up and down. "I said do you understand?"

"I do."

"Good. I hear your husband was awarded his Iron Cross First Class. Where is he now?"

"I don't know."

"You don't know."

When he was gone she carried down a pitcher of water and two glasses. The men drank thirstily, sitting up in their foul strawbeds. The one with grey hair reached for the spectacles by his side and put them on. He looked up at her. He said something in Polish, then he said, "Thank you" in English.

She had Anna boil soup bones and vegetables, and she fed them the broth and gave them slices of dark bread. She pressed apples and fed them the juice. One night near the end of the first week she put on a dark coat and in the co-operative orchard at the end of the street she filled her pockets with apples that lay on the ground and took them down into the cellar. The prisoners bit into them gingerly because their teeth were loose in their jawbones.

And the two that had been ill did get better. The fever lifted and before long they departed in the mornings with the rest and came back at night.

But she kept giving them fruit, sweet plums and apples, all of which she collected by stealth at night. When she took down her gifts, Willa stood at the open basement door with her hair parted and tied in two little side plaits and watched.

The one with grey hair and glasses told her he had been an English high-school teacher in Warsaw. As if to prove it he said, "*If one advances confidently in the direction of his dream and endeavours to live the life he has imagined, he will meet with a success unexpected in common hours.*"

He stood proudly in the cellar under a bare light bulb quoting this, a gaunt man with glasses and a wild beard. He stepped back.

"Henry David Thoreau," she said. She handed him an apple.

One other night he said to her, "What is a loon?"

"A loan?"

"Yes," he said. "I quote: *In the fall the loon came, as usual, to moult and bathe in the pond, making the woods ring with his wild laughter before I had risen.*"

"Ah. A *loon*. It's a North American kind of duck with a black-and-white spotted back and a very pointy beak. Its eyes are nearly red, and it makes a sound like no other bird. It laughs like a crazy person, which is perhaps where the expression *loony* comes from. It may also come from *luna*, the moon."

"Loony," he said, and tasted the word. "*Loony.*"

The others spoke to her through the professor. Some weeks later, one of them asked for a knife. "You don't have to," said the professor. "But he is a good boy." He pulled down his lower eyelid with his forefinger. "I will watch."

She let them have the paring knife, even if Anna's eyes were round and still when Clara took it downstairs. Three nights later, when she went down into the cellar, the man spoke to the professor and the professor replied. They were all standing on the dirt floor in their cracked shoes and torn clothes, looking on expectantly, and the man reached under his strawbed and handed her something.

It was a small duck carved in wood. It had wheels turning on wooden dowels and an optimistic upturned beak. Individual feathers had been carved into tail and folded wings. Under the body, set into the spinning dowel, was a small tongue of wood that made a clacking sound when the wheels turned.

The man said something and pointed at the door at the top of the stairs, and the professor said, "He says it's for the little girl. He hopes she'll like it."

THEY BECAME the nearest thing to friends, and when any of them got sick again, she and Anna made them well. She put plasters on their cuts, she gave them fruit for their teeth, and she let them have Albert's razor. The guards saw them clean-shaven but made no comment to her.

September passed, and October. The days were sunny and warm, and the harvest that year of 1940 was the best in years. The grapes were sweet and heavy, and when the first nightfrost came it concentrated the sugar in the grapes still on vines, and the warmth of midday and early afternoons turned them rich and golden. Ice-wine was made from them, and a local Tokay, and the golden Burgenländer in brown bottles that travelled from there by rail and in the holds of ships to London and New York and Sydney, war or not.

By then she already knew that she was pregnant again. She had spoken to Anna, who had handed her a glass jar to urinate into. Anna had taken the jar to a woman in the village who kept cages of certain kinds of rabbits just for that purpose. Within days Clara knew.

And as soon as she knew, she became still inside, and happy. Her mind and her body both understood and knew, and they prepared for the event. She smiled more often, and she moved more slowly and was more careful on steps. And since the rabbit woman knew, so did the neighbours. The women came to the door in their kerchiefs and their long skirts and wooden mudshoes, and they smiled with embarrassment as they offered reed baskets with eggs and garden tomatoes and golden grapes, heavy and sweet.

One morning, as she sat at the sunlit table, the grapes in the bowl and the time of year and her very mood reminded her of something, and she looked up Rilke, and there it was: *Autumn Day.*

> *Lord, it is time. The summer was immense.*
> *Lay your shadow on the sundials now*
> *and in the fields let loose the wind.*
> *Order the last fruit to be full;*
> *give it two more southerly days,*
> *urge it to ripeness, and drive*
> *the last sweetness into the heavy wine.*
> *Whosoever has no house now will not build one anymore.*
> *Whosoever is alone now, will remain so for a long, long time,*
> *will stay awake, will read and write long letters,*
> *and walk the tree-lined streets, restlessly back and forth,*
> *while leaves are blowing.*

AND AS SHE CALMED, she rediscovered her love of reading, writing, and thinking. She described the men in the basement and what they meant to her, and she typed the pages with carbon copies and she placed them into files she was keeping for Willa and for the new baby. She updated her journal, and she began making notes for future essays and of ideas for poetry, even a longer work of fiction that she might tackle when all this was over. She knew she was preparing the ground for creative work to come; not for the present, because all her love and energy in those weeks went into Willa and into the new life inside her; it went into every thought of Albert, and it went to the men housed in her cellar who were so strong a human presence and responsibility in her life. It went to Anna, and into every passing moment of every day.

One weekend her friends came to visit, all of them, Mitzi, Erika, Cecilia, and Daniela. It was November, but still sunny and not too cold during the day. They went for walks and exchanged news, and she told them of the prisoners and her illicit help for them. On Saturday they prepared a fine harvest lunch in the garden, a long trestle table and wooden benches, and she invited all her neighbours and everyone brought something to share: wine and cider, meat and casseroles of chicken stew and roast pheasant and venison, bread still warm with wood ashes stuck to the crust, and bowls of fruit. Whatever food was left over they put away and when the prisoners were home and the trucks had left she and her friends carried it down to them in the basement.

On Sunday evening she took the women to the train station in a taxi, and on the way home she felt a sudden sharp pain in her abdomen. In an instant the day was no longer fine, the fields as they passed no longer rich with black soil. She sat still and afraid in the backseat of the car, and at home she went straight to the bathroom. She locked the door and pulled down her underpants and immediately in the cotton fabric saw the smear of bright-red blood.

TWENTY-SIX

※

ANNA SENT HER straight to bed and there she remained for several days. The bleeding stopped and gradually her hope and confidence returned. Three weeks after that Albert came home to rotate out the garrison crew. He arrived with only forty-five men. The rest of the battalion remained in France, marshalled and rearmed, and still attached to Rommel's panzer units.

Within the hour he had commissioned a military ambulance, a medic, and a driver. They headed west at speed, then south into the mountains and along the snowbound valleys on chained wheels toward St. Töllden. They drove all night, and when the sun rose the mountains stood deep orange along their edges against the cloudless sky.

Dr. Mannheim made a thorough examination, internal and external. He took smears and blood and examined them under a microscope for hostile bacteria. He consulted a colleague in Innsbruck, a specialist, by telephone. Albert sat in the doctor's office, and he could hear one side of the conversation murmured through the door to the examination room. The telephone was put down and he could hear the doctor speaking to Clara.

The doctor came into the room. He put his stethoscope on the desk and sat down in the chair. "Clara is getting dressed," he said to Albert. "Let's wait until she can join us. You're just back from France?"

"I am."

"It's all completely unnecessary, isn't it?"

"Unnecessary?"

The doctor sat and studied Albert's uniform in the combined light from the desk lamp and the blue window light of morning: the rank insignia of silver stars and oak leaves, the tank badge and the Iron Crosses, the wound badge; the face above the collar, unshaven, gaunt, the skin drawn tight and windburnt.

"Yes," said the doctor. "Unnecessary. Even mad. Mad. I was a young surgeon in the first war. I know."

Albert moved his head in acknowledgement of that, but he said nothing.

They sat in silence and when the door opened they stood up as Clara sat down. She glanced at Albert. "Dr. Mannheim says I'm fine."

"Not quite," said the doctor, and he went on to explain that while Clara was organically strong and the bacterial counts were normal, her nervous system was nevertheless attacking her. He said the situation was similar to last time, a weakening of certain functions by anxiety. More research was necessary, but his recommendation was for her to rest as much as possible. Rest, he said; no excitement, good nutrition, and perhaps no sexual intercourse. Just to be on the safe side.

WHEN THEY ARRIVED back at the base, SS Obersturmführer Bönninghaus had already made a report to his superiors. He was recommending a court-martial for Albert. The charge was going absent without leave and abusing his rank to requisition military transportation for personal use.

At first it seemed a petty thing, no more. A complaint by a political officer of subordinate rank against a senior military officer. But the problem grew, perhaps because someone in Berlin saw it as an opportunity to damage Rommel. A complaint was launched, and Field Marshal Paul von Kleist told Rommel to fix the problem. Rommel ordered Albert to France by the next-available transportation.

Eight hours later Albert stood before Rommel's desk, and the general asked what this complaint was all about.

Albert explained and Rommel listened without interruption. They were standing in the salon of the small castle that served as Rommel's headquarters at Toulon. A harpsichord with its legs removed lay in one corner, and on the wall above it hung oil paintings of men in lace and powdered wigs.

Rommel said that at the very least Albert should have checked with his office. "To protect yourself and me," he said. "In Berlin the knives are out for all of us, so don't give openings to the SS."

Albert said there had been no time to check with anyone. He said this had been a personal emergency regarding her, and he had made a decision. He gave no apology but he said he regretted having caused problems for the general. He accepted full responsibility.

Rommel stared at him for a long time. For so long, Albert told her, he grew uneasy.

"So be it," Rommel said finally. "Go back to your base now and wait at your office there. You'll hear from me."

Halfway to the door Rommel stopped him. "Colonel," he said. "Off the record, you did the right thing. Assess, decide, and act. Never hesitate. Now go and accept the consequences."

Next day Albert was back at the base in Burgenland. He called her, and she was fine. He called his mother, and Cecilia told him that Sissy had given birth to a girl. He had a tiny niece now, she said. Caroline Gottschalk, seven pounds and a pair of strong lungs.

In the morning Rommel's chief of staff called to say the general had been able to convert the court-martial to seven days of brig, beginning immediately. Albert was to hand over pro-forma command to his major, and the major was to submit the proper documentation and to see that Albert was kept behind bars in the jail on the premises.

It was clear that Rommel must have called in some favours to convert a court-martial to only this. Albert sat behind the bars of the lockup in his own base, and Anna's home-cooking was brought to him, and blankets and a proper jug, towels, soap, and a washbasin. Out the window from up high he could see all the way to Hungary across the plain covered in snow that swirled and rose and fell and rose and danced in the constant wind.

She came to visit him every day, driven by Corporal Fuchs. She brought Willa, who played with her duck and with a puzzle of wooden blocks made also by the Polish prisoners. The cell door was open, and they played together, the three of them, on the wooden pallet with the blanket folded away.

Once, SS Obersturmführer Bönninghaus saw the car on the road and he flagged it, and he looked into the backseat through the window. He shook his head at her and walked around to the driver's side. He motioned Fuchs to lower the window, and when it was down he said, "Do you have authorized orders to do this, Corporal? Are you a taxi service for civilians now?"

Fuchs did not know what to say, and Bönninghaus leaned close and stared at him. "I'll be reporting this," he said. He straightened and stood back. He waved them on. She saw him from the rear window, his black outline on the white road with his fists on his hips, until the car turned a corner.

When the sentence was up, Albert returned home

feeling rested and relaxed. They had four more fine days together, then he had to return to France. The small complement of men left at the base included Corporal Fuchs, whose job it would be to look after the remaining vehicles.

She and Willa saw them off at the station, all these soldiers climbing aboard the train, Albert waving from the lowered window, blowing them kisses, leaning out so they could see him for as long as possible.

In France, General Rommel assigned him additional tanks, among them the new Type IV/G with improved armour and cannon. All ammunition was by then filled with the new type of propellant that drove the heavy 88mm projectiles at unprecedented speeds. As fast as rifle bullets, Albert had told her.

By January 27, 1941, the main body of the Afrika Korps was ready to go. It was a relatively small force consisting of the 5th Light Panzer Regiment and of various special units, including Albert's Landshut Black. They entrained, men and equipment, in long transports for the ride south, and at 2300 hours on February 12, on ships under full blackout, they left Sicily for North Africa.

TWENTY-SEVEN

❖

ROMMEL JOINED THE Afrika Korps two days later in his Fieseler Stork airplane, and that night he addressed his men. He stood on the closed turret hatch of one of the wide-tracked desert tanks and told them their job was to stop the British 8th Army from gaining any more ground in North Africa. He told them it would be hard work because the British were tough soldiers under good leadership, but that was the job.

As Rommel spoke there was no moon at all, but there was enough starlight, Albert said, so you could see him clearly up there in his baggy old leather coat, talking with his hands in his pockets. The desert sky was more sprayed with stars than any of the men had ever seen. A carpet of light, Albert said, some of the stars bright as searchlights. Albert's second-in-command, Major von Rhenold, had studied celestial navigation, and he told the men that some of the brightest stars did not even exist any more. That they had died years ago and now it was just their light like a memory that was still travelling for this generation and perhaps many more.

THE NEXT TIME the obersturmführer came to her house it was two o'clock in the morning. He pounded on the door and when she opened it sleepily, just a crack, he smiled at her with wide thin lips.

He said, "There is a serious charge against you." He shoved the door against her body and stepped inside. "Your husband, Colonel Leonhardt, is presently in North Africa, yes?"

"What?"

"I know he is." He studied her breasts and seven-month belly under the night gown. "Nice," he said. "To think it's all his."

She stood hugging her elbows, then she turned abruptly, went to the bedroom, and put on her robe.

"I'll report you," she said from there. "I don't think you're allowed to just walk in here."

"I'm allowed to do whatever I consider to be my duty," he said and followed her. "This is national security. The powers we have, you have no idea. I haven't called the SD, but when I do they'll just take you away and no one will ever find out what happened to you. Or the child," he said from the bedroom door. "I can guarantee that."

"Don't come in here!" She stared at him in his blacks

and silvers. At the silly little death's head on his cap. She hoped Willa would sleep through this in her own room down the hall.

"What sort of charge is there against me?"

"Are you fraternizing with the prisoners?"

"No, I'm not."

"The guards say you are. Are you giving them extra food? Treating injuries for them?"

"Is that fraternizing?"

"Yes. Are you?"

"I've given them fruit, yes. Is that bad? A plaster once in a while."

"Remember the first day, I told you not to."

"And some time after that, when two of them were sick, I was told to give them extra water and broth if I had any. I did, and I gave them fruit and they got better."

He stood in her bedroom door, solidly in his black boots, his thumbs in his gun belt, his eyes narrowed. She knew precisely what he was thinking, how close she was to disaster.

"You should go," she said softly. "I won't give them anything any more. I won't fraternize."

For a long moment her fate and the fate of all of them just hung there; it swayed and trembled; it was completely out of her hands and it might have tipped, but for some reason it did not.

"Show me the basement door," he said.

She held her robe closed as she squeezed past him. He

raised a finger and she felt the hard broad tip of it on her belly, then she was clear of him. She walked ahead into the kitchen and turned on the light.

"There," she said and pointed. The door was closed, the long black key stuck in the lock.

"It has to be locked at all times." He strode up to it, yanked down the handle, and pulled.

Behind him the door to the lean-to opened and Anna came out barefoot in a nightshirt nearly to the floor. She blinked in the light, looked at the man in black and from him at Clara.

He pointed at the open door. "Go back where you came from," he said. "Go and close that door."

When Anna did not move he took two quick steps and slapped her casually, left and right. "I said leave!"

Anna backed away and stood again. He lunged and pushed her away hard into her open doorway. "I said go, old woman." He slammed the door. To Clara he said, "I have made out a report, but I haven't sent it yet. It is up to you." He stepped closer. "Have you heard of the Cheka?"

"Lenin's secret police," she said.

"Yes. They're abolished now but they live on in Stalin's men. Much more ruthless than any of us. Some weeks ago a few of us went on a course in Russia, and they taught us things. About interrogation. Tricks with sharp knives. It was fascinating. They taught us how to stand at just the right distance with the nagaika and to snap the wrist near the end of the swing. Two lashes and bone is laid bare, Mrs. Leonhardt. Four lashes and flesh and skin will never heal. Never."

He reached out one hand to touch her face and she stepped back. They stood like this for a tense moment, then he lowered his hand. He turned and she heard his heels on the hallway floor. The door opened and remained open until she'd heard the car engine and found the courage to go there and close it.

She fought for inner calm for the sake of the baby. She washed her stomach where his finger had touched her, even if it had only been through layers of cloth. In the kitchen she pulled open the door to Anna's lean-to. Anna sat on the bed and she sat down next to Anna and neither of them spoke.

On the wall behind the headboard hung a small cross fashioned from sticks of birch, and a framed communion picture of Christ with a long blond beard, an aura of golden rays, and a red heart on fire in his open hands.

She thought of Professor Freud's X-factor in the human equation, psychological health or sickness, and who was to say which was which, by whose rule and by whose morality. Aristotle with his good for the many before the good for the few, or Nietzsche. Hard and factual. Godless, accountable to none but himself, but still fully accountable.

Over the next several weeks the obersturmführer came many more times, often late in the evening, and each time she felt more afraid. It was as if he were building momentum to do something, gathering his recklessness.

She wrote letters to Albert, not knowing that they never arrived because all mail was routed through the district office where it was steamed open, read, and censored, or more often simply discarded. Nor did eight of the nine letters that Albert wrote in those weeks arrive, in their case because of sinkings in the Mediterranean where the Royal Navy was more and more in control. The one letter she did receive had lines crossed out with heavy black ink, but she carried it with her everywhere and read it over and over again, like a child, savouring the comfort it brought.

Defiantly she kept giving apples to the prisoners, and some evenings she invited the professor up into the kitchen and she spoke English with him, discussed American and English writers at the table there; their boldness, the absence of fear or caution in their language. The clarity of their characters. Once in a while, and one by one, she allowed the men to come up the basement stairs and use the bathroom, use the soap and shower there.

Anna saw all this and shook her head in disapproval. But Anna cleaned, Anna found food where food was increasingly hard to find, Anna helped with Willa. Anna spoke Hungarian to Willa, and Willa for nearly three years heard German, English, and Hungarian.

Clara told the professor of her fears with the obersturm-führer, and he listened and thought about it, and then he told her not to lock the basement door.

"What if he checks?"

"We know he did the first few times. Has he checked lately?"

"No."

"So risk it," said the professor. "If you need help, scream."

She delayed going to bed so as not to be in her nightgown when his knock came. Even when she was fully dressed he stared at her stomach, and once when Willa came out of her room, barefoot and in her nightgown and rubbing her eyes, he stared at the child in a way that froze her blood. She stepped between him and Willa and without turning around she said, "Willa-dear, please go back to your room. I'll be there in a minute."

He leaned to see past her.

"Willa, now. Back to your room."

They heard the door click shut, and he said, "Maybe next time I'll bring some candy." He smiled and put on his cap and walked out.

That night she stood at the chest of drawers, and she opened the second one, reached under the stack of Albert's shirts and took out the pistol.

Sitting on the edge of her bed, she wept as she held the gun with two hands and studied it. She put it down, dried her eyes, and picked it up again. The safety catch. She could not remember what Albert had said: should the safety be up or down?

She pushed the gun under the pillow. Then she remembered. Of course: he had stored it with the safety on, and had told her simply to shift the lever and the gun would be ready. She took it out, slipped the lever up, and put the gun back under the pillow. She held up her hands in the fading light and willed them to stop shaking.

During the nights that followed she dreamt she found Freud in her house, in his spats and vested suits and gold fob, researching a book on Women Cloaked in Madness, he said. She dreamt that Dr. Mannheim was in her living room, holding forth on glandular activities and their effects as yet poorly understood. And she saw dear Anna standing at the stove, shaking her head, and stirring a large pot of chicken paprikash with the steam rising and condensing in her grey old hair.

And early one morning in a terror dream she glimpsed Albert's face under a helmet at the very moment something fast and hard struck him from behind. The helmet slipped and his head fell forward, out of the picture. Only a landscape of sand dunes remained, sand blowing off the crest like spume torn from ocean waves.

She woke and sat up. Her heart was pounding.

She rose, padded heavily into Willa's room, and bent over her bed. The girl was asleep on her side, her two little hands close to her face as if they were holding something. She turned and left, and had almost reached her own bedroom when there was the familiar pounding at the door.

MUCH LATER, when she had calmed and could see things clearly again, she would eventually understand that there had been all the signs and the veerings of paths to this hour. A bending of fatelines to this point by energy fields, of which perhaps one might be controlled, or two, but never all.

In some way her body understood this, or some snake-brain part of her did, and when she opened the door it was already nearly all decided, it was written if not done. But he pushed his way in, locked the door and turned, and this time there was something new in his face: violence, she felt, and the fixed stare of the goat in heat, the cloven-hoofed thing.

He snatched her wrist and pulled her toward her bed-room. He put his finger to his lips. "Not one sound," he hissed. "We don't want to wake the little girl, do we?"

With the door closed and by the light of the bedside lamp he said, "Take off your nightgown. Stand there and let it drop." He stood with his legs apart in black breeches and boots, the flap of the pistol holster unfastened with the holed strip of leather curling away.

"Now," he said, and he took off his cap. He let it sail playfully onto the bed and reached up to smooth his blond, thin hair.

"But . . ." she said. In supporting her belly her hand was tightening the material of the nightgown. Her belly was round and enormous.

"But nothing. Let's see."

"I'm eight and a half months pregnant." If there was another way out, she prayed it would show itself soon. She would remember this later; she actually prayed, reverted to her childhood and appealed to some well-meaning power to come to her aid.

He grinned. "I know. How exciting. Let's see."

"See what?"

"Don't talk. Take it off."

And something did come to help her then. Some strength or inspiration she would never know, but it showed her a way and it gave her courage.

"You just want to see," she said.

"Yes. Stop talking. Take it off."

"You won't hurt us?"

"*Us?* How quaint." He shook his head. "Don't be afraid. Take it off."

"So go sit on that chair," she said, and there it was, that help from somewhere. "Sit over there." She waved him away, moved past him to the lamp.

He squinted at her, suspicious for a moment. He opened the bedside table drawer, stirred the few contents with his hand, and closed it again. He backed away and sat on the chair.

"Go ahead," he said.

She slipped out of herself then, and from some safe distance could watch herself unbutton the gown at throat and breasts, taking it off like an open shirt, shoulders, arms, and lowering it to her waist now and slipping it down over this enormous belly to drop and pool on the floor.

He sat staring, with his face flushed, his mouth open. He licked his lips.

"Turn," he said.

And she turned like an artist's model in the yellow light, looked down, and saw the shifting shadows of her heavy breasts, her nipples large and dark, her stomach with the uneven bumps of the baby, perhaps an arm here, the bottom there. She moved her thighs and belly, the breasts sideways now, a monstrous shadow game, at the tips of her nipples the tiniest droplets catching the light. She watched his face, his greed. She felt advantage and became hopeful.

Until he moved abruptly, as though he were shaking something off, and he stood up and said, "Lie on that bed. On your back."

When she hesitated he gave her a shove that sent her backwards heavily onto the bed with her belly swaying. "Don't move," he said and raised his hand at her. He took off his tunic and unbuckled the gun belt. The trousers then, his fingers fumbling with the fly.

Coldly she shifted and moved over, inched her hand under the pillow. The moment his fingers forced their way between her legs and his staring face came down she brought out her hand, put the gun to the side of his head, and squeezed the trigger. It was not difficult at all. She felt a wild and reckless satisfaction.

In the noise and flash she saw his head jerk sideways while the other side exploded. He sagged on top of her and now she screamed and struggled out from under him.

She slapped at the blood and gore on her face and body.

She was holding her nightgown in front of her with one hand, the gun still in the other, when the prisoners came running. She dropped the gun on the bed, and the men spoke rapidly among themselves.

"Is this your pistol?" said the professor.

She nodded.

"Put something on," he said. "Just the nightgown, or a robe. Don't wipe his blood off."

Anna came and stared, and in her bedroom Willa was calling out. "Go look after Willa," she told Anna. "Keep her door closed."

The professor handed her pistol to one of the men. They found the empty shell and the man hurried away with both. The hole in the mortar on the stone wall was surrounded by specks of blood and pale matter, and they talked about it. One of the men ran down into the basement, and the professor tapped the floor in the corner by the armoire. The man came back up and nodded, and they shifted the heavy armoire aside. They took the obersturm-führer's gun from its holster and the professor stood close in the corner and covered his face with one hand while he fired the gun into the very corner of the wood floor there. He picked up the shell and wiped it, and they moved the armoire back where it had been. The professor calculated the way the shell might have been ejected and tossed it onto the bed.

He took the dead man's hand, pressed his gun into it, and folded the fingers firmly around the butt. The hand fell to the bedsheet and the fingers relaxed and let loosely go. The obersturmführer's pants were undone, his fly open. Pale flesh and hair showed there.

"He killed himself," the professor said urgently to her. "Look at me. Listen!" He shook her by the shoulders. "He killed himself. He was trying to rape you, and perhaps he became ashamed. Or something. You don't have to understand his reason. Do not wash your face or anything." He let her go. "All right? We're going back down. Talk to Anna and Willa. No one has seen us. We weren't here. Do you understand? Say yes."

She nodded. "Yes."

"When we are back downstairs, lock the basement door, and call the police. Your gun is buried in the cellar. No one will ever find it."

THE POLICE CAME, and because this was an SS officer they were afraid and called the district office. By then it was early morning. An SD major came, and Gestapo drove down from Vienna. They stood in her bedroom in their boots and bulky coats and looked at everything. They stepped here and there and examined the blood and the dead man. They whispered among themselves. A photographer took pictures of the scene, and the popping of his flashbulbs was loud in the room: the bed, the SS man's state of undress, the gun in his hand, the blood on her face and body as much as the nightgown allowed. No one closed the man's fly.

The SD major allowed her to bathe and get dressed, then he sat her down in the living room for a more detailed account. She tried not to stray from what she had said earlier.

He listened. He made notes. "I have your file here, Doctor Leonhardt," he said and held up a folder. "The Gold Party Pin, the Blood Order in your family. Your husband a decorated colonel at the front."

"Yes?" she said. "Please understand that I never applied for—"

He waited. He sat watching her. "Applied for what?"

"Never mind. Go ahead." She hid her face behind her hands for a moment. "This has been – you understand."

"Of course," he said. "And the Motherhood Cross for what you had to endure for your unborn child seems inadequate for this. I will put your name forward for the Civilian Medal of Honour."

And so it went. In time she would have to explain all this and it would be nearly impossible.

But eventually that day the house was hers again. Anna came with bucket and brush and scrubbed the bedroom. She filled the bullet hole with toothpaste, washed the blood off the wall, stripped the bed, and did the laundry. All the while Clara sat with Willa, and held her and talked to her.

Later that day Anna made the rounds among neighbours. She came back with a bulging bag and in the late afternoon she made a large pot of chicken paprikash.

It would always be one of Clara's favourite memories, how that night they fed the men in the cellar, using every cup and plate they had, and how she and Anna and Willa then sat on the lower steps of the basement stairs and watched them eat.

TWENTY·EIGHT

❖

TWO WEEKS LATER she gave birth to Emma, right there in her bedroom, with Anna more capable than anyone else she might have had by her side. Emma was fine and healthy, and soon she even slept through the night. Clara wrote regularly to Albert, even if she heard back only once more. The battles of Tobruk, Gazala, and Mersa Matruh were reported on the radio and in the newsreels, and on many Saturdays when the previous week's newsreel reached the cinemas she took Willa and later Emma too on the train to Vienna and they sat in the dark movie house, hoping to see news from Africa. Once for a few thrilling seconds they saw Albert on the screen in a *Welt im Bild* newsreel, walking with General Rommel around a destroyed tank all blackened with jagged metal sticking up.

One day in May 1941 the SD major arrived with a driver and a ceremonial clerk to present her with the Civilian

Medal of Honour. After he'd left she tossed it and its documentation into the same drawer as the Gold Party Pin.

She told the truth about the night of the obersturmführer to no one at the time. Once in a while she considered placing an addendum page into the journal of that day, beyond the factual notation of SS man †, and she still might. But probably not. It was part of what had made her. Her and no one else.

Two weeks after the killing she had the professor dig up the pistol and show her again how it worked and how to take it apart. She rinsed off the dirt in stove oil, wiped it well, and reassembled it. Because it had given her an entirely new sense of what she and the world were capable of, she treated it with respect and from then on carried it in her purse wherever she went.

The months following the birth of Emma brought a fine summer and fall, and the fields around the cottages were golden with wheat. Robins and soldierbirds fluttered and trilled, and sunflowers were the size of platters. Birds sat on fences and in berry shrubs; birds clung to sunflower faces, hacking at seeds. The apple and plum trees in the orchards bore more fruit than they had in years, people said. Fruit was rotting on the ground, and in backyard stills the local women made slivovitz and apple brandy and a brandy compote that supposedly did wonders for a man's desires, to put away for when their men came back. The compote was jarred piping hot and sealed with wax or cellophane and elastics, and with luck it would keep.

Not far away at the lake the new factory was being commissioned and some of the prisoners in the cellar were taken there to work. The factory made long cardboard tubes that came in three different thicknesses and lengths, and in three different colours. They were made from paper mash that was extruded in tube-shapes by enormous machines, then cut to length, dried, and shipped.

Her friends came often to see her. A weekend at Clara's was country bliss for them, and they went for walks and boatrides and they played with Willa and Emma on blankets in the backyard. They tucked flowers into their hatbands and collected small bird feathers they found on the ground. Come evening they'd look out for the prisoners.

The men would arrive at the end of daylight, and the women would watch behind curtains from the darkened room, watch the trucks and the guards, and when the outer cellar door was locked and the trucks were gone, the prisoners would put on the clean used clothes from Red Cross supplies Erika had brought, and on those nights a kind of salon took place in that dirt basement, with candlelight and sweet apple cider, and the professor would be the Mr. Speaker of conversation, and questions would be directed at him and he would translate them, as in polite society. The men explained to Mitzi what a village in Poland looked like. They spoke of their families.

One who had been a pastry chef at a hotel in Warsaw described in detail how to make a good chocolate layer cake and pavlovas, which had been his specialty. In over-large clothes he stood under the light bulb and made all the motions, and he spoke of the great care that had to be taken with batter and temperatures, and with the fillings. He described how to melt chocolate in a double boiler and then how to pour it criss-cross into the form, not too soon and not too late, when thickness and temperature were just right.

"You test it on the inside of your wrist," the professor translated. "The way mothers do with baby bottles."

The women and men sat on the basement stairs and on a few kitchen chairs brought down, and they sipped cider and nibbled on sun-dried apple slices, and they listened to the fine points of making chocolate cake.

On her second or third visit there Mitzi fell in love with one of them, a blond, pale young man who had been a journalist in Warsaw. He was the one who played the har-monica, and Mitzi would sit next to him in the dark cellar on those evenings, and once Clara saw them holding hands, like children sharing a secret.

Erika had her Ph.D. by then, and she was working for the Red Cross full-time. She told of reports from Poland, of camps there that were hopefully holding the people who had disappeared in night and fog so they could be released after the war. This was the official line, and it was still credible then. It was before the Wannsee Conference of July 1943, before Hitler's decree of the Final Solution.

DURING ONE VISIT Mitzi reported that there was no gasoline now to be found anywhere in Vienna, and the next day Clara bicycled with Mitzi on the luggage rack to speak to Corporal Fuchs at the base. They found him at work under a truck in the yard, and he would have seen the women's nice tanned legs there in the sunshine, the hems of their printed dresses and their feet in cork-sole strap sandals.

He dollied out from under the truck, wiped his hands on a rag and grinned at them, and listened. He said he might be able to spare a jerry can or two, but no more or he'd be in trouble. That week he drove into Vienna in the Mercedes to meet Mitzi where her car was stranded in the Red Cross garage. Fuchs filled her tank and then he put a board under the seat where the battery was, and he hoisted three canisters of gasoline onto her backseat, at twenty litres each.

"Panzer fuel," he said to her and grinned. "I hope it's not too high octane. A type four on the run would burn that much in a few minutes."

He said fuel ran into a revving panzer engine like from a hose tap wide open.

Next Sunday all the women came along to watch Mitzi cut the hair of every last soldier on the base. They lined up and laughed and joked with her and with the other women. It was like a party, with the man whose hair was being cut at the centre, sitting on a steel typing chair with a bedsheet over his shoulders, clearly loving Mitzi's hands on him and her nice woman's body nearby. She worked with comb and scissors, then used a razor on their necks, and in the end sprayed scented water from a blue flacon.

The three jerry cans of petrol and the full tank lasted Mitzi for nearly seven weeks. When it was all gone, she acted on a notion she'd had earlier. She spoke to one of her clients, a Mrs. Schmitt, the wife of an SS sturmbannführer attached to the Gestapo office, and boldly she proposed the kind of a contra deal that had worked so well for the plastic surgery on Erika's ear.

The deal would be for free gas for Mitzi in exchange for free hair, face, and nails for Mrs. Schmitt. The woman, who liked her hair and nails just so, spoke to her sturmbannführer husband, and from then on all Mitzi had to do was drive up at the pumps on Himmelpfortgasse and show the official piece of paper. The young men in their service blacks would salute and snap into action. They'd fill her tank and they'd polish and fuss and check her tires and once in a while change the oil and respectfully show her the mark on the dipstick.

ALBERT NEVER CAME HOME all that time. For the Afrika Korps supply had become the main problem, with their lines stretched so far, at some point nearly all the way to the Suez Canal. The newsreels said the British were making temporary gains; they mentioned the names of Generals Auchinleck, Montgomery, Ritchie, and Morshead. She received no mail from Albert, but she still wrote at least once a week. Because he had yet to meet Emma, she sent pictures Erika had taken with her Agfa-Click.

In the summer of 1942, when Emma was one year and two months old, the first bombs fell on war-effort sites and railroad points near Vienna. The Ostbahnhof was hit, and near Schwechat a munitions depot kept burning and exploding for a full day and night. Not far from the cottage and the base four bombs barely missed the new factory, causing enormous craters that filled quickly with water and attracted families of ducks. She drove there on the bicycle, with Emma on the handlebar seat and Willa on the luggage rack. They sat in the grass and watched the baby ducks paddling after their mother.

That August, her father died. She spoke to Anna, packed up the children, and left for St. Töllden.

There was a small graveside service. Her mother and she and the children stood under umbrellas in the rain, all in black on wooden boards around the wet hole in the ground and the earth piled in mounds at the feet of the angel. The ministrant held an umbrella over the priest, who stood with black robes trailing. He waved the censor and made crosses with his hand and he said, "*Memento homo, quia pulvis es, et in pulverem reverteris.*"

The memorial service took place not at the Benedictine chapel but at the main church because there were so many mourners. The family sat in the first pew, and her mother never moved, never even stood up or knelt at the liturgical points, only laid one bare hand on the bible rail and crossed herself with the other.

Peter was not there. From Norway he had been ordered to Holland, and from there someplace east. He had been home only once, for a one-week leave. According to Daniela they'd spent it all in the kitchen and bedroom.

That night her mother asked if she could possibly move back to St. Töllden. Clara sat on the chair in her parents' bedroom, in an emptiness so enormous it expanded the room and made them lower their voices.

"Move back here," she said. "I don't know. It depends on Albert's situation, I guess. It's his base there. Mama, I couldn't just . . . I can ask him when he comes home on leave. How much longer can it be?"

Her mother who had lived through one world war already said nothing to that.

He returned some three months later, a full colonel now, and with the Knight's Cross under his collar. He had been brought back by High Command along with General Rommel and other senior officers, after the second battle of El Alamein, where after many successes the tide had turned. It was now apparent that the war in the desert could no longer be won, not with the lack of petrol and ammunition and basic supplies that Hitler was refusing to address.

Once after a morning conference Rommel had told Albert that Hitler had lost interest in rescuing Mussolini's disappointing armies again and again. He'd lost interest in North Africa and was expecting the final collapse there any month now. Until then, they should do what they could to slow the Allied advance, Hitler had said. If they ran out of artillery shells, they were to use rifles and bayonets.

Through Rommel, Albert requested permission to bring his 14th Armoured Battalion home to be used elsewhere; to rescue it, essentially, rather than see it wasted, but Hitler refused. Rommel told Albert that he was no exception. Hitler was refusing all such requests for strategic relocation, not even to save an entire division from being destroyed. It was difficult, Rommel said, to listen to the man's rants on the telephone about not yielding an inch of soil and defending to the last drop of blood.

One month later, Hitler had ordered Rommel and Albert and other senior officers to hand over to their seconds in command and to return to Berlin. And not long thereafter, the Afrika Korps, outgunned and outsupplied by the Allied Forces there under General Dwight Eisenhower now, was history. More than half the men were dead, the rest were behind barbwire in the desert.

BACK IN EUROPE Albert was given command of an Alpine battalion of special units and ordered to Yugoslavia. He was home just long enough to enjoy four days' leave and then to hand over the base to an artillery unit.

Those days and nights again she never once left his side. It was November 1942, a cold November with early frost and snow that then melted and froze again so that roads and fields became sheets of ice. Again there was so much to tell that for the first few hours they could hardly speak a word. Emma was a year and a half old, and it was the first time that he saw her. The second night, when the children were asleep and the house was quiet, she whispered the truth to him about the SS man, Bönninghaus. He was stunned. He sat up in bed. He asked questions, and he whispered that he was proud of her. She described what had happened afterwards, the professor and the pastry chef and the journalist and all the others who had come to her help, and then the SD major and the medal.

The next evening, after the guards had left, he put on his full uniform, cap, and boots but not the pistolbelt, and she and the children went down ahead of him into the basement. She was carrying a candle because one of the two light bulbs was burnt out and she'd not been able to find a replacement.

When they saw him coming down behind her, first his boots then the uniform, the prisoners sat up in their strawbeds and stared. She told them that this was her husband back from Africa, and she indicated the professor and mentioned his name, and then one by one she indicated the other men, their white astonished faces in the gloom, and she mentioned their names. Albert took off his cap and clamped it under his left arm and he walked up to every man and shook his hand and thanked him.

Two days later he left. She and the girls saw him off at the train station. They embraced and kissed, and he knelt and kissed the girls. In the cold, the steam from the loco-motive was low on the ground and white, and there were harsh metallic noises coming from the next track. The girls must have picked up her mood because they were crying.

THE NEW BASE COMMANDER and his family would be taking over the cottage, and so she had to leave; Anna had the option to stay or to move with her and the children to St. Töllden.

Anna sat in the lean-to and thought about it. Walking past the half-open door, Clara saw her sitting on the bed, round and sad and looking down into her lap.

Half an hour later she came out and touched Clara's sleeve. "I'll go with you, Frau Doktor," she said. "I want to help with the children."

And so she and Anna packed up their belongings and they took a box of candles and some matches and some apples down to the Polish prisoners to say farewell, and for the boy who had carved the duck and the puzzle she brought the sharp paring knife wrapped in a strip of cloth.

On the morning of December 15, 1942, they climbed into the grey Mercedes car still with Corporal Fuchs at the wheel. Fuchs touched the horn and the truck carrying their belongings pulled away. They followed. Neighbour women stood outside their cottage doors and waved. Anna wept driving past them, but she tried not to show it. She sat in the front seat in her best clothes, with her grey hair in a tidy bun that day. Clara sat in the back with the girls nestling against her under blankets because the car's heater was broken.

There was a light snow falling and the fields were white and black. The mountains when they reached them later that day stood nearly blue with ice, with frozen runoff like sculptures showing between trees and rock, hanging from granite lips in enormous creations.

TWENTY-NINE

IT WAS REMARKABLE, the speed with which Mitzi was recovering. Some days she had pain in that hip and at the back of her thigh, but Dr. Gottschalk said it was natural that some tissue would have been offended during the procedure. The pain would disappear in time.

Three weeks after the operation she was able to walk with only one cane, and on that Sunday Clara took time away from the manuscript and she and Mitzi rode the cable car to the restaurant at the top of the mountain. They had coffee and pastry, and they sat and looked out the picture windows at the valley below with the afternoon sun low and orange skimming the faces of mountains as far as they could see.

From a cliff to the left of the restaurant, hang gliders were jumping off, young men and women laughing and kidding each other, dressed in ski clothing and helmets and goggles and gloves. They clung to the frames of their brightly coloured wings and took running starts at the cliff, and they leapt and sailed away in slow spirals and long ellipses descending to the valley floor a thousand metres below. On the sunside slopes some of them caught the updrafts and climbed to begin all over again.

"Look at those two," said Mitzi. She pointed at a couple in bright clothing kissing and touching barehanded before they put on gloves to leap off the mountain.

"Were you ever in love?" said Clara abruptly. "Forgive me. I'm not sure what I'm asking."

Mitzi turned and studied her. "What a question. What brought that on?"

"I find myself thinking back a fair bit these days. Don't you?"

"I try not to. You know I was in love. That blond little Pole. Don't you remember?"

"I do. What I meant to ask was, *how much* in love? What kind of love."

"Enough and in different ways. A few men. Cecilia, what a fine woman. Erika. Your brother Peter, that noble man. Danni. You. Does that count? Albert, of course."

"It all counts," she said.

She was remembering that when she was young and had little past, she could not wait to leap forward into the future, leap off just like these young people with the full confidence she would be able to control and shape her life; now when she looked into the mirror and accepted what

she saw, she knew that her past was all she had. And how
was it? How did it feel?

She knew of old people who were terribly plagued by
their past, by what they had done to others, or not done
for them. Mistakes made, wrong turns, and no way back.
Old people in homes, their lips moving all the time,
explaining, justifying, remaking conversations and actions.
Looking back all day long through the merciless and
warped telescope of hindsight.

She thought about this all the way down the mountain,
and later that day she finally understood in her heart the
genesis of a core Christian idea. A myth like most, but
what a useful one.

And something relating precisely to that, something
from literature, cutting right to the heart of it.

Late that night, she calculated the time difference and at
one o'clock in the morning she called Willa on her camel
farm in Australia and gave her the gist of it. Willa, an
English major before starting all over again to become a vet,
Willa knew it.

"William Butler Yeats," she said. "Look it up. It's got
to be in his *Purgatory*."

She looked it up that very night, and there it was.
Nailed down, perfect:

They know at last the consequence of their transgressions,
either upon others or upon themselves.
If upon others, then others may bring help,

if upon themselves, there is no help but in themselves
and in the mercy of God.

SHE GOT SOME SLEEP that night, not much. She kept thinking that as a child she'd been simply able to confess sins; speak them into that patient ear behind the grille. Then go to the altar, rattle off her penance, and walk away, go skipping home, feeling free and relieved. What magic. What simple pleasure, that lightness.

But there was also something else, something quite to the contrary. It would come to her; not now perhaps. It was some mature thing, bone-hard and far beyond the simple lightness of a myth.

Next day the van came from the provincial archives, and a young man in jeans and a T-shirt and windbreaker carried down the file boxes.

"Just those six," she told him. "Not the ones with the red labels. They should go down to the basement, if you wouldn't mind. I'd be grateful. Just set them down by the door and I'll put them away later." She slipped him a ten-euro bill.

He looked at it and nodded. "Mr. Hofer said he'd call you later today or tomorrow morning to discuss things."

"Fine," she said.

By noon she was back at the computer, at the manuscript. Just another hundred pages to go. Then the revisions, the word-for-word checking. Some rewriting, and finally sending it off to Frankfurt.

THIRTY

❖

OVER CHRISTMAS OF 1942 she and her mother would leave the children with Anna while they went to see the newsreels at the small movie house at the back of the post office in St. Töllden. She never caught another glimpse of Albert and she had no idea where he was now, but on the screen it was always good news on all fronts. Their soldiers were gaining ground everywhere and liberated people were welcoming them and tossing flowers at their tanks. The war would be won any day now, the announcers said.

"I know a man that's hiding on a farm," whispered Mrs. Dorfer, the milkwoman. "He walked away from the eastern front, imagine, all that way and he says the war in Russia is going very badly. He says the entire sixth army is surrounded. No medical supplies and no food. They don't even have fuel for their tanks, he says."

The radio reported that a student organization called White Rose had been secretly distributing anti-government leaflets. A brother-and-sister team had been behind this act of treason. The Gestapo had found them all and executed them. Nearly a hundred students in their early twenties, said the radio.

In June 1943, she recorded in her notes that banks had to report all private money, and unless one was well connected to the party, all money was confiscated in exchange for War Bonds. Food was scarce, even with stamps, and all manufactured goods were of ersatz quality. Bread came blended with sawdust, coffee was made from dried figs and acorns, clothing was of the poorest cotton mixed with wood fibres, buttons were of pressed cardboard. Glass, steel, wood, and metal were unavailable.

In St. Töllden two men came to the house, showed official papers, and said that everyone had to hand over whatever gold they owned for the war effort.

"Your wedding bands," they said. In exchange they gave them small iron rings with an inscription that said, *I gave gold for iron.*

Two days a week she toured on her bicycle from farm to farm to trade cigarette stamps for goat milk and goat cheese and for the rare piece of meat, mostly rabbit.

In Italy, in June, Mussolini was deposed by the Fascist Grand Council. He was arrested and taken as a prisoner to the Gran Sasso Hotel in the Abruzzi Mountains.

"The Italians at least have the sense to get rid of these

people," said her mother. "Why can't we do the same?"

But no sooner was Mussolini locked up than he was rescued by German paratroopers and taken to northern Italy to live in hiding.

The Allies landed in Italy in September, and Italy capitulated. The radio said that unemployed Italian soldiers had formed gangs of partisans and were fighting their former allies from the rear. Those same partisans later found and arrested Mussolini near his hiding place at Lake Como. They killed him along with his mistress, and they hung them from their heels like game in a market square in Milan. The public spat at the corpses and threw rocks at them.

The Americans built bomber bases in Italy, and from March 1944 on the raids came regularly. Oil refineries were hit, and railroad points, and factories of any kind.

For the St. Töllden file she noted that in the beginning it seemed that homes were not being bombed on purpose, only by mistake. But six months later smaller urban centres too were set afire in planned raids, day and night.

On March 23, 1944, the cardboard tube factory in Burgenland was hit. Also hit in that same daylight raid were Albert's former base, and three of the cottages in the village, including the one she and her family had lived in. The munitions depot and buried gasoline tanks exploded and not much was left of any part of the compound. The cardboard tube factory, it turned out, had been making rocket parts, and it burned to the ground. The Polish prisoners there all died; the ones working in the fields, including the professor and the thin blond one who had played the harmonica, survived and were taken that night to another basement in the area.

IN JULY 1944, the generals' plot against Hitler became the sixth known attempt on his life. People learned the name of Colonel Stauffenberg along an underground chain of rumours and whispers.

"A hero," Mrs. Dorfer said, leaning on her bicycle. "Finally. Thank God." She put her finger across her lips. "What a brave man. And did you hear? Blind in one eye and one arm gone."

But the thing had failed, and in its wake perhaps a thousand army officers and their families were killed by the SS.

"Shot, hanged, stabbed, garrotted, their heads hacked off," the announcer said firmly on the radio, and she wrote it down word for word, for what it said about the spirit of that time.

When in later years the assignments from Dr. Hufnagel in Geneva gave her access to Nuremberg files, she spent weeks at the warehouse where the files were stored. She sat at one of the small desks in the research room and went through box after box of records and sworn depositions that gave a clear picture of the event.

Stauffenberg had placed his explosive briefcase under the conference table at Rastenburg and had left the room. Someone kicked the briefcase over, and the bomb went off but the heavy table acted as a shield and Hitler suffered barely a scratch.

Many officers had been involved in the planning of the plot and of the subsequent surrender to the Allies and the running of the country. The more famous ones were Generals Speidel, Fromm, Olbrecht, von Witzleben, von Böck, Höpner, and a dozen more. Even Field Marshal Rommel was accused of having known of it. General Fromm, who was the one coward and the weak link, switched sides when the bomb did not kill Hitler. He betrayed the plotters to the SS.

All the generals involved were killed, as were many of their subordinate officers, and in many cases their wives and children and parents also. Stauffenberg on Fromm's orders was shot dead in the ministry yard. In his punishment of the men whose acceptance he had always craved but never received, Hitler ordered some generals to be beheaded. He brought back the broadaxe for that purpose, and the hooded axeman dressed in black.

"A block of wood from some mythical five-hundred-year oak," said the sworn deposition. "In a basement room, with tiered benches for those who were ordered to watch."

Rommel, because of his fame and popularity, was promised that his family would not be touched, and he was given the choice between a pistol and poison. He swallowed cyanide, did so in the passenger seat of the staff car, not far from his house.

Other officers chose the handgun, the standard Walther P38 9mm parabellum. A pistol like Albert's. They filled their mouths with water and stuck the barrel in there, and the bullet and gas expansion combined with the hydro-static pressure left almost nothing of their heads for Hitler's deputies to ridicule.

And Albert, because he had been one of Field Marshal Rommel's favourite officers, was sent from Yugoslavia straight to the Russian front, where the average survival rate for newly arrived officers was one day and a half.

Such was the year of 1944. By then SS Obergruppen-führer Reinhard Heydrich was also dead. He had been the mastermind of the Final Solution, of the death camps in the East, and of the SS Einsatzgruppen that had murdered Jews in the occupied territories by the hundreds of thousands. In 1942 he had been killed by a team of partisans, and in revenge for his killing the SS had destroyed the Czech village of Lidice and murdered most of its population.

She never knew that Albert had been sent to Russia. She had no idea where he was, and never heard from him after they left the base in Burgenland. She wrote to the last field post number she had for him, poured out her heart and sent the letters off like messages in a bottle.

Writing was still saving her. Even just getting ready to set pen to paper forced her to think clearly. The discipline of following one thought in linear ways past all distractions to its conclusion. The absolutely all-important attitude of As-if.

But what she thought late one evening in November that year had nothing to do with Heidegger, Nietzsche, Kant, or Husserl. Nothing to do with any of the poets and writers she had studied and learned so much from, these kings and queens of words and ideas and emotions. It did not even have anything to do with her own notion of philosophy as a mental structure and house to live in.

What she thought had to do with the churchbells. She realized that all this time they had been faithfully tolling the hour, tolling Vesper, tolling Sanctus, tolling the hours of the healing of souls. And it struck her that somehow from the thousand-year stretch and more when Christian religion had been at the centre of lives in the western world, had been the source of most art and music and morality in western civilization, it had come to this.

She thought this, sitting in the children's bedroom, the two of them asleep with the blackout blinds pulled all the way down and pinned to frames and crossbars, and not so very far away the sky was filled with the drone of squadrons of B-17 bombers flying toward the cities in the valley.

It was too far away to hear the air raid alarms, but before long she could hear the bombs, could feel them more than hear them by the rumbling and trembling of floor and windows.

THIRTY·ONE

⬥

LUNCH WAS DELIVERED by a caterer whom she paid on a regular basis, and every day she put the white cloth on the kitchen table, and linen napkins. Mitzi spooned the food from the plastic containers onto plates and rinsed the containers and stacked them for the driver to collect the next time.

They ate and made plans for the afternoon.

A moth fluttered by and they watched it. It rose up to the pantry and sat on the patterned metal screen. It folded its wings and crawled inside.

From old habit, perhaps as insurance against those times returning, she kept staples up there; items like flour and rice and beans and sugar in small paper sacks, and dried lentils and peas and breadcrumbs and rolled oats and coffee still in her mother's little metal tins shaped like mosques. What treasure those things would have been then, along with jars with lids, and plastic bags. Or aluminium foil; unthinkable. For years when it first came out she would iron aluminium foil smooth and refold it to be used again; she would wash out and reuse plastic bags over and over. Hang them upside down on the line to dry.

Another moth, or perhaps the same one, crawled out, fluttered around the room as if for exercise, and then went back inside, through the stencilled holes shaped like tiny flowers.

Mitzi said, "Somebody will have to clean all those cupboards out someday. Should we do it?"

She said nothing to that.

MITZI HAD COME TO ST. TÖLLDEN in the spring of 1944, after she and the other women were bombed out in Vienna. By then bombing runs on civilian targets were flown in three waves: the first with high explosive bombs to blow up buildings and expose their interiors, the second wave with phosphorous bombs to set fire to structural wood and furniture, and the third with anti-personnel bombs to kill firefighters and people who'd left the shelters too soon.

One night after one of those attacks on Vienna, the women made their way back from the shelter through dust- and smoke-filled streets to the apartment. When they turned the corner, they saw that much of their building was gone. Floors hanging, rooms with furnishings still on fire. Walls still collapsing in clouds of dust and ashes.

They spent that night in the archway that had been the entrance to their building. The women and four-year-old Caroline huddled under Cecilia's coat and a Red Cross blanket of Erika's, and all night long they heard rats. Once, Sissy felt one walking on her leg, and she leapt up and screamed and snatched Caroline up off the ground. They caught glimpses of looters poking through ruins, filling jute sacks with whatever might be worth money on the black market.

In the morning they made their way up to the apartment. It was mostly burnt out, with entire walls and some floors gone. The dining room had more or less survived, but looters had taken paintings and the silver and whatever else they'd been able to carry. The four-day Silverbell Napoleon clock was still there, and the upright piano in the small salon. The grand piano had burned and fallen partly through the floor.

By noon that day Erika had been able to find temporary shelter for them at the Red Cross, and by midafternoon Cecilia and Sissy had located a man with a horse and farmwagon. Somehow with the help of his son they had hoisted the upright piano and the wallclock onto the boards. Sissy said that when they rumbled away, her mother sat defiantly upright on that piano stool in her battered and balding Persian lamb coat and cap and heels, her feet tucked away and crossed at the ankles, while around them there was nothing but smoke and ruins.

Two blocks away people were hauling sodden bodies from a shelter that had been hit, and where, when firemen had put out the flames, those who had not died from the concussion or from the smoke had drowned.

Erika remained in Vienna, living in one of a few hundred cubicles behind blankets on ropes in the main system of barracks. Great red crosses on white ground had been painted on roofs and walls. Mitzi's car had by some miracle survived at the Red Cross garage, and she just left it there for Erika to use if she needed to. The tank was nearly full but most streets had become impassable.

A week later, Mitzi, Cecilia, and Sissy and Caroline arrived at St. Töllden. There was enough room if some of them doubled up, and it was still safe. The hydro-electric station and the salt processing plant in the valley had been bombed, but St. Töllden itself had so far not been targeted.

A household of all women now, like most. It was tense at first, especially because the differences between her mother and Cecilia had never been resolved. She sat with them in the kitchen and made them talk about it, would not let up until they did. Mothers with a dead son each, both lost to the same empty cause. What now? As soon as their shoulders softened and the first few words about loss had been spoken, she left the room. Eventually she could see their heads in outline in the etched glass in the kitchen door moving closer together.

They lined up for ration stamps and bartered with

shopkeepers and farmers. She hunted for food on her bicycle, and Mitzi cut hair in exchange for one potato or half a cabbage or ten coffee beans. Sissy sewed and altered clothes, and Cecilia still had a deerskin pouch of 18 carat gold jewellery. In it were necklaces, French brooches, and three diamond rings that she had not given for iron. It was illegal, but nearly everything required for survival was.

With the frequency of firebombings in the larger cities, the radio gave cheerful advice. "In case of phosphorus bombs," the *German Mother's Listening Hour* said, "quickly pull down all curtains and throw bedding and cushions out the window. Put the children in a bathtub filled with water up to their necks and push them under when needed."

The first air raid alarm in St. Töllden was heard on September 15, 1944. The siren was mounted on the roof of the town hall. It looked like a great tin mushroom, and since its installation it had been tested every Saturday precisely at noon. It made an unnerving rising and falling wail, but after a while people got used to it. It made them feel safe, and soon when they heard it they'd look at their watches, pull out the crowns, and set them.

Since there was no air raid shelter in town, bills had been posted telling people to use the area known as the Christian Caves in case of an alarm. They were the very caves her father had restored and opened up as part of the museum with wooden stairs and platforms.

It was a good twenty minutes from the house, but at the first alarm they all hurried there: her mother, Cecilia,

Anna, Mitzi, Sissy and Caroline, and she with Emma and Willa. Many of the people in St. Töllden were gathered there that night, like at some pilgrims' place of miracles. The caves were not nearly large enough to hold the entire town, but they held several hundred. The rest huddled against the mountain, behind boulders and slabs of fallen rock.

In the dark sky they could see nothing since the bombers were blacked out. A few searchlights stabbed up from some distant place that had air defences, but not here. They craned their necks, and people in the caves crowded the stone entrances while those in the back sat covering their ears.

Those in front and down by the rocks could not see the airplanes, but they could hear them, a drone like a thousand bees and the very air vibrating with engine noise. They could not see the bombs falling, but they saw them exploding, enormous firecrackers in their old town, outlines of buildings momentarily black against the flashes, the church steeple black against an explosion, then darkness again. They stood and stared, and when the airplanes were gone some people left to run home, but a warden in a tin hat shouted at them to wait for the next wave.

It came within minutes, and this time they saw the containers exploding in midair to scatter their chips of phosphorus, and as soon as these were touched by air they began to burn bright blue and white, and so they rained down on St. Töllden, mid-air explosions scattering tongues of fire that fell on roofs and trees and everywhere, like piñatas scattering gifts for children.

There was no third wave that night, and the house when they reached it was fine. That fall and winter saw several more attacks, and eventually many of the older women simply took cover in their basements. Anna, Cecilia, and her mother did that, and neighbours came to join them since the house had a good vaulted basement. They sat on the stone floor there by candlelight and listened to the explosions.

One old man, a World War One artillery major with a medal on his chest and one trouserleg pinned up, for that leg was missing, told them that you never hear the bomb that gets you, since it comes straight for you with no sound at all.

"Bombs," he said, and he reached out to touch Cecilia's coat sleeve in the candlelight. "Listen," he said. "You'll find this interesting."

Those were two-hundred-kilo bombs with delayed fuses, he told them, and delayed fuses were invented for just this purpose, to allow bombs to penetrate the house from top to bottom, right down to where they were hiding now, before the thing detonated. And bombs, he said, did not come down straight but fell in a lessening arc as gravity slowed their horizontal speed from the moment of release. He leaned to the candle and showed them with his hand pretending it was a bomb. And he told the women whether they wanted to hear this or not, that bomb fragments at the outset travelled nearly at the speed of gas expansion, some eight thousand feet and more per second.

"That fast," he said and nodded.

And one night in January 1945, one such bomb smashed through the top of the house and exploded at the rear. It killed her mother and Cecilia with flying bricks and bomb fragments the size of axe heads, and it killed three more old women and the invalid man. That day there were no fire bombs, and no third wave.

THERE WERE PICTURES of the bomb damage in the St. Töllden files, and pictures of women all over town dressed like men in boots and baggy men's pants cinched tight with ropes. They were called the rubble women, and while Anna looked after the children, Mitzi, Sissy, and Clara joined their brigades, cleaned bricks, and stacked them for reuse.

With a crosscut saw they'd found in some ruin they cut down two of the pine trees in the garden and they stripped them and used the trunks to shore up the housewall; they even made a sill beam from a heavy piece of lumber to go between the bricks and the shores. Over time they were able to scavenge enough boards and other materials to patch the worst of the other damage, but all that winter and spring the women and children lived like ghosts in the damaged house, grey, empty-eyed people with dust on their faces and broken fingernails tapping on the table.

They fetched water in buckets from the river, and they took whatever food they found in other ruins, and they traded the last of Cecilia's brooches for a scrawny goat that they kept in the basement. Anna took charge of the goat, and several times a day she led it outside so it could scratch for grass and twigs from the hazelnut bush. The milk from that goat was drunk mostly by the children.

And still writing like a gift was saving her. She would sit daily at the kitchen table and write in her journals and on loose pages for her folders of notes to herself and to Willa and Emma, describing the essence of these days. She could feel herself slowing down then, could observe herself taking control, sorting ideas and problems, putting them in perspective. A fine clarity came to her in those moments, and an ability to step back and see things in a light she could understand and accept.

Without much hope that the letters would reach them, she wrote to Albert and to Erika in Vienna.

Once, she received a letter from Erika describing her own life. She said that David Koren was well and still living in Sweden. He was writing for an English paper, and she was in touch with him through the Red Cross courier. When the war was over, he would come to Vienna, and they'd be together again. Erika wrote she was still using Mitzi's little car and some of the wider streets were passable again.

They had painted red crosses on it, on roof and doors, and for gasoline she was able to access the Red Cross emergency depot that was guarded day and night.

And she was seeing Daniela quite regularly, Erika wrote. Peter had been home on a short leave from somewhere. He was at the eastern front now, Daniela had no idea where. Not in Russia, they hoped.

THIRTY-TWO

❖

LATE IN MARCH as the snow was melting even on the shade side of the garden wall, and as white and sky-blue crocuses were coming out and the first green pokes of gladioli, Mitzi had another appointment with Dr. Gottschalk. In the early afternoon on that day she and Clara sat in the waiting room, and through the connecting door they could hear the doctor talking to someone in her office.

"No," they heard her say. "I want you to take two of these in the morning . . ." and she lowered her voice. It was like listening to Cecilia taking charge and making things very clear so that there could be no misunderstanding.

"Sissy never spoke like that to people," Mitzi said to her. "Did she?"

"Maybe she did as she got older. Maybe it skipped a generation."

When it was Mitzi's turn, Dr. Gottschalk said to Clara, "You could wait out here," but Mitzi said she wanted her to come along.

In the inner office she sat and heard Dr. Gottschalk's instructions to Mitzi behind the examination screen. "Take off your skirt, and lie down on your front," she said. "Where is the pain?"

"That whole right side sometimes," said Mitzi. "Yes, down along there."

Silence, then. Rustling noises.

"And this?"

"That's fine."

"All right. You can get dressed now."

Then Dr. Gottschalk stood next to her. "And you? You look pale. Is everything all right?"

"I'm fine. Maybe the long winter."

"Maybe. Come and see me sometime. Or are you seeing Dr. Kessler?"

"I'm not seeing anyone as long as I can help it."

Dr. Gottschalk took her wrist, found the pulse, and looked at her watch.

"How are your parents, Caroline? Where are they now?"

The doctor shook her head and kept counting. "In Florida," she said then. "You knew that? Sold the house in Nova Scotia and retired down there."

She shook her head. "I didn't know that. I haven't heard from Sissy in years."

"We talk on the phone," said Dr. Gottschalk and offered nothing further.

Mitzi joined them. Dr. Gottschalk reassured her and spoke of exercise and a low-salt and low-sugar diet. She wrote a prescription.

Out in the street, Mitzi said, "I'm sure she's a good doctor."

"What else did she tell you?"

"You heard her. Nothing too useful. To keep moving."

"But the pain?"

"It's not there all the time."

"We could get a second opinion from Dr. Kessler."

Mitzi shook her head. They walked home, and in the mid-afternoon they sat in deckchairs with their faces turned up like wrinkled heliotropes. They sat in their coats and gloves and hats feeling warm and peaceful.

"Like at a ski chalet," said Mitzi with her eyes closed. "All we need is the smell of that lotion, what was it called?"

"A coconut smell," she said.

"Coconut, yes."

THE NEXT DAY WAS SATURDAY, and as usual they walked to the Golden Goose for lunch. They sat at a table for two by the leaded window where the light came in golden and bright on china and cutlery, and they enjoyed their meal.

On the way home Mitzi stumbled and her knees gave way crossing the street. She knelt and reached up for

Clara's hand but then fell forward onto the asphalt and slumped on her side. Cars stopped and people rushed to help. Someone with a cellphone called an ambulance.

At the clinic she sat waiting in one of the chairs by the milk-glass door, and eventually Dr. Gottschalk came and sat down by her side.

"A heart attack, I think," she said gently. "Maybe a thrombosis. We can do a postmortem and find out, if you want to."

"Don't. Could it have been caused by the operation? Maybe a blood clot breaking free?"

"It's not impossible. Even though I'd put her on blood thinners. We'll never know. I'm calling it a heart attack." They sat in silence with the door puffing open and closed and people in white walking past and looking at them and then quickly away.

"Sorry," said Dr. Gottschalk after a while. "I loved her too."

For the memorial service the Benedictine chapel was full, pews and standing room, even along the walls with the stations of the cross. The air was dense with cold and incense, and out the ancient sandglass windows you could see the mountains still covered in snow, and the blue river-run where the glaciers were melting in the warm days and freezing again stone-hard at night.

The coffin sat sideways in the small apse before the altar, and candles burned in great candelabra of brass and silver. Her white roses lay on the black wood.

When they had sung the hymn, Father Hofstätter took the censer from the ministrant and he swung it in cruciform above the coffin. He said what she had asked him to say, which were the Latin words her mother had chosen for her father, about human beings and ashes: "*Memento homo, quia pulvis es, et in pulverem reverteris.*"

The ministrant was the very girl who not so long ago had taken them up the stairs into the bell tower. She stood clear-eyed and young with her hands folded in front of the red surplice over jeans and running shoes, and she found Clara in the first pew and smiled at her. It was only then that she began to weep.

SHE CALLED EMMA and spoke with her, and she called Willa on Skype. She used many tissues, which she balled up and stashed in the plastic shopping bag hung from the pull in the desk drawer.

"If you were to get a call," she said to Willa. "Say you had to come quickly, how long would it take?"

"Mom. What are you saying?"

"How long, dear?"

"A few days, I'd say. Four or five at the most. Why? Do you want me to come now? Are you all right?"

"I'll be fine. Don't worry. There was something else. The lawyer, you know him, Doctor Haas, he has all my stuff. The will, the insurance."

"Mom. What are you talking about? What is this?"

"Just let me. Oh yes. Maybe, when you have a moment

. . . A quote, I do think it's a man speaking, and he says something about enduring rather than curing."

"Enduring rather than curing. The rhyme is yours?"

"Probably. It may not be those words, just the sentiment."

"The sentiment. Where do you think I would even begin with something this vague?"

"You're good at it," she said. "You'll find it."

She told Willa she loved her, always had, and Willa in faraway Australia over airwaves and satellites impossible to see said that she loved her too.

FOR DAYS AFTER MITZI'S FUNERAL she was puzzled by the degree of comfort the ceremony had given her. After all these years. The very puzzlement opened up a new field of research and study for her. She could begin all over again with Rilke's famous and towering line of *dennoch preisen*. These poor two words, no more than a fragment of an idea, and yet enormous in what they opened up, especially when read in the context of the reminder to be just that preceded them. They had been studied and interpreted by countless scholars and translators, but to her mind none had gotten them right. The word *dennoch* was part of a transitive phrase, and like the English word *regardless* it needed something more. It needed both a target and the bow that had launched it. To praise *what*, regardless of *what*, was the great question here.

She had been there before, at university as a student, and later as a professor of literature, but now she went deeper.

Probably the thing needed not understanding but feeling, not a frontal but a sideways approach. As she had once told her students, the work itself was the answer. "*And yet*," she'd said to them. "Let's say to praise life regardless of . . . Begin with that notion and then go deeper." *Dennoch preisen*, she'd said, was a cut diamond that sparkled differently depending on the light you shone on it.

One night in bed she remembered primary school, the catechism class when Protestants and Jews had to sit out the hour in the hallway, banished there to wait until the rest would include them again. She saw little girls sitting on low wooden benches painted and scratched and painted many times, bright blue in her days. Little girls in dresses and sandals, with barrettes in their hair, playing hopscotch or penny-to-the-wall until some teacher poked her head out a classroom door and glared at them.

And later, at university, the joy at being free from all that, being absolutely in charge of her life and fully accountable and responsible for anything that might happen to her, and for any meaning whatsoever her life might have, fully accountable only to herself and to her conscience.

Many years after the war Professor Emmerich had come back as a guest lecturer, and he had recognized her. This had been in the hallway at the end of their lectures, and they had gone downstairs for a coffee.

"How did the war go for you?" he said. He still looked much the same, except that his shirt now had a collar, an

American button-down collar at that, and the bicycle clips were gone. His brown eyes were untroubled and clear, and he still looked as though he might be able to sit in this very chair with one cup of coffee and spend a lifetime pursuing only the thoughts he chose.

"It could have been worse," she said. "I began teaching soon after the war. First in Innsbruck, then here."

"I know. I looked up the register."

"I married, I had two children. *Have* two children."

"You were here all this time? In Vienna?"

"More or less. A few years in Burgenland, then in St. Töllden, and in Innsbruck. And you?"

"England," he said. "The United States. On lecturing contracts." He sat watching her. "You published. Seven, eight works, I believe."

"Nine. The first paper was banned here, but we found a copy in Geneva in the archives. They burned it in 1938 along with many others. Too many references to Jewish writers, as I found out later. They burned yours too, probably." She pointed. "Right out there in the courtyard. It made me proud to think I was among the ones they burned."

"It did?"

"It did. Like belonging to something important."

"Was that the one on moments of faith and power?"

She smiled. "You remembered."

"It's on the required reading list for my second-year students. It's good. A bit raw in places, but good."

It had been the most cherished acceptance anyone had

ever shown her, and they became friends after that. Sometimes in the summer and in the fabulous falls, Professor Roland Emmerich would come to St. Töllden by train and stay in a bed-and-breakfast there. Albert and he got along well, and often they'd all go hiking up into the Italian saddle or along the river. They'd watch ibex and chamois through binoculars, and on Sunday evening or Monday morning Professor Emmerich would take the train back to Vienna.

THIRTY-THREE

❖

IN RUSSIA Albert had been in command of a division
that shrank from nine hundred tanks to just sixty-five.
There was one battle, he told her one day long afterwards,
one single battle that alone had cost the Germans some
three hundred thousand dead and wounded. There were
no words to describe the fighting, he'd said to her. Biblical
proportions. He'd seen none like it before. Even if you
survived it, it murdered your soul. People went crazy on
both sides. They climbed out of tanks and ran and were
shot down.

The Russian T34 tank had better armour and bigger
guns, he said. And the waves of men that surged behind
them were endless. Soldiers as far as you could see. Then
came Kursk, which was even worse, and Stalingrad was
worse still with maybe eight hundred fifty thousand dead
all told. You cannot imagine, he'd said.

In January 1945, he was replaced in Russia by an eager Waffen-SS colonel. Because of his alpine experience, he was sent to Italy to command an infantry division in the Apennines that was battling the U.S. 10th Mountain Division. He had not yet reached his destination when the SS colonel who'd replaced him was already dead, shot by a sniper.

That spring in Italy, Albert's division fought American, British, Canadian, and Polish troops, and Italian partisans. The Germans were on the run, he said. The Allies had more airplanes, artillery, tanks, and troops than he had ever thought possible. And his men, while they had machine guns capable of firing nine hundred rounds per minute, were by then counting their shells.

Albert summoned Guido Malfatti, the boy on his peg leg, and he gave him some letters for her and a few supplies. He made out a *Laissez Passer* and a request for transportation, and he sent him north toward Austria.

On April 19, 1945, when the situation had become hopeless for his unit, he took it upon himself to sign honourable discharge papers for his commanders, who then did the same for their men. He shook the hands of his officers, and that evening he was taken prisoner by a young captain from the U.S. 5th Army. The captain climbed down from the jeep, saluted, and said what he had to say. Behind him two soldiers were at the Browning machine gun on its post in the jeep, and the windshield lay folded forward for clear fire.

Two days previously Albert had been injured in his left thigh, and at an American field hospital they looked to the wound, bandaged him up, and returned him to his captor.

On April 29, 1945, General Heinrich von Vietinghoff signed the articles of surrender, and the war in Italy was over. By then Albert was in a vast POW pen near Bolzano, he and several thousand officers and men.

IN VIENNA Peter had somehow made his way home from Romania. He'd received two field promotions and was a captain now. But he'd taken a grenade fragment in the arm, and it had shattered the bone and torn out muscle. They'd patched him up and, with his arm in a sling, he fled the camp on a truck going west and he kept going, showing written orders he'd issued himself. By the time he reached the apartment in Vienna he was delirious.

His beloved Daniela was there; she had been there most of the war, waiting for him, somehow surviving the bombs and the shortages. Part of the building was gone, and with it the bedroom wall of her flat. She put him in her bed on the living-room couch, and then ran through the streets to find Erika and to plead with her to send a nurse. Daniela told her all this later, how they'd driven through the ruined city in Mitzi's little car, the three of them: Daniela, Erika, and the nurse in her blue coat and white cap with the small red cross in front.

The nurse swabbed the malodorous wound with iodine and she sprinkled Salvarsan powder. She applied a fresh bandage. Peter had lost consciousness.

"Water," said the nurse. "When he wakes up. We don't want his kidneys to fail. Sugar, if you have any. Dissolve it in warm water for the glucose in it. About the infection, we'll just have to wait. Maybe we can catch it."

For the next six nights, Daniela slept on the floor by the couch, curled up there on a blanket like a faithful dog. During the day she sat for hours with his head in her lap, wiping his brow and spoon-feeding him a broth she'd made on her camping stove with potatoes and tomatoes from her corner patch in the garden.

On the credenza stood a copy of that picture of him as a young man on his laughing horse, in his uniform at the end of the First World War. Proud and dashing. His lieutenant's star, the braid, the lanyard, the sabre.

Peter died the day the Russians took Vienna. Not that there was much left to take. The city lay in ruins and there were no soldiers, no defences, hardly any men. The shelling and the bombing was over, but the raping and casual murdering by Russian soldiers was only just beginning, and it increased and multiplied as if becoming crazed on its own scent and its absolute and triumphant lawlessness. To get rid of the bodies, mass graves were dug all over the city and people carted their dead there and dumped them. Lime was shovelled on them in white and dusty layers.

"Rats this big," said Daniela and held out her hands to show her. "They tunnelled among the dead. And dogs running mad-eyed and snarling in the streets."

Daniela spent two days in the apartment with Peter dead on the couch. Against the smell she said she sprinkled kerosene on a handkerchief and held that to her nose. But no mass grave for him, she had decided, and so during the second night she rolled him into a rug and dragged him down flights of stairs in the dark. She hoisted him cross-wise onto a wheelbarrow and pushed him to the place she had chosen in daylight, a small park around a few corners from the apartment, the flowerbeds full of soft soil. She dug a hole there and she rolled him into it, and covered him up and tamped down the soil to discourage the dogs.

She would go there often during the next few years to plant flowers or just sit in the grass and read or smoke a cigarette.

Ten years later when the Russian occupation finally ended, she had his remains dug up. She put his bones in a bag and brought them on the train to St. Töllden. The stonemason made a small box of slate for them, and Daniela borrowed a shovel and dug a hole in the ground in the monarchist grave with the plumed helmet.

There was no official memorial service at the chapel that day, just Daniela, Mitzi, and Clara. They lit a candle and sat remembering. No incense for him, no old words in Latin, but a funeral just the same.

WITHIN A MONTH after the Russian invasion of Vienna, the war in Europe was over. The Allies had come from three sides and met in the middle, and the Nuremberg documents and depositions from survivors made accurate and shocking pictures of what happened then.

She sat reading them in that research room partitioned off at the warehouse with the oiled floor and the plywood walls, sat for days at the desk as if in a trance, walked to the hotel to sleep, and came back the next morning. Each time they checked her personal identification and the documents issued by Dr. Hufnagel under the distinctive blue United Nations letterhead.

Some days there were American and British journalists in that research room with her, but most days it was just her and a younger woman. Her name was Faith Stinson, and she was a postgraduate student from Cambridge University, a redhead with freckles and a bright, spontaneous smile.

"The only reason they're letting me in here," said Miss Stinson, "is that my father is a colonel and he was on some of the panels. He fought in Italy." She was working on a degree in political science, she said. Something on the self-destructive nature of dictatorships. The other big topic was Communism. But there were too many people doing work on that already, she said.

"Communism is back?"

"Well," said Miss Stinson. "Socialism, kind of. Embracing the common fate of humanity. Helping those who cannot help themselves. Welfare. All that."

They read in silence. They moved papers and made notes.

"And you?" said Miss Stinson on another day.

"I'm doing research for one of the UN archives, the Human Rights section in New York. What used to be the League of Nations."

"Interesting. On what exactly?"

They were just the two of them in the room that day, with the door closed to the photocopy room and the counter with index files, long metal boxes one after the other. There was an elderly female clerk with rhinestone glasses in there who did the copying at the light table and the actual search in the stacks.

"Specific topics," she said. "They want abstracts, condensed seven-page versions of a topic. Like the July coup, or the end in the bunker. Or denazification."

"I've done the July coup," said Miss Stinson. "The bomb and the aftermath. All those generals. Rommel slumped dead in the front seat of his car, with his cap slipped into his face. My father says he would have liked to know him."

"Many would. But forget that image, him dead from poison. I can give you better ways to see him."

And over soup and sandwich in a place just up the street she told Miss Stinson about that dinner after the horse race so long ago. She described Rommel raising his glass to horses and humans, and his calm face across the table, studying her.

"My God," said Miss Stinson. "You go back to all that? That's so interesting. Tell me more."

"Some day, perhaps."

Back at the document warehouse, once they were past

the security checks and back at their desks in the research room, Miss Stinson said, "But it's also such dark and terrible stuff. Don't you think? I'm just doing the bunker file. How they all killed themselves. Shot, poisoned. Can you explain the dead Goebbels children? The marks on the older girl's face."

"No. There is no explaining those things. An explanation would come close to a justification, but there must never be one. We can try to reconstruct their thinking with mythology and madness, but do we need to?"

"And him and Eva Braun in the end. And she, just married."

"Yes. I've done that box."

To ashes! Hitler had ordered. *Not one bone left of me! Nothing. Nothing. Nothing. Nothing.*

The fate of Mussolini and his mistress had terrified Hitler, strung up by their heels and spat at in death, so utterly despised that he had ordered his chauffeur to have enough gasoline on hand to burn their bodies beyond recognition.

And on the last day, while all the country was on fire, SS on Himmler's orders went through the many Gestapo cells in Berlin and shot dead every last person in them, a thousand and more civilians vaguely accused of words or actions not in the interest of the National Socialist German Workers' Party.

Thousands, hundreds of thousands, millions, seventy-five million and more dead. Among them millions of Jews across Europe, and in the end by Red Cross and League of Nations estimates easily twice as many civilians as soldiers.

In some ways for women and children the first years of peace were worse than the war had been. Allied Command had issued a directive that the entire civilian population should be made to feel guilty not just for the war but for Nazi atrocities as well. It was called *The Doctrine of Collective Guilt*, and posters were printed and displayed everywhere of the death camps that read, *You Are Guilty of This! These Atrocities: Your Fault!*

Women and children were at gunpoint marched through death camps, and one day in September 1945 Erika and Daniela on trucks with many others were carted east by Russian soldiers to an SS Einsatzgruppen death pit and forced to drag up the dead and lay them out for viewing, and then to take them down again and bury them.

But among those accused and caught in the net of retribution were also most of the actual criminals that had thrived in Hitler's shadow, and most of them were hanged.

"You've seen this one?" said Miss Stinson one day at her desk. "It should be cross-referenced in the Generals' Plot file. I don't think it is."

"What?"

It was a page on the fate of General Fromm, the one weak link and traitor among the plotting generals. It turned out that even though he had tried desperately to show loyalty to Hitler by having Colonel Stauffenberg shot, the Gestapo arrested him too. They tortured him and tried him before a mock People's Court, and then hanged him at Brandenburg prison on March 19, 1945. *Hanged by the neck until dead*, the document said.

Faith Stinson had been finished with her work one week before her. The day she left to take the train to Frankfurt and then from there to fly back to England, Clara had walked with her to the guard house at the main gate. They hugged.

"Maybe I'll do something on Communism after all," said Miss Stinson. "Socialism as the new hope. Human kindness. Do you know what I mean?"

"Oh, I do."

Miss Stinson stepped back and studied her face. "You mean it?"

"I do. Hope of any kind. Old, new."

Miss Stinson wore a trenchcoat and a fashionable black beret that day. Her lips were full and red, and she looked young and lovely. "Keep in touch," she said. "Come and visit. We have a big house with peacocks in the garden. And quince bushes. Do you like quince jelly?"

"I've never tasted it. You have my address."

She had stood hugging her arms because she felt cold even though it was June. Miss Stinson had rolled down the window and smiled and waved as the taxi drove away.

She waved back, then stood, missing her children.

THIRTY-FOUR

❖

LONG BEFORE THEN, and for months on end in the winter of 1945 after the bomb and into spring and summer, she had stayed up nights and wandered the shattered house, looked in on the children, sat in their darkened room, sat with Mitzi and Sissy in the kitchen. She read to them from Eliot's *Wasteland*. It seemed almost kind and warm now, almost hopeful in a human, accepting way. Like the words of a friend who understood about hope, that April indeed was perhaps the cruellest month, breeding lilacs like hope out of the dead land.

Anna had grown old and vague, but she still did the cooking and the cleaning. One evening after saying good night she walked down the stairs to her room with the cracked walls, and in her room sat on a chair and died as quietly as she had lived.

Clara and everyone else had to submit to the denazification

routine. She sat before the Truth Commission in the dining room at the Golden Goose, and she knew not one person on the board. Some were locals, but most were brought in for the process. They had her file and they kept passing it up and down the long table, whispering.

The chairman of the commission was an American major with grey hair and a trim moustache who had been a lawyer before the war. It was difficult to explain the Gold Party Pin, the Blood Order, and the Civilian Medal of Honour, impossible to explain them out of context. And so into the exceptional silence in the room she told her story from the beginning, and she told the truth about the death of the SS man, Bönninghaus, in her bedroom. The American major made detailed notes and asked questions as to specifics.

It took all morning. She had Mitzi there as a witness already cleared, and she had signatures on her question-naire from the head archaeologist and the priest. The commission broke for lunch and ate the roast of venison with gravy and rice and sweet peas, and a dessert of California tinned peaches that was on the menu that day. She and Mitzi were served at the scrubbed cook's table in the kitchen. It was the best meal they'd had in years.

After lunch the major dismissed Mitzi and he made Clara repeat her story from the beginning while he com-pared painstakingly what she was saying now with what she had said before.

Afterwards he sent her into the other room while the commission debated her case. It took forty-eight minutes by her watch. At times she heard raised voices, but in the end when they called her back into the room she was exonerated.

With the document she applied at Innsbruck University and was asked by the rector to prepare a sample first-year curriculum and four lesson plans in English Literature. They searched for her paper on *Moments of Faith and Power*, and fortunately found the copy at Geneva University.

While she waited for them to decide, she applied for an interpreter position at the district commander's office. St. Töllden was on the border between the British and the French occupation zone, and district command was held by the British, supported by Canadians.

Of Albert, she knew nothing. He might be dead. She knew only what Guido Malfatti had told her about the fighting in Russia and then in Italy. And she'd read the five letters from Albert that the boy had brought. She was reading them for weeks, again and again. She took them to bed and read a paragraph a night before going to sleep so as to have his words as the last thought of that day.

She and Guido had sat at the back of the house one day in June 1945, on the big smooth rock there, the boy with his peg leg straight out and a chip of iron at the end of the peg like a small horseshoe. A boy maybe fourteen, with bright eyes and dirt streaks on his face. She had found some bread and cheese for him, and milk, and he ate and drank with enormous gratitude while he told how Albert had taken him on as a mechanic's apprentice in

Russia and later filled out papers for the transfer to Italy.

He asked about the Norton, and she showed it to him, in the garage. There was rubble on it, and a dent in the tank, but no other visible damage. He ran his finger through the dust on the seat and asked if he could clean it. He knew about motorcycles, he said. Two-stroke and four-stroke engines. A few weeks later he'd found work as a mechanic with the British.

ONE OTHER GOOD THING that occurred in those months was that Sissy met a nice young Canadian officer, the lieutenant in charge of the Film and Propaganda Unit. She met him at a viewing of the film made at the Mauthausen concentration camp. Sissy was there with five-year-old Caroline. There were perhaps twenty women in the Canadian Armed Forces tent that day, the younger ones in their good dresses, with their hair pinned back on the side with combs, some with small children on their laps.

All were there because in order to receive ration cards and the prerequisite rubberstamp in their ration book they had to sit through these films on a regular basis. In case they missed the point, a finger uncurled from a big fist onscreen, and the finger pointed at them while a man's voice told them that the atrocities they were about to see were all their fault.

The Canadian lieutenant watched Sissy, and when the film was over and the tentflaps had been rolled up, he came up to her and gave her two Hershey chocolate bars.

"One for yourself and one for the little girl," he said. "Is she yours? What's her name?"

Sissy already looked much like her mother, Cecilia, beautiful, proud, and contained. Most of her clothes had been her mother's, and with some adjustments here and there they fit not too badly. More importantly she knew how to carry herself, and she spoke English.

"Yes, she's mine," she said. "Her name is Caroline. Caroline Gottschalk."

Sissy and Caroline came home with chocolate on their breath, and Clara waved Sissy into her study and closed the door. "We saved some for you and Mitzi," said Sissy, and Clara told her that was not the point.

That same afternoon she and Sissy with Emma, Willa, and Caroline in tow marched to the town hall to speak to the military district commander. He was Captain Hamilton, and she knew him because he had interviewed her before counter-signing the denazification document made out by the Truth Commission.

"Not our children," she said to the captain once they were in his office. They stood there, all of them, the children embarrassed and Sissy worried Clara might say the wrong thing.

He shook his head. "What? Don't I know you?"

"You do. That is why I feel I can make this request. We would have brought our mothers too, but they were killed in the bombing."

"Were they?" he said. "Sit down." He stepped to the door and called for more chairs. To her he said, "Write down your name on this piece of paper."

He sat behind his desk and looked at her name. On a coathook hung his belt and canvas holster with his pistol. He was a nice-looking man her own age, with brown eyes that looked at you straight and steady.

"Back up, if you would," he said. "What's this all about?"

Behind her Sissy poked her and hissed, "Don't. Clara. Let's go."

He looked from her to Sissy and the children, scrubbed and bright-eyed all of them and with decent haircuts thanks to Mitzi, but in clothes handed down again and again, and Emma's blue wool jacket overlarge and bare to the weave except in the creases.

"Well?" he said.

She said it was completely unacceptable for children, these children for instance, four, five, and seven years old, to have to sit through these films on the death-camps, however terrible, terrible no doubt, the facts were. But to accuse these children and any and all children of those atrocities was completely wrong. It was insane, she said angrily.

He stared at her. He said, "The orders are no food stamps without seeing the films. Orders. It is not for me . . ." He stopped.

"But can you see how unacceptable that is for a mother?"

"These are orders from the top. From the Psychological Warfare Division. All civilians and military alike are to be held responsible for the actions of the Nazi regime. For the war and for the atrocities."

"I understand that, even though it is ridiculous. One of the cleverest tricks of the Christian Church was the idea of the Original Sin. That everyone is born guilty. So devious. The never-ending burden, the unredeemable debt."

He sat watching her. He pulled the paper close and studied it, tapped her name with his finger, a clean finger with the nail cut short and slightly rounded.

"Your degree is in Theology? Or Divinity?"

"No, it's not," she said. "Captain, if you want justification for having dropped all those bombs on us, find another way. Not by pretending our children are criminals."

He said nothing for some time. He looked down at her name on the piece of paper and back up at her.

"I think you should go," he said then.

"All I am asking is, not the children, Captain Hamilton."

"Under the age of one they can be on the mother's card and they don't have to watch the films."

"You need to stop and think about a sentence like that. I'd rather feed my children twigs and leaves. I'd rather . . . I'll dig latrine ditches for blackmarket money. I will. But I won't have them accused and burdened like this."

He looked away from her eyes. He sat back in his chair. Beyond the closed door they could hear voices. They could hear a typewriter. Out the window the sun was shining on the old house fronts opposite. A truck went by.

"You should go," he said. "Thank you."

The next time Sissy saw the Canadian lieutenant he told her that children under twelve could now get food stamps without having to sit through the films. It was an experiment, he said. The age cut-off was now up to district commanders. He was glad about it. He put his finger to his lips and said that Captain Hamilton and three others including two Americans had travelled to Frankfurt and made their case.

By early winter the screening program, food-for-blame as it was commonly called, was abandoned altogether, except in parts of the Russian and French zones.

But that was how it began for Sissy and her lieutenant from the Annapolis Valley of Nova Scotia. The way they got around the fraternization ban was that he hired her as the official interpreter for the unit.

UNTIL CLARA HAD her university post in Innsbruck, she too worked as an interpreter for the Allies. For weeks in the fall of 1945 she would go around with two Canadians, the one a lieutenant, the other a corporal. They would go from house to house, the Canadians in their sharply ironed uniforms and she in her print dress with the puffed sleeves and her one good pair of shoes, low black heels they were, and ring the bell.

"Are there any guns in this house?" she would ask them, mostly women and a few men on crutches or missing an arm. "You have to hand them over," she would say. "Any kind of gun."

The people would hesitate, and she would say, "Come on now. In the French and Russian zones they are shooting people for it. So just give it to the lieutenant."

This was a hunting community with a fine gunsmithing tradition, and so in every other house there would be a rifle or shotgun, and the lieutenant would weigh it in his hand. If it was nothing special he would pass it to the corporal, who would stick it muzzle-first into the nearest sewer grill and lean on it hard and stomp it until the barrel kinked and the stock snapped off. If the shotgun or rifle was a good piece handmade in Ferlach or in Steyr, the lieutenant would write a receipt for it by type and serial number, and the corporal would put it in the cart he was pulling and they'd move on to the next house.

ONE NIGHT in the spring of 1946, when the moment of David Koren's return from Sweden was only weeks away, Erika in Mitzi's battered old Steyr was driving through Vienna on a Red Cross assignment. She was turning a corner onto Burgring when she was stopped by drunken Russian soldiers. They shot her dead and dragged her out and left her there on the pavement. They took the car for a joyride and crashed it.

Clara found out only four months later, from Daniela. Two civilians had witnessed the shooting and reported it to the Red Cross.

THIRTY-FIVE

❖

NEAR THEIR END, she knew, Blake and Rilke, Nietzsche and Goethe, Eliot and Schopenhauer, and probably all who had spent their lives examining and summing up had come to the conclusion that it was important to question, yes, but that in the end it was just as important simply to accept.

With Mitzi gone she felt lonely. Or not *lonely*, she decided, but alone in a final way; different than she had felt in her youth when she had used her aloneness to hone her strength, the way an athlete uses weights for her muscles and stamina. The discipline of living successfully in one room and in one mind while building forward. She still had that discipline, even if it was infused now with a sense not of loss but of closure, and she used the discipline to finish the translation and to review it and then to pick through it word for word, and through each sentence and paragraph echo for echo. Again and again. Hours and days and weeks at her desk, pushing herself: a writer's chosen life.

"It's what helps us through," Martin Heidegger had said to her. "The discipline. Putting the mind in harness and staying with the load."

This had been after he had come back into acceptance and then even into fame in France and Germany, years after the war. She had spoken to the rector, and they had invited Heidegger for guest lectures in Vienna, long after her years in Innsbruck, and he had come. Older, wiser, slower, but with even more steel in his thought. Yes, he had been of the opinion that the early National Socialists had some good ideas. But then of course . . . one knew now what came after.

At the time of his guest lectures he had been able to foresee the social and cultural pendulum swinging toward some new kind of socialism. All noble intentions, he'd said, very democratic, but bringing with it a continuous lowering of standards in order to be ever-more inclusive and accepting. It too would pass because it would run out of energy and money. It would swing back and forth, he had predicted, always in search of some humane and economic centre.

None of it really mattered, he said, and it did not alter the fact that one had to get through one's life somehow and build courage and structure within oneself. That took work, but there was no other way.

———

WHEN ALBERT came back from the war he was not able to walk very well because of his leg injury and because of his weakness due to malnutrition. But the latter was no different for any of the returning POWs. For months and months they came home from all over the continent, from the camps in France and England where the more fortunate ones had been allowed to work on farms. They were lucky to come home at all, since of those overrun by the Russians few did; no one knew exactly how many had died in the Russian camps. Hundreds of thousands. More than a million, said one statistic.

Albert too had to go through denazification, and there the only thing that was held against him were his brother's politics. By then denazification was done in civil courts, and in Albert's case the foreman was a one-time monarchist who stood his ground against the board and refused to exonerate Albert. The best he would agree to was the classification of "Less Incriminated."

The five classifications were:

1) Major Offenders (most of whom were hanged)
2) Activists, Militants, Profiteers, and Incriminated
   Persons (many of whom were hanged)
3) Less Incriminated
4) Followers
5) Exonerated

As a Less Incriminated person, Albert did not have to go to jail or, worse, to Nuremberg, but as a punishment he was not allowed to make his living at anything other than manual labour for one year.

Guido Malfatti had serviced the Norton and he'd been able to find some petrol. And so on his motorcycle like in the old days Albert drove looking for work, but this time, perhaps because the war had changed things and half the men were dead, he was quickly successful. A farmer, Mr. Richard Pachmayr in the next valley, wanted to start raising horses. Not saddle horses, he said, but coldbloods. Black Belgians. Albert said they weren't his specialty, but a horse was a horse.

Mr. Pachmayr hired Albert for room and board and a small wage, and Albert slept in the groom bunk there and ate in the kitchen. He exercised his leg daily by climbing the hayloft stairs, faster and faster each day. He had limited movement in his left shoulder from the French bullet, but he learned to live with that. She and the children often went by train to visit him. At cider-pressing time the girls helped with picking apples and pears, and they were allowed to sit on the big workhorses. They'd be nearly lying on the broad backs, hanging on wide-armed to the horses' necks. Once, when they were allowed to assist at a foaling, Emma became afraid and ran away when the vet had to reach into the mare and arrange things and pull, but Willa stayed to watch and help. Afterwards she helped rinse the foal with warm water and then rub it dry with hay. It was coal-black and rough-coated, and it soon stood on wobbly legs and took milk from its mother. Willa and Emma were allowed that night to sleep in the hay in the stall next to the foal.

In the spring of 1948, Mr. Pachmayr was hauling logs when a load slipped and crushed him. He left a wife and a fifteen-year-old son, and after the funeral the widow offered Albert a substantial raise and she asked him to help prepare the boy for his coming responsibilities as the owner and breeder.

For weeks during those summers the girls lived on the farm. They slept in the hay and helped with chores. Albert taught them horseback riding on the one saddle horse there, and he took them trout-fishing. He would kneel behind them and hold the rods with them, and let them swing back the line and count one, two, three, and let them bring the rod forward just so far for the fly to settle gently on the flat water of the millpond. And in May and June when the bark was soft and the sap fresh, he showed them how to make flutes now with six fingerholes out of willow branches.

In the end his love of horses found no lasting echo in Emma, but it did in Willa who in later years, halfway through her studies, decided to backtrack and sign up for Science and then for Veterinary Medicine while Emma was studying for her teacher's degree.

ONCE THE NEUTRALITY PACT was signed, Austria was permitted to develop a small army. Albert was offered reinstatement at full rank and a post in the defence ministry. He spoke with Mrs. Pachmayr and the son; the farm had earned itself a good name for its black Belgians, and the son was twenty-three by then and a good worker. Albert said it was time for him to take over. He would move on, but he'd be glad to help and advise whenever they needed him.

At the ministry, Albert was put in charge of rearmament, and for the next several years he and his team travelled all over Europe buying American surplus equipment, from helmets to GMC trucks and Sherman tanks.

The main infantry weapon he commissioned was the Belgian-made FN/SG assault rifle; a revolutionary design, he said, and he described it to her. A switch for single-fire or full automatic, a gas port and a clever piston return system.

Later he was promoted and put in charge of the army in the western provinces. From then on he was both a soldier again and a horse trainer much in demand by private owners.

By then, Guido Malfatti had passed the exam as a master mechanic. Albert had lent him the money for a jointed prosthesis, and young Dr. Kessler measured him for it. The thing arrived six months later in a wooden box all the way from America, from a factory in Seattle. It was perfect. With it Guido could not only ride motorcycles, he even began to race them. And when he started his own dealership, Albert asked her if it were all right with her if he donated the Norton. As a showpiece, he said. A classic. She agreed. Guido gave the Norton pride of place in his showroom, among red and gleaming Ducatis and Yamahas and BMWs. He even had an electrician install a spotlight that shone down on its deep black and chrome, and on the leather seats and the bulbous rubber horn on the handlebar.

In St. Töllden all the old-timers knew Albert. Early on some had rumoured about his past, but after a while few knew exactly any more what that had been. He had a certain aura, and he never lost his military bearing. People respected him, and many, when they saw him in uniform walking home from the train station, nodded and said General.

But not the young people in his own family; Emma's kids and Tom's kids, or their friends for that matter. They made fun of Albert behind his back; of his military history, of his attempts to teach them things; of his old-fashioned values. They viewed him with a mixture of grudging respect and condescension born of ignorance. In the end they rejected him, and he, them. Her, they treated much the same way; Oma, with her endless scribbling and her boxes full of files. With her tiresome reminders to think before speaking; with her stale cookies in doillied tins and moths flying in and out of her cupboards. She knew all that, and she did not mind. It made no difference to her whatsoever.

———

WHEN SHE HAD FINISHED the translation, she sent it off to the editor and waited for the confirmation of receipt from Mrs. Neumann's assistant. She shut down the computer and sat with her hands in her lap and her eyes closed.

Now what? she said to him. Tell me.

It was late evening, and for the next half-hour she wandered through rooms, opening armoires and drawers, making mental lists. She shivered and put on a cardigan. She thought she might eventually do some housecleaning, hire someone with a truck to take away things to the various recycling depots. So the girls wouldn't have to wade through all this some day.

In Mitzi's room she opened the drawer in the bedside table and took out the small black-and-white photograph of the pale blond Polish prisoner. So young. Just a boy. Erika had taken it, with her Agfa-Click. She put it back and closed the drawer. The leather couch was still in the study, and the matching chair. Count Torben's sword was gone, his duelling blade. Gone for a bit of flour in 1944, to some travelling black-marketeer.

She remembered the boxes with the red labels marked *Personal* in the basement. The notes to herself over the years. What to do about them now?

The next morning she was tempted simply to stay in bed, but mindful of As-ifness she did not. Instead that day she fetched the pistol from its hiding place and she unwrapped the pieces and put them loosely into her purse. She took the noon train into the side valley and from the station walked to the waterfall.

When she had still been at high school and Peter a junior partner with a law firm in Innsbruck, he would come home on weekends in the summer and fall and in his black Citroën motorcar would take her into the mountains as far as they could drive, and with their rods and satchels they would hike to one of the rivers, water that came rocketing down from the glaciers, fast and ice cold. Water so clear you could look down from high rocks and in the shallow parts see trout, brook and rainbow, facing the current, slow ripples of fins to stand still, then a lightning dash for food.

They were using his English dry flies with the barbs pinched flat according to sporting rules, so that the hook could be removed without much injury to the fish. That day he tied on a brown fly and with it hooked a rainbow that leapt four feet in the air and ran with the reel screaming, and it leapt again and again. It took him fifty yards or more downriver and it forced him into fast currents where he tripped and fell and floated for a while, but he managed to keep the rod up and the line tight. In the end he was back in the shallows and he called to her for a hand with the net.

That rainbow was the biggest she'd ever seen. They agreed it was much too beautiful to kill, and so they let it go. Afterwards they lay in the sun to dry their clothes. They lay on the white gravel bank by the falls, both of them basking in the warmth that struck down from the sun and up from the clean white riverstones. Her ears and her entire body were filled with the ceaseless roaring of the falls.

She could look upriver now and see those falls from the footbridge that the Alpine Club had built some years ago, to go with the new trails. There had not been a railroad into this valley until long after the war.

She turned and looked carefully to both sides, but there was no one about. A wet spring day, the river high; not yet weather for hiking.

She snapped open her purse, and one by one she took out the pistol pieces and threw them into the deepest part of the river below her, into the pools dark green and full of air bubbles and turbulence. The barrel, the grip, the magazine, the slide. The box of shells. They sailed out in a flat arc through the cold air and sank without a trace. Gone. She felt nothing. No guilt, no relief, no regret.

She looked down at the river, downstream to the rocks. For a moment she saw tall Peter balancing there, casting the line with a looping sideways motion, because of the trees behind him. He'd learned that rollcast from a river guide in Scotland in the 1920s.

On the way back to the train station, already near the small supermarket, she tripped over something and fell to one knee. A young tourist couple helped her up.

"Take a hold," said the girl. "Are you all right? Is your knee okay?"

For a moment of confusion she thought this might be Willa home from Australia, but of course she was not. This one was blond and quite young. She had a small stars-and-stripes pin on her windbreaker.

Clara thanked her. The young man was unwrapping a chocolate bar and he peeled back the silver foil and held out the chocolate to her. "Have some," he said. "It's very good."

On the train back she felt cold. She felt close to tears much of the time but did not want to probe the reason why. The mountains moved past, their peaks orange in the setting sun. Flocks of crows rising and settling, and in the distance the great steel cross already flashing on its peak.

In St. Töllden, on the way home from the train station Father Hofstätter saw her and he crossed the street. Wordlessly he offered his arm and walked her home.

"Too cold to be out, Doctor Herzog," he said near her house. "The damp from the river."

He waited until she had unlocked the gate and gone in, then he raised his hat and nodded a greeting. He turned back the way they'd come.

Upstairs she switched on the computer, loaded Skype, and put on the headset. She called Willa. There was only the answering machine.

"Call me back, dear," she said. "Soon. Call any time."

That night she dreamed of Romans in togas and tooled leather breastplates, some of them with laurel wreaths like crowns, poking through the remains of a fire, some enormous conflagration it must have been, and they were going through it, spearing things and holding them up, giving them due consideration and talking to each other and shaking their Roman heads. And in her dream she finally understood what they were looking for: they were looking for clues to themselves, trying to understand what it was that had made them who they were. In some places there was smoke still rising, in tall thin columns widening near the top as if to hold up the pale eternal sky.

Willa called in the dark of night. She picked up the bedside telephone. She dropped the receiver. She fumbled and found it and pulled it up by its cord. She felt hot, she shivered. She felt on fire herself.

"Mom? What is it? Are you all right?"

"Can you come home, Willa?"

"What is the matter? Has something happened?"

"No. Just come home, dear," she said. "Come soon."

"Mom, what is it?"

"Just come home now."

She woke to the first pale light and made herself get up and put on slippers and robe, and then holding on to the rail with both hands she descended to the basement one step at a time.

She dragged the two boxes with the red labels from where they sat on the cement floor into the old laundry room and she pulled up the washer bench to the firebox under the laundry cauldron. She balled up the first few pages and set fire to them. The flue had not seen warm air rising in years and there was a great deal of smoke, but eventually the flames caught. They flared and rolled out of the firebox and were sucked back inside.

She sat on the bench with her hair wild from the pillow, sat with her elbows resting on her knees and fed her notes to herself into the flames. Hers and hers alone. She felt the heat on her face and eyes, and on her bare shins and hands. Two banker's boxes full of paper. It took a long time.

AT MIDMORNING that day Caroline Gottschalk looked at Emma and motioned her out of the room.

"I think your mother has pneumonia," she said in the kitchen. "A temperature of forty-one and a half. We'll have to see whether it's viral or bacterial. Keep her cool with damp cloths and change the sheets often. I'll get her into the hospital."

"She probably won't want to go. She hasn't seen a doctor in, I don't know how long."

Dr. Gottschalk shrugged. "She needs chest X-rays, maybe infusions of antibiotics. A cardio monitor. A number of things. You talk to her. When did she call you?"

"Just this morning. I came over and found her like this."

"Stay with her. I'll take the blood sample to the lab and get them to run it."

"Why so suddenly? How did she get it?"

"It would have started a day or two ago," Dr. Gottschalk said. "Like a cold. Maybe a sniffle, then it hits you in the night. Your mother is old, Emma. I have to go, but call my cell if you need to."

THIRTY-SIX

OF COURSE SHE REFUSED to go into the hospital. Her fever peaked at forty-two degrees Celsius, and she nearly died then. It seemed to Emma that Dr. Gottschalk was more angry at being ignored than she was sad for her mother.

At the height of her delirium Clara saw her parents standing at the foot of her bed, beckoning for her to get up and come along. They looked carefree and relaxed, her mother for once not in greys and blacks but in a nice sky-blue dress with long sleeves and lace at collar and wrists, and her father in a fine suit and with the kind of upturned moustache he'd worn when he met her mother. They looked better and happier than she had ever seen them.

She said so to Emma when she woke up. Emma in short sleeves was leaning over her with sponge and basin, wiping her brow.

"Could be the fever," said Emma. "Remember what Willa said with Dad."

"Willa?" she sat up. "Did Willa come? Where is she?"

Emma put the sponge in the basin. "Mom. I'm the one that's here. Look at me."

"Emma-dear. Of course. God, I'm hot." She fanned herself.

Emma put basin and sponge on the floor, stood up, and pushed them under the bed with her toe.

"Lie back. Sleep," she said. "Caroline says that if the fever comes back, you will have to go into the hospital. She can get you into the small one, the Catholic sisters, the what's-it-called."

"It's called the Merciful Heart." She lay watching Emma. "Sit down. First prop up my pillow and then sit down. Not on the bed. In that chair so I can see you better. And cheer up. I am so very grateful for everything you've done. You do feel that. I know you do."

Emma sat back in the chair. She stood up and put on the cardigan.

"Emma, your father loved you very much. He loved you just the same as Willa. We all did."

"I never doubted that." Emma sat in the chair with her elbows held close and her hands making fists in her lap.

"Be happy, dear Emma. Please let me see you being happy. You don't depend on anyone else for that. I think your husband is a good man, but he needs to get a bit of an edge. Take action. Something."

"What about the museum?"

"Yes. The museum. I did speak to Mr. Hofer a few days ago and I mentioned Tom. He can call. I have no idea how that'll go. He really should retrain for something. Tell him I have some money. I'd help."

"You would?"

"Yes, I would. I've thought about it. Be happy, my dear Emma. That's what a mother wants most of all, for her children to be happy. For her children finally to understand that their happiness is up to them. Life becomes so much easier once you accept that."

"Dad never liked the kids much, did he?"

"Oh dear. Not true, Emma. He loved them. For the longest time. We both did, but as they got older, instead of growing up, they became opinionated and rude. Disrespectful. Especially – you know who. I won't name names."

"Because he called you Nazis? Was that why?"

"Well, no. That was just ignorance. Anger. All your dad and I ever expected were decent manners. And that Nazi word has become so misused as to be meaningless. Some day take them to the archives. The facts are all there now if they care to know them. But, Emma . . . the pages I wrote for you and Willa when you were small, the ones I gave you years ago? That was something special. That was between you and me, and it came straight and pure from our lives in those times. Don't let anyone spoil it."

"I won't."

For a while they were silent. In the street, the ten o'clock bus went by, and then the old man who was still grinding knives rang his bell. The sound came from the distance, passed in the street, and faded again. The day then was so still they could hear the river, which was running high from the glaciers and snowfields.

"I'm hot," she said.

Emma reached for the sponge, soaked and squeezed it, and wiped her brow.

"I loved your dad. So much."

"I know you did."

"And it was so very easy, Emma."

Emma said nothing. She stood up and went to the window. She used a tissue and stood looking out for some moments.

"There's something else," said Clara. "Come and sit down again. The angry boy we were talking about. Man, I guess. He stole the Knight's Cross. He of all people. Isn't that interesting? I saw him holding it up to his collar and grinning at what's her name. His wife."

"Katrin, Mom. You should really know their names by now."

"Oh for God's sake. I *do* know her name. I just couldn't remember it. Anyway, Willa wants it back."

"Why didn't you say something sooner? He may have sold it."

"He'd better not."

"Why can't he have it?"

"Because he doesn't *deserve* it. It stands for something. A famous general recommended your father for it, a man he admired, and so it has a soul. Willa reminded me of that and she is right. He has to give it back. I have decided. The rest of the medals – you and Willa can work it out. It's all yours anyway, split straight down the middle. Now don't . . . listen to me. Don't fight over one single thing. It is not worth it. Never, ever. You are sisters."

Emma sat looking at the small silver-framed pictures on the bedside table.

"Emma-dear," said Clara. "Look at me." She waited.

"What?"

"When you were born in that cottage in Burgenland, you've seen the photo album. It was such a lovely warm summer, and Mitzi and Daniela and Cecilia and Erika, they would all come out some weekends, and when your dad came home, from Africa it was. When he came home he was so very happy with you, Emma. He was only there a week I think, but he'd have you on his lap, you looking at him with your big eyes, and so serious. There were moments, Emma . . ."

Emma was sitting very still. "Go on."

"And later," she said. "The weekend hikes we would go on. Backpacks with blankets and food and stuff, and we'd sleep in some mountain cabin and in the mornings we'd make a breakfast of pancakes on the alcohol burner. Do you remember that?"

"Of course I do."

"Good. But enough of all that. Come give your mother a hug. I love you."

Later that day Dr. Gottschalk came by. She listened to Clara's heart and lungs. She took temperature and blood pressure. She inserted a feed into a vein in the back of Clara's hand and taped down the vial there.

In the kitchen she said to Emma, "I am getting a bit worried. She has viral pneumonia, and it's far from over. It progresses in waves. I've put her on antivirals now. Sometimes they help."

"But she seems fine now. We had a long talk."

Dr. Gottschalk nodded. "Good. You have your talks. Is Willa coming?"

"Why? Is she that sick?"

"Yes. At the very least I want her in the Merciful Heart. They have good nurses there. Work on her, Emma. Do what you can."

In the other room, Clara lay in bed, weak but the calmest she had been in a long time. She felt at peace and lucid, and in this mood she lay remembering. She could see Albert's face so clearly before her. His eyes, his smile for her. She could see the girls when they were small. Easter bonnets on them. Willa on a horse. She could see Professor Emmerich sitting on the desk, and Martin Heidegger lost on that park bench. She could see Freud poking the air with his cigar.

She tried to decide which had been the most helpful thing she had ever read or heard, and that was hard because there had been so much of it.

Which? she thought, and the words that came were Rilke's:

Lord, it is time,
The summer was immense.

She called out for Emma, and Emma came to her side.

"Sit with me," she said. "Is it very hot in here? Can we open the window?"

Emma opened the window and cool evening air blew in, the scent of the cold river water, the scent of wet earth, the scent of the mountains, pine and wet rock.

That night, the fever came back, and Emma called an ambulance. While she waited, she packed a small bag of toilet essentials. She folded the little hinged picture from her mother's night table and put that in too.

Clara was dimly aware of being on fire, and that fire she thought must have been caused by the embers she had been sheltering in her cupped hands much of her life, carrying them as her secret flame wherever she had gone.

She was aware of being taken down the stairs by men in uniforms, and then being loaded into a van. She saw her parents again, she saw Willa; she saw Albert, she saw dear Mitzi and Erika.

Later she was dimly aware of people standing and sitting by her bedside in an unfamiliar room. There was nothing she could do for them. Women in blue and white hats like small wings wiped her brow and tried to feed her, but she kept her lips closed and turned away.

Perhaps the next night or the one thereafter she spoke with Albert and he told her happily that he had bought a new motorcycle for them. A new Norton, he said. And on it they could ride through the hills again, together again, just the two of them, she snuggling up to him with her arms around his middle. He was waiting for her, he said.

She wanted to kiss him and hold him, but he was moving away.

Wait! she called out. Wait for me. I want to be with you.

WILLA ARRIVED AT NOON by taxi from Innsbruck airport. She was tired from the interminable flights and the lineups, but she was also excited. She was pleased because she had been able to find the quote her mother had been looking for.

It was from a collection of letters literary friends had written to one Mme Louise d'Épinay in the mid-eighteenth century. The quote was from Abbé Ferdinando Galiani: "*The important thing, Madame,*" the abbé had written, "*is not to be cured, but to live with one's ailments.*"

She arrived at the house and used her key. She hurried up the stairs, opened the door and called out. "Mom! Where are you?"

The door to the bedroom opened and there was Emma, pulling sheets off the bed. She was weeping.

Later at the Catholic hospital, Willa stood at the open door and looked into the empty room. She had needed to see, to help her understand.

But there was nothing. Bright daylight on the bare mattress. The glass-topped bedside table. The cheap wooden chair. All empty except for the silver pictureframe still on the table.

A nun in a blue and white habit came along the hall carrying an armful of laundry. She saw Willa and stopped. Looked at the number on the door and then at Willa.

"Our patient number seven," she said. "She was not with us for long. We hardly even knew her name."

"She was here only a few days. I missed her. I flew in from Australia as soon as I could."

The nun nodded and waited. "That's a long way," she said then. "And you are?"

"Wilhelmina Leonhardt. Her other daughter."

"Ah. I see. Your sister was here."

"Not when Mom died. None of us was." Willa wiped her cheek with the inside of her wrist. "I spoke with her just a few days ago."

The nun stood watching Willa's face. After a while she said gently, "The dying often choose their time. It's as if they came to a place where the dead need them more than the living, and they want to let go. I've seen it when they ask people to leave the room so they can die unobserved. They close their eyes. They make the decision. They withdraw."

"They do?"

"They do."

The nun stood a moment longer. "Don't forget that little picture," she said. She touched Willa's arm lightly and walked away.

AUTHOR'S NOTE

❖

I'D BEEN COLLECTING MATERIAL to write *Clara* for years. I had drawers full of notes on conversations with people living in Vienna and New York and London and Tel Aviv. The oldest man I spoke with had seen Emperor Franz Joseph strolling in a Vienna park in 1904. Others had fought in the First World War and seen the end of the Dual Monarchy, and many remembered the Great Depression and what came after: the street battles in Vienna of the early 1930s, the years that finally gave way to National Socialism.

One by one these people passed away and took their stories with them, and I still didn't know what to do with what they'd given me. What I felt I needed was the thick folder of documents that I knew existed in my own family. I'd seen it and we'd talked about it: letters handwritten in the old style and giving a flavour of social and private life; photographs and documents from the key years between 1930 and 1950; official forms full of personal questions and threats; Gestapo documents signed and sealed *Heil Hitler*; birth and death certificates; Work Passes and Marriage Permits; Certificates of Racial Purity. All this documentation rubber-stamped with eagles and swastikas, without which you were nothing.

The way men once planted trees so that their grandchildren might one day enjoy their shade, various family members over two generations had assembled these papers into a kind of Lest We Forget Archive for those to follow. Over the years the folder became more mythical than real, and when I needed it for my research I could not find it. Then the house was sold and an era was clearly at its end.

For periods in 2006–7 I lived in Austria on a teaching contract with the Institute for Economic Development. I rented an apartment in a small city with a long history, and from there I travelled by train and road to my seminars.

The apartment was in a castle that had served as a defensive position during the peasant uprisings and the wars of religion of the 1600s and before. Parts of the walls and burial tablets in them dated back to the Romans. The best thing about it was the view, which was of an eighth-century stone church right across the street. That church and creative elements relating to it are in the story.

To furnish the place I used some Biedermeier pieces I'd inherited, and while I was cleaning out drawers and compartments I found the document folder. It sat back on a lower shelf, three inches thick, bound with bits of frayed string. Like a nod from fate. A gift, really.

I spent months checking my own material against the documents for historical accuracy, and I experimented with form and voice and the dramatic arc of the work I was planning. I was dealing with a generation that had experienced so much: the end of the Austro-Hungarian Empire, the First World War, the Great Depression, the rise of Nazism, and the Second World War and its aftermath.

Eventually I created as the main character for my story a young woman I named Clara Eugenie Herzog, a student at Vienna University in 1932. I would use her stubborn and true love for a man whom everybody in her family disapproved of as the mainspring, and her intellectual, professional, and moral development as the backbone of the novel. Once I'd made those framing decisions, it became quite naturally Clara's story and the material began to flow.

Clara is a novel inspired by actual events set against a background of recorded history and documented fact. Nevertheless, it is a work of the imagination, and except for persons known to history, the names and incidents in the story are either imaginary or are used fictitiously.

K. P.
Summer 2011

ACKNOWLEDGEMENTS

MY SPECIAL THANKS for support and encouragement with *Clara* go out to Heather, to Aunt Thea in London, and to Laverne Barnes in Vancouver. Thanks also to Michael Tait in Toronto, and a big Thank You to Ellen Seligman, my publisher, and to Lara Hinchberger, my editor on this novel. All the people who over two generations have added documents and photographs to the file mentioned in the Author's Note have now passed on; I am indebted to them all.

Heather Chisvin

KURT PALKA was born and educated in Austria. He began his working life in Africa where he wrote for African Mirror and made wildlife films in Kenya and Tanzania. After moving to Canada he worked on international stories for CTV and GLOBAL TV, wrote for American and Canadian publications such as the *Chronicle Herald* and the *Globe and Mail*, and worked as a Senior Producer for the CBC. *Clara* (originally published in hardcover as *Patient Number 7*) is his fifth novel; it was a finalist for the Hammett Prize.

A NOTE ABOUT THE TYPE

Clara is set in Monotype Van Dijck, originally designed by Christoffel van Dijck, a Dutch typefounder (and sometime goldsmith) of the seventeenth century. While the roman font may not have been cut by van Dijck himself, the italic, for which original punches survive, is almost certainly his work. The face first made its appearance circa 1606. It was re-cut for modern use in 1937.